Kabria
Not until I die

By
Arvind Parashar

ISBN 978-93-83952-72-4

First published in 2015

Pre-Press & Distribution:

Wordit Content Design & Editing Services Pvt Ltd
Quest Offices, C38/39, Parinee Crescenzo Building,
Bandra Kurla Complex, Mumbai 400 051,
India T: +91 8080226699

Cover Design by Rathi Varma

Publishing Partner

To my mom and dad.

Acknowledgements

First and foremost, to all my readers- A Big Thank You.

To my family- Manasie, Madhav, Preya, Chiya, Tintin, Jaanhvi, Cdr Nishant, Komalbir.

To all my dearest friends, without whom I will cease to exist.

To my Facebook family. Every friend and family member that I am connected on Facebook has truly inspired me and motivated me to write.

To all my ex-colleagues in the corporate world, who I learned a lot from.

To my ex employers- GE, Dell, Genpact and Altisource. My corporate experience helped me plan, strategize and execute well in life.

To Mr. Rana Raj Singh, Mr. Vivek Bajpai and Mr. Rajiv Gulati for the literary inspiration.

This certainly would not have been possible without all the support that wonderful editor, Roona Ballachanda, provided. She has been instrumental in the entire editing process. Without her, the book would certainly have not taken the shape that it did.

The backbone of this piece is the publishing team led by Malini Nair, Publishing Project Manager Rinky Gopalani, Publishing

Editorial Head Niyati Joshi, and the Crossword team led by Anup Jerajani.

Special note of thanks to Rinky for being a great support in managing it all so well.

Had it not been for the support of my adorable mom, sweet sister, and my lovely wife, for giving me space and tolerating my absence during this period, I would have never become an author. We all feel dad must be pleased in heaven now.

References-

Working paper of Vasiliy Mitrokhin, former KGB archivist, work of Kabir das, Mirza Ghalib, Gibran and Rumi.

When you are holding this book, you must know that this is written in earnest, with a lot of passion and love. This is a work of fiction, and I hope and wish you enjoy reading it. That said, I would like to wish you happiness in life. I offer my gratitude for purchasing my book, and shall continue to entertain you through my writings. My next two books, 'Hooked, Booked and C(r)ooked' and 'The Manhattan Mahatma', are in progress, and every attempt is being made to publish one of these by early next year.

Hope you like the book. Do send me a Hello at author@ arvindparashar.com, authorarvindparashar@gmail, or my pages on social media, if you wish and I will try to respond to you. Please leave a book review on Goodreads. Thank You.

Best wishes

Arvind Parashar

Prologue

"Maya mari na man mara, mar mar gaye shareer,
asha trishna na mari, keh gaye das Kabir"
"Neither your wishes end, nor your heart satiated
But your body ends, with no end to hopes and desires."

IT IS EVENING, ARID JULY MONTH OF 1990, and the Prison of Charkhi in Kabul is riddled with the usual activities, that involved the inmates. It housed some of the most dreaded criminals and also some who were falsely convicted. And, then, there were those who were in prison even though they were not accused of any crime and so were not even eligible to be tried in court. Life, at times, gives the most unexpected and shocking outcome for the most ordinary person, leading to extraordinary tales. Kabir seemed to have preempted it. He called it an Epic to unfold, much before it was inscribed. An Indian, from Bombay, he had lived in Afghanistan for thirteen years now; three years of a gloriously free and exceptional life, and then, ten years in prison, where he still remained.

Kabir was all set again to impart training on photography to his fellow prisoners. Added to this training, there was another aspect that kept Kabir and the prison gang active; it was the weaving of rugs and some fine intricate craft work. This earned great revenue, and kept the prison in-charge and the internal security pleased—very pleased, and rich too. In return, the prisoners too received favors that kept them going in torrid conditions.

He spent the initial part of the previous ten years of his captivity in training the prison administration in English and Russian languages, as well as photography. Afghanistan had experienced huge Soviet control throughout the eighties, and hence Russian language came in handy. All these skills set him apart from the rest of the prisoners, and hence a reason for his long survival too; in such a prison, anything more than a few months could easily be termed long. To some extent, he had been lucky as far as death was concerned, for once, in 1981, he survived a bomb attack that destroyed the prison in Kandahar, the place where he was initially taken. It is a different matter that he was announced to be released a day before the tragic event took place. In the event of prison destruction, a day later, when three people including Kabir were found alive, they were taken to Charkhi. All the records that existed in the Kandahar were destroyed and, hence, for the previous eight years, he was locked up in this prison without any case against him. This certainly was the unfortunate part.

In the previous ten years, this man had seen the worst, as he recounted the horror at every given opportunity. He had suffered betrayal at the hands of some people that left him with an ineffaceable mark. So far as the innocents go, there were a few more like him within the confines of the prison building. On the other hand, many civilians outside were either executed, or had lost their lives fighting the enemy. The definition of enemy changed, however, the war still continued. The war that saw putrid convolution of atrocities, killings and mass destruction. Millions lost their lives, and the survivors from the unwinnable Soviet war in Afghanistan had deep horrifying memories and scars. Unhealed.

Most of them just survived to die every day. The prison was their hell home.

Amidst such a traumatic life, some still carried a hope. Kabir was one of them, who believed he would sleep under the stars once again before his death.

Why did I leave you alone? Why did I break my promise? Kabir thought in his head, his face darkened with anger at himself. And, that day, during his usual photography classes, he broke down completely. After a long time, he cried in the open. Most of the prisoners would do that in private, and so would he, but that day was an exception.

Upon being asked by one of the fellow inmates, he simply said "I wish to sleep freely under the billion stars." Then he went quiet and, after a momentary pause, "And I want to be with you," he said softly to himself, as he remembered Noosh. He had never appeared so weak and hopeless before. He would be the one to instill hope in others, however, today was not his day. His instinct told him that his time to go free had come, and, therefore, the fact that he was still behind bars haunted and bothered him much more than ever before. As a matter of fact, a few years ago, one of the prisoners who claimed to be trained in palmistry had looked at his palm and stated that his life would turn around after the age of 35. He continued to believe him till date.

The long day came to an end, as the prisoners gathered in the small yard, where they would usually huddle up to do their daily work. After the classes, they got together to discuss much more. Like all other days, yet again, discussion broke amongst the inmates, mostly about the fiendish practices in the country and how they had witnessed the grotesque theatre of pain and loss during the war.

"I was once offered a deal. My release was promised, if I fought against the Guerrillas, however I refused. Though, some accepted the offer and may have died fighting," Kabir sighed looking at the fellow prisoners around him.

They were oblivious to whatever was happening in the outside world. Kabir even believed, by now World War III would have erupted. There were no news channels for him. He wrote many letters to be posted. He was always assured that they would be, however, none of them even made it outside the prison walls. There were no postal services in order. The only few things that made out of this place to their destination was the rugs and crafts. Nothing else.

Around the same month, a decade ago, Kabir and his wife Noosh were separated in the bloody war. That was the most painful and unfortunate part of their life. All these years Kabir knew that Noosh had made it successfully to Bombay, however, Noosh and Kabir's parents were informed that he had died.

With the Soviet withdrawal of troops being initiated in 1989, things were beginning to look better. Human Rights Organizations were more active and in control. Release of prisoners was part of the rightful decision. A roadmap was planned, and the implementation had begun early part of 1990.

The same evening, head of the prisons announced the release of a few prisoners. The date was set for some time in the winter. There was excitement in the air. I just hope nobody brings the prison down this time, Kabir thought and laughed aloud, expecting his name to be there in the list. God bless you, palmist, he said to himself. The names were not announced yet, and the prison head's inscrutable face dropped no hints either.

Chapter 1

"Kabira kiya kuchh na hote hai, an-kiya sab hoye
Jo kiya kuchh hote hai, karta aur koi."
"By my doing, nothing happens
What I don't, does come to pass
If anything happens, as if it is my doing
Then truly it is done by Almighty."

IT IS ONE OF THE MONSOON EVENING OF JULY, in 1990 in Bombay. The tri level house of Colaba, just a few hundred meters inside of Colaba Causeway was brightly lit up. That particular day, this house, where Kabir's family lived, had many guests arriving to celebrate some occasion. The maddening rush, the furor and people tripping all over created a nice scene for one or two youngsters to capture in their camera.

This house merited Victorian and Gothic style architecture. The facade blended well with the neighborhood. The interiors boasted of Medieval Indian and Central Asian touch. The house smelled of the wood, and the décor primarily included materials that Kabir had been fond of. There were ornate teakwood screens as ventilators. The showcase in the living room flaunted Kabir's favorite possession, a 70's Nikon Camera and it was placed strategically to form the heart of the room. All this beauty that this house carried diminished, as beloved Kabir was always being missed around here. The housemates carried his fond memories.

This was a very close knit society. The locality included friendly and warm families, shopkeepers who would not mind wrapping gifts from their own shop in beautiful wrapping paper, and the felicitations would come from the entire clan, so that even the space in the gift tag would fall short.

Mrs and Mr. Boxerwala appeared in their best costumes, which was designed by Mohan Lal and Sons from Calcutta a few months ago on their wedding anniversary. Their present had three gift tags, since the compliments of the entire clan could not be written on one. This family was one example of settling here eons ago, but the clan was spread across the world. Some of them wouldn't even know who Noosh was, or even her in laws who have been living there for more than half a century.

"Where is our Sehar?" asked Mrs. Boxerwala with a curious pair of bespectacled eyes.

"I have no idea, Aunty, I am also looking for my son," said Noosh, in despair.

The kids were running around, and the seniors caused equal commotion. There was nobody who would control anything, as the house was divided; there were kids who were doing their own thing, then there were elders who would not stop talking.

All these activities formed an integral part of the evening. As darkness prevailed outside, the locality appeared much brighter, and inside, the décor looked very neat with its touch of Persian deco and the best artifacts from the world over.

A tall good looking man in his 50's came out to the living room, holding hands with his pleasant looking wife. The aura brightened further as Mr. Devraj Prakash welcomed all the guests.

He met and greeted everyone, with a firm handshake to all men, and a customary Namaste and Salaam to all the ladies. The younger women preferred a handshake though. And then, he recited a verse-

Arz Kiya hai (Here I say something)

Irshaad (Go ahead)

"Khushiyon ka waqt bhee, Kabhi Aa jayega
Gam bhee to mil rahe hain, Tamanna kiye bina."
"The moments of joy and good times shall strike again
For, the sorrows that we have, struck us without a desire too."

The house resounded with *'wah wah'*, and there was an apparent hidden pain behind the verse.

Sehar was seen playing with a few boys, mostly his age, in one corner of the house.

Devraj in his manly voice "We raise the toast, To you all, in celebration of 10th Birthday of our grandson Sehar, the son of Kabir and Noosh."

At this point, Sehar began to shoot pictures with his newly gifted camera.

"Not today, my son," said Devraj warmly. "It is your day. May the Almighty bless you with all his love and wishes. Your father would have been so proud of you today," Devraj wiped his moist eyes, and Sehar hugged his mother before turning to his grandfather. Some sort of silence gripped Noosh's eyes, as the tears began to rush like a stream of pearly water.

"Don't cry, mom. Please don't," Sehar reached out to get some tissues, but Noosh resisted.

"I miss your father so much. I wish he were here with us today."

Sehar kept looking at the photographs on the walls, when his grandmother came in, "I did not wish to come in between you both earlier, but Noosh, your father and I are worried for you. How long will you continue to cry like this?"

The relationship Noosh shared with them had always been like that of parent and child. She was the angel, and they were the guiding stars. In this world of warm relationships, Sehar was growing up to be the best son in the world. Also, their neighbors, friends and relatives had always been there for them through the years.

"Happy Birthday, once again, my son." Noosh said, and ran out of the room in an emotional state.

Mr. Boxerwala turned up, trying to control the situation and he was joined by Devraj.

Devraj had more wine than he usually would. He turned to his wife, "Look I had an extra glass, and hence, you need to take care of me now."

Noosh, on over hearing the conversation, bursted into tears, yet again. It triggered many memories in her mind, as she kept transcending into the past; a past that would never leave her. It was leading her into the future. Everything, including the extra glass of wine and the photography by Sehar, was history replaying itself in front of Noosh.

Most of the stuff was known to the Devrajs and the neighbors. Some of it kept unravelling further during the conversation.

Noosh had never been able to share the past in detail with Sehar. She knew and thought that the tales of his father might weaken him, and disturb his growing years.

She wanted to keep him strong and, hence, always maintained that his father might have died in a plane crash, but they weren't sure as the body had never been recovered. She never gave him the details of war episodes, nor was it ever revealed by his grandparents. Sehar was aware that about ten years ago, when his parents lived in Afghanistan, even before he was born, war had struck that country.

Far from the deep etched painful saga, some of the guests were eating and enjoying themselves thoroughly.

"What a sumptuous meal, this yum chicken, pulao and phirni, nobody can cook the way Noosh does," said one of the guests.

"Is the situation still bad over there in Afghanistan, or has it improved now?" asked Mrs. Vithhal.

"I do not follow much news anymore, owing to the hurt and grief and sad memories, Aunt," said Noosh.

"Oh, I can understand. Just hope, now that the Russians have withdrawn their troops, things improve over there."

"Sorry, Aunty, but I do not know anyone out there and it does not matter to me anymore; that war took its toll on me, I am still not able to come out of my husband's loss," Noosh choked.

In between all this, Devraj came and apologized to the guests, "See we wanted to celebrate, and you have always witnessed our celebrations, and you know they aren't void of tears."

By now, the guests were very much aware of the emotions that struck the family. Mrs and Mr. Pandit were moist eyed too, and the same applied to the Sharmas, Vithhals, Siddiquis, Singhs, Bajpais and even the younger Joshis and Sens.

"This is so much about us human beings that the next thing after yawning, that is contagious, is tears. One person cries, everybody else, starts to cry," said one of the guests.

"Mr Devraj Prakash Saab." Somebody called out his name from the door. Devraj's wife went to the door.

"Who was at the door, my wifey? And at this hour, it is 8:30 P.M."

"He was the postman from the head post office to deliver a letter to you, and I did not want to bother you. He wanted you to sign the paper. He shall come again, tomorrow."

Mr. Prakash turned sad at the mention of the posts; for many days and months, he had waited for some news from Kabir.

"Oh, okay, now shall I go to my room and retire? I hope the guests will not mind it." Suddenly, at the mention of the post as he turned sentimental too, he wanted to be aloof for some time.

On the other hand, Noosh and Sehar spent some time alone in the balcony. "Mom, you have to take good care of yourself."

Sehar came across as a more mature boy than most of the boys his age. He had also learned to hide his emotions to a great extent, something that he picked up from his mother.

This time, he wanted to know everything that took place to change their world largely.

"Mom, please tell me how it all happened. I am a grown up boy now. I beg of you, please do not stop in between this time, you know it, you end up crying and then you stop talking, and then the point shifts."

In the past, on two occasions, Noosh had gathered her courage to share with her son the events that happened more than a decade ago. One was the time when Kabir's cousin, Akash, had passed out of National Defence Academy, Khadakwasla, and the entire day the topic, under discussion was the Indian Army and the Battlefield. The other time was when the Soviets had begun to withdraw their troops in Afghanistan. These were two historically significant events; one event became historical in the family circles, and the other needed no mention as it held global significance. It was not hard to figure out the common factor in these two events. The Battle field. The War.

"Epic. Yes, Kabir used to call it an Epic, much before it happened," Noosh said. Many poignant memories seemed to be repressed in her mind.

The house was back to its silence.

The conversation between mother and son was interrupted as the most talkative of the lot, Mr. Boxerwala, arrived in expectation of a see off to all the guests.

"*Arey, wah*!! *Aaj toh maa beta.* I do not want to disturb you both, rarely do you both talk so much. And, hence just to let you know, it was great to be here as always. Take care of Devraj saab."

After all the guests had left, the domestic help, who had stayed late because of the party, began to put the house back in order. "Mangla, beta, you must be tired, too; first eat some food, then do everything else." Mrs Devraj did not forget this ever. In a few weeks, Mangla would be getting married, and the entire arrangement was being done by The Prakashs and The Sens. The good part was that she was getting married to their neighbor's driver. Nur had been driving their car for four years now, and was a smart young man.

It might sound unusual that their marriage was a big discussion between the Prakashs and the Sens. In this party too, this topic was discussed a couple of times. They were insistent that the marriage should take place in full steam. After a long time, there was a wedding to look forward to, and Mangla had always been considered an integral part of the family.

In particular, so far as Mangla's wedding was concerned, Noosh played a huge role in getting it fixed. When the Sens asked her for her point of view, she simply said, "His name is Nur; do not think twice about it."

The marriage was all set for December of that year.

It could have been set for an earlier date too, however, Noosh wanted Nikita, her old friend and ex- colleague, to be there personally as she had specifically mentioned that she wanted to witness an Indian wedding.

While they spoke of celebrations, everybody in the family also felt a sense of hollowness. But, the elders considered themselves fortunate to have their daughter-in-law and grandson with them as a blessing from God.

The day after the party was a little relaxed. For the Prakash family, the celebratory get-together of the previous day was a bit emotionally draining as well.

Noosh was seen cleaning the couple's photographs on the wall, and also cleaned the pictures in the photo album as it had gathered some dust.

"This is where you exactly go on your father. You will be a wonderful photographer, too."

"One day I hope I will be able to take brilliant photographs like dad. I always tell my friends that artists earn a lot of respect."

"You talk just like your father, Sehar."

"Like father, like son."

"Yes, God bless you. Are you stepping out now?"

"Yes, mom."

"Okay, I want you to give this food to Bajpai Aunty, and the other packet to Sen Aunty."

"Mom, why don't you go? if I do, they will again chew my time and share the same story again. I have heard it so many times, especially the expressions that Sen Aunty gives, when she narrates—Oh, son, when Noosh came here, you were inside her tummy; your mother is a strong woman; she has braved a lot, and so on and so forth. And then, mom, I would rather prefer to hear it all from you." Sehar sounded like a typical ten-year-old.

"Yes Sehar. Can you do me a favor and pull out the album from the almirah? Let us go through these memories together. Well, before I do, let me ask you; do you remember them all?"

"Not all; I mean, of course, besides dad, I know your two friends Nikita and Jemima and your other friend too, what's her name, ya, Lisa, all those aunties definitely. Nonetheless, time and again, you keep talking about them."

While Sehar went to the room to fetch the photo album, the doorbell rang.

Noosh got up lazily and opened the door.

"*Ji, appka post hai…main kal bhee aaya thha*, and even you can sign and take it."

"*Oh, haanji…ek minute.* Sehar, please get my id also. Not sure why would she address this post in dad's name, anyway."

"No, no id required. I know you, and also this seems to be just a letter from America."

"It is from Nikita."

"Mom, what does it say?"

"Let me open it. See, this is her daughter. Isn't she pretty? Ah, she knows about my collection of hard prints. She keeps sharing her family pictures with me, like this; how beautiful."

"Yes mom, indeed, she is pretty. Why do you ask this every time?" asked Sehar shyly.

"She is turning ten in December, so Nikita wants to see us all. It's been ages; the last time I met her was during Rain's 5th birthday, these guys had come to Bombay, and we planned a trip to Goa. You were at your cousin's then."

"Mom, are you not in touch with Lisa and Jemima Aunty?"

"Not as much, Sehar, just once in a while. See, Nikita aunty and I have been fairly close," Noosh smiled.

"See this photo from our album," Noosh pointed at the one taken in the lobby of a hotel in Herat, that had Nikita, Jemima, Lisa, Kabir, Noosh, their associates Babu, Salem, Meer and Singh, and a couple of hotel staff in it.

"This was a very special day for your father."

"Really?"

"Yes, and, well, it was special for me too."

"Now, this sounds exciting; tell me more mom."

"This was the day your father had taken me out for a ride on a Royal Enfield. Someone from the hotel staff arranged for the bike, I believe, it was Mr. Singh the manager who got it for us, and that day we did some sightseeing and had a lot of fun. That was the beginning of our relationship." Noosh continued, as she was lost in her thoughts, and did not even realize that she was talking to a ten-year-old.

"Oh, really, so you and dad were super romantic." Sehar said, contrary to what one would have expected of a ten-year-old—to understand romance.

"Yeah, our romance was woven in nature, for it was so beautiful, you would want to be alone and happily engulfed in nature. It used to be a very beautiful country, and it holds some beautiful memories for me."

"Hmmmm, and?"

"Yes, and that day I was drunk on wine. I was all by myself in the room. After your father dropped me back to the hotel, then I had some more by myself, but this picture was taken when we returned from our ride. That day it was all official that your father was going to lead the crew. The intention was positive; who knew what lay in wait for us; who knew that danger was setting foot on the land."

She continued.

"I was in my early 20's, and it was the semester beginning of our first year in engineering college, in the University of Moscow, early 70's, yeah, 1971 Fall, to be precise.

I was not able to find the office of the dean, and that is when it all started. Kabir showed up like some God-sent gift, and from that moment onwards, till we last saw each other, he had always been like that to me, he was my messiah."

She got up to get some water.

"I always liked your father, however, my priority at that point was to finish my studies and go to Afghanistan to serve the country. To be engaged or married or even see a man was the last thing on my mind. After I finished my engineering, I moved back to my native land while he continued to pursue an advanced course in journalism; then he landed a job in Kabul."

Sehar was keenly listening to her, and got up to draw the curtains, and began to look at the rest of the photographs.

"And, why were these pictures taken? I mean, look at this one; these are just your hands, and there are many of your close ups too. Well those are self-explanatory. What is the story behind these hands, mom?"

"Yes, that is another long story, for another day. I will not stop crying otherwise. These were the last pictures taken, for now that is all I can say."

"….Mom, you never complete it."

Mrs Prakash came in at that point.

"Sehar, he came home to our old house, where we used to live earlier. We last saw him in 1979 when he visited us for a few months. He had then promised us that next time he shall come with Noosh; we even discussed their marriage plans. We wanted to go to Kabul and plan the wedding, however, he stated that Noosh was interested in getting married in India."

Noosh kept looking at her while she was speaking.

"During his stay, he shared many heroic tales. He even told us about your father and how loving he was."

"Yes my dear mom, you always praise my father this way. I wish we could turn back time. I wish we were not living this horror of missing the most important man in our life. And Sehar, coming back to your earlier point, I am not insipid. I am just trying too hard, I believe."

Mr Prakash also joined them in their conversation.

"How could we forget the day Noosh arrived here? It was the winter of 1980; pass me the bottle of water, *beta*."

"Here you go."

"She was carrying you inside her tummy then, gracious, pleasant looking, exhausted, and lost. I remember being told that she was dropped home by a few cops. We used to live in our old house then."

"Yeah, Grandma mentioned the old house, too."

"We tried very hard to find out about Kabir; just a few days later, we heard the news from the Embassy that Kabir was nowhere to be found, and, then, another set of news that he died in the war."

Noosh intervened, "Dad… that was the most unfortunate day of my life. I wish I had not left him."

"So, the story of the plane crash never existed?" Sehar was baffled, "Mom, can you answer me?"

The melancholy of the moment gripped the family more poignantly than the day before.

The next moment, Kabir's cousin Akash arrived on the scene. He broke the news of his selection to go to Afghanistan and work with the U.N towards restoration of peace. Being an Army man, it was a matter of great pride for him to work on this critical mission. He was already recognized for his excellent work in the Indian Armed Forces.

The news received a mixed response from the family members. Sehar seemed to be the only one excited about it. "Chachu, please find my dad's enemies and crush them."

Akash could understand and comforted everyone. Devraj seemed a little worried, and asked him to take care of himself during the stint. He was close to the family, and sat down as Noosh began to think back and narrate the series of events that took place since the arrival of Kabir in Jalabad.

Chapter 2

"Kabira khara bazaar main, mange sabki khair
Na kahu se dosti, na kahu se bair"
"Kabira in the marketplace, wishes welfare for all
Neither friendship, nor enmity with anyone at all."

IT WAS IN MAY 1977, KABIR HAD SPENT CLOSE TO A WEEK in Afghanistan already. He had travelled across quite a few cities to discover the vast beauty of the country, and also do his groundwork for the coming days.

After finishing his education in engineering, followed by journalism in March 1977, Kabir underwent a four week rigorous training program in Moscow. This training was unrelated to his college studies, as he was picked as a recruit in Russian Secret services agency by his college professor who had deep connections in the agency. He was trained as an Illegal resident, the term used for an illegal spy by the Chekas, agency which later on went on to become KGB.

So, when Kabir arrived in Afghanistan, he was fully aware of how the intelligence system worked. His training in gathering information had equipped him well to do tasks that were beyond ordinary. All of what Professor told him and he learned in these four weeks was indelibly fixed in his memory. He was on a mission to achieve the extraordinary.

"Something is different here," he murmured, and then folded his hands only to scream into space "Whoaaaaaaaaa." Kabir was excited, and he was peeping out of the window of the truck. For him, this place was beyond belief, and he expressed it in no less form, true to his young age.

The 50-year-old Volvo truck from the 'Moscow Kabul Transportation Affairs' kept moving forward as Kabir tightened his knuckles on the jumping seat in the front, capturing all he could in his Nikon FE, which was fondly gifted to him by his favorite professor in Journalism School in Moscow.

An avid photographer, nature lover, and a mystic, he was here to unravel and capture the beauty that existed from Bamyan to Jalalabad, Herat to Kabul, across the beautiful terrain of Afghanistan.

"Aha!! Hard to believe this wonderful week is already over. This country is amazing. Who would know that they produce tons of dry fruits here, pomegranates, and what not, and did I just catch a glimpse of the bulbous vegetation? Prohibited. Perhaps, that is where Noosh is working with a US NGO. In time, in time, I shall see her." Kabir had his soliloquies as he tumbled down the super strong war-friendly body of iron.

As he departed into the evening dust, he folded up his sleeves in lassitude, and unhurriedly sauntered into the pack of roughly 200 traders who, far from the nature in mystic terrains, were busy striking chords with the buyers or potential ones, or people like Kabir who had no clue what to do except look for that one perfect shot in his Nikon. And, in the process, carelessly dropped his camera and damaged the lens.

What did I just do? Why the heck would I drop my kit lens, my sole lens!? Seems broken. I need to go 100 miles to Kabul to find a new set or pair, darn!

He screamed at himself.

"Mister, can you help me clear my lens?" asked Kabir as he spotted the first shopkeeper in the busy Bazaar.

"I have yet to begin my sales, and it is evening already," said the shop owner in broken English.

Kabir was still lost in translation; in his own sorry state of mind due to the probable loss. Given the frenzy that this place was running into, he decided to retrace his steps.

After a week on the road and the tragic camera episode, he finally arrived at the hotel in Jalalabad.

Upon reaching the hotel, he took a brief look at the reception area that was surrounded by some dignitaries from the western part of the globe; he turned back, and spotted a man with a Nikon. A local man with a Nikon! Kabir exclaimed to himself.

"He is my man; he is my man; I got him," Kabir was as hushed as he could be, but seemed to have left some traces of his echo in the camera man's ears. He thought he might get some help, but was well ignored.

With his battered lens, backpack and a near torn look, he looked like a journo in town, which he was, and some kept him at an arm's length while others feigned ignorance.

"Welcome to Jalalabad, ladies and gentleman," a husky voice boomed from within the sea of humanity, and addressed these immaculate men.

And, as Kabir inched towards this camera wielding figure, trying hard to conceal his despondent state of mind, this bearded professional pulled up his equipment, and started taking pictures, as he was the photographer for the occasion.

Kabir lost his only chance for the evening, as he walked dissatisfied towards his room in 'Cabool', the Hotel.

The iridescent light bulbs on the stairway walls were flashing, making the entire setting perfunctorily visible, impressing the ones raising the toast, but this man had lost interest. He simply went into his room and closed the door.

The doorbell rang.

Two men carrying a trolley stood straight for a moment, followed by the customary salaam. "A*apne shorba, afghani chicken and naan order kiya?*" asked Salem.

E "Did you place the order for Soup, Afghani chicken and breads?"

"*Aap sahi kamrey main aaye hain*", E *"You have come to the correct room."*

Said Kabir with a sign of disbelief that they spoke his language. "Do you speak any other language?"

"We know a little Persian; we are from Calcutta. We came here to sell dry fruits and spices from India, but 'Golden Traders' owner cheated us and ran away to some other place, as we were told."

Kabir did not reveal where he was from yet.

"Did you not file a complaint?"

"Yes, we called up our parents, and they asked us not to return as the agent had charged them seven hundred and fifty rupees to get us here."

"Oh! So this is a nexus. You have been fooled."

"Yes, and we are not the only ones."

"People from Iran, India and Pakistan came here for various employment opportunities, mostly in trade."

There was silence, no further questions. But, Kabir registered key points of interest.

"Who is your Hotel owner here?" he quipped.

"Hahaha," they burst with laughter. "Are you serious? We are hardly connected to anybody here; how will we know?"

By this time, the room was filled with the aroma of food, and Kabir had to try hard to control his hunger. But, this topic was more than an appetizer for him; now he was beginning to thoroughly enjoy this conversation.

Meer, the other steward, now found a suitable place in this conversation, as so far, he felt side-lined in this tete-a- tete.

"*Saab*, our owner is a rich business man in the main town of Jalalabad, and I have heard he runs a major trade in the Bazaar and also owns a small time transport company. He is fondly called Sheikh in the circle."

"Oh, okay, this is very interesting. I want to meet him Meer. Do you know where I can find him? Can you arrange it?" said Kabir feeling the crisp notes of the Afghanis in his hand.

Kabir was inquisitive for a variety of reasons. He wanted to find out more about this country, and also thought he would be able to build up a network here that would help him at some point. He never ignored anything.

"*Saab,* are you a hotel owner in India?"

I am from Bombay. My name is Kabir, and I am a Journalist. I am here for a long term assignment.

"If you talk to anyone, tell them I am a photographer. Please do not mention that I am a journalist and, if your boss is wealthy, he can show me around and I can impress him with my work and also gift him some pearls from this town in India, called Hyderabad. Since he's a trader, it might interest him. I got a few from Mangat Rai in Hyderabad."

"Hahahaha. Saab, why do you want to believe Meer? He seems to have cooked it up."

"I did enquire with the reception guy about him," said Meer.

"And, what did he say?"

"He told me all that I told you, in addition to the executive suite that he has for himself over here as Room 407, where we were never permitted to go."

"This sounds very interesting Meer. Thanks for the information," Kabir said.

"But, Kabir *Saab* from Bombay, why are you so keen in knowing about our boss?"

"I wish you were also as keen, you would do something big in life. You know, I learned a lot during my engineering in USSR, and one of it was to be aware about things. I learned further during my course in Journalism, outside my classes, too."

Kabir continued the lecture, as if these guys understood it all.

"You got fooled, not due to your innocence, but due to your foolishness."

"My lord, stupidity is another term for innocence, isn't it true? But we still don't know what you mean."

"Good night, innocent people."

Salem and Meer were unmoved. Kabir understood as he saw 'please help us' signals in their eyes.

"Yes, guys, what do you want?"

"I don't know what Meer had on his mind, but I want you to hire us temporarily for your assistance on the go."

"I could somehow sense that you will ask something like this."

"Really, so can you please do something?"

"Look I am not the final decision maker here. But, yes, we can plan it well. Why don't you ask this when I am with my group? Let us play it by ear and see where we land. I shall try my best to influence when needed tomorrow. Okay now. All the best, and let me sleep."

As Kabir closed his door, he thought that the boys looked completely charged up and were probably waiting for the night to get over soon.

Back in the room, with a hectic day gone by, he tried to fit his 6'2" body on this 6' bed, legs curled up and despite the noise of Kirloskar compressor, fitted in General air-conditioning system, that was barely two feet away, he was still able to sink into sound slumber.

The hotel was 10 miles off the airport and Arfina airlines was mostly seen with Indians and westerners coming from Delhi, Jordan and other places.

The planes would cut across the moon glazed skies of 'Cabool', mostly during midnight. A few years later, the skies would be busier and smoke-filled. Kabir wouldn't have known this at that time, nor did Mohammad Daud, the president of the country foresee this turn of events.

Chapter 3

"Aisi vaani boliye, man ka apa khoye
Apna tan sheetal kare, auran ko sukh hoye."
"Speak such words, sans ego's ploy
Body remains composed, giving listener a joy."

THE NEXT MORNING SEEMED to foretell an action packed day ahead.

Curtains were drawn, room still appeared dark, and the clock kept on the mahogany wooden side table showed 7:35 a.m. Afghan time.

As Kabir peeped outside, he could see some turban headed fellows gather for a morning huddle, planning the day that lay ahead. The sun was bright and Kabir seemed late, but he wasn't noticed by anyone in town except for the staff, or so he thought.

Whoops, I forgot to turn the TV off. I Love this lady journo. I love Canada broadcasting corporation that shows for an hour every day, Kabir said to himself, stepping out of the room for breakfast.

The breakfast lobby had a few people who broke into somewhat of a revelry, the moment Kabir alighted the stairs. He wasn't a bit surprised, or was he? He knew it, but thought to go ahead with the pretentious air.

"Hey Kabir, Hope you had a good sleep, and are ready to take on from here." said Jemima, a newly arrived Journo, head of Kabir's team.

Kabir's expressions shifted rapidly, and, before Jemima could catch it, he was shaking hands with the crew of The Daily Times.

Jemima and Nikita had arrived late last night to join Kabir for the assignment.

"Niks, grab your coffee, pronto, and pick up your assignment from Jemima. This is a perfect day for us. Let's get the stuff," said Kabir.

"Did I just get demoted?" Nikita chided.

"Jemima asked me to take on from here, so I thought she will hand over my promotion soon," Kabir said with a smile.

He continued.

"I know, guys, this is my first job, but I can assure you I have done this during my internship in the USSR."

Kabir continued to share his experience in Russia during his internship days there.

"You know, last time around, I witnessed that from cold tundra regions to high grasslands; there was a vast expanse in which to lose yourself. You could see the reflection of the coniferous forests in the temporary pools, and that would seem like skyscrapers covered in soot."

He gave a brief pause and saw both the ladies were dumbstruck; Kabir assumed they were keenly listening to him. Without seeking their confirmation, he kept on talking, "And, you know what, I wondered every moment, catching such glimpses…while, during the day, you could capture pink flamingoes wading about with their heads, on the other hand, at dusk, you had to be weary of the deadly arachnids queuing up for a warm hiding place in your bag."

"Hahaha, come on, Kabir; that is from the course book," teased Nikita.

Kabir and Nikita seemed to have hit off well, from the moment they met.

==========

Nikita was a Brit, born and raised in London, and had everything that she needed. That's how she came across as well. She hailed from an aristocratic family but she never wanted to live as an heir to the throne. Her parents knew she was meant for tougher terrains, and hence let her decide her own course in life. Being their only daughter, she was always given the freedom to choose.

She loved people and the abundant beauty offered by nature. She took great interest in finding uninhabited virgin landscapes, and this place had a lot to offer. So, she had a lot to grab with both hands.

Having grown up in the busy urbane streets of London, all this was a distant dream. To move a few thousand miles away to the most extraordinary, mountainous country in middle Asia was a phenomenon one got to live once in a lifetime.

Today, Nikita was living it, like all the others with her. She was experiencing it, in and out. She loved to venture out, even during her college days. Now this was her profession. Her happiness was not driven by the locale fact alone, it was also to do with the kind of people she was with. They all had one thing in common. Passion. They could go to any extent to build their dreams. Not castles; dreams like a fresh whiff of air. That charm of living life under those billion stars, covering the stretches, terrains, mountain ranges, big bulky pomegranate trees and the umbrella palms that dotted the road side. What also got her kicked about was the loose white sand moving surreptitiously in the wind, occasionally forming small twisters that seemed to be doing the shimmy.

"To be a travel journalist here brings us a lot closer to a different universe that would have been a far-fetched wish for us. I am glad we are here to make the best of these days ahead.

The world must know what this land offers. And, now, it will through our special edition." Jemima was lost in her imaginative world. She knew that there was a lot more to it than what meets the eye. It was not by any means a cakewalk.

And, she was often reminded by Kabir, how Patricia's crew was lost in the deep forest of Africa a year ago. "This is going to be dedicated to them. This is a small gift from us. We shall pledge to keep this in the spirit of binding the world together, and in the name of mankind."

Jemima, of the entire crew was the senior most and highly experienced in terms of years in the industry. She was a very warm person, intensely emotional but wore a tough exterior. She had grown up in a cosmopolitan environment; her father was Polish and mother Italian. She was born and brought up in New York, and went for her higher studies to London.

She knew she was fighting in this male dominated world to succeed and, therefore, this assignment could not go wrong in any sense. Nevertheless, she had fears. She had her inner demons to silence.

She had seen her father dominate her mother over everything. She did not want to be subservient like her mother had been. She wanted to carve her own identity. She wanted to be known as Jemima, a fiercely independent successful woman.

But she would never confide in her peers. She would never show nor reveal her deepest fears. She was mysterious on occasions. Knowing her was a tall task.

Jemima and Nikita studied in the same college in London, before Nikita went to Queen Mary's College for masters in Journalism. She was fondly called Niks by her classmates, and that continued till date.

"Salaam Kabir Saab," two voices in one tone hurled out of nowhere. "Can we join you?" They carefully noted the right time to utter their voice, as planned.

"Kabir, this was supposed to be a dead bolted secret. You spilt it, didn't you?" asked Nikita.

"Oh, come on, are we some undercover investigative crew? Still, I did not tell them anything. They just know me as a guest in the hotel."

Salem had already spoken with the hotel manager. He was convinced that Kabir would be able to influence his boss, in case it was needed.

Discussion with the manager was also not very rough. After some persuasion, they were granted a month's leave and were paid for the days they had worked at the hotel. The only condition was that they needed to return after a month. In lieu, their documents were taken into the manager's custody now.

On seeing Kabir getting cornered, and driven by a slight hint of guilt, Salem stepped aside and quickly revealed the reason. "Will we get more money? We want to hold your tripods, serve you nice meals, and can also offer you some foot reflexology, just in case you need it. And, yes, today is the beginning of our month long leave; we do not mind some extra money to be sent across to our parents."

This got Jemima thinking. Never in her past had she invited anyone for special services. This seemed like a treat.

She immediately got back to Kabir, "What are you waiting for? They are hired."

"Am I still retained?" Nikita was at it again.

"Yes, girl, you are leading us today. Both these newly appointed gentlemen are yours for all your assistance."

As the 60's Toyota throttled, it had some small boys chasing to say good bye, leaving behind a few scratches on the side door of the old transport.

"I am super excited as we embark upon this terrain trail. I want to capture it all. I want to experience it fully," said an overjoyed Nikita.

Singing in chorus

It is the will, it is all in May
It is the Daily Crew, All the way
And we are the Sultans of swing
And all we do is sing sing sing….

"Thank goodness, Mr Dire Straits isn't around." Kabir said.

"Kabir, what happened to your lens? Is it broken?" Nikita screamed.

"No no, it is not, it is just pretending to be broken."

"Oh, that is bad news. This is not your first time experience, so you can still fix it and take photographs, can't you?" asked Jemima.

"Saab, don't mind. We got this spare lens for you. And a camera body too. Just in case you end up breaking your camera too."

There was complete silence. Atmospherics stopped. Brakes could be heard loud, like a roar.

Everybody was down. And nervous.

"Guys, how did you know about my camera lens? Who got these? How did you manage these? Where did you get these from?" A fountain of questions against similar surprising expressions had the crew in a limbo.

Jemima kept staring from a distance at these two, "I told ya, we can't trust them. They have been spying on you, and now us too. This, to me, appears to be an ulterior motive. They might take our skulls back and hang them for a show. Do you guys also carry guns or daggers or anything that is like a weapon?"

"Ladies and gentleman, my owner, now please hear me out. My ex-owner gave this to me in the morning. Apparently, he knew you had broken yours from that evening's gathering. He was also there, and he noticed you."

"Why were you quiet all this while, Salem?"

"I tried to save the best for the last, but all of you seem to be some kind of maniacs here. Pardon my honesty," said Salem, with a guffaw.

The atmosphere had lightened up by now.

Kabir wondered why the owner did not mention this to him when he had met him in the morning. He had had a brief chat, as a step to build a local network. He knew, the owner was highly influential and, him being a Journo, broke the ice without much problem.

This crew was handpicked for the assignment on central Asia, and this country was the focus. 'The Afghan Frontiers' was their dream in the making, and they needed to explore this part of the erstwhile Great Khorasan. Nobody had ever been able to conquer the Khorasan. There was a lot to discover, and so much to see; so much to remember. The crew was high on their excitement levels.

It took Kabir some days to help Nikita pronounce 'Afghan' correctly. It will take him a few more days now to help her pronounce 'Khorasan'.

"What made you join us at the last moment? You were to cover the Swiss Alps, weren't you?" asked Nikita with much curiosity.

"Well, Niks, there is someone more beautiful; more fascinating than Swiss Alps who resides here. I am here for her, and, of course, work too, but, yes, my primary reason was her."

"Oh, my goodness, really; this sounds so much like a movie. Tell us more about her," Nikita asked.

Salem looked at Meer, "See, I told you, Kabir Saab and Nikita are just good friends and colleagues. He loves someone else."

"Okay, okay, hold on guys, I want you to meet her in the coming days. You would know it all in time. She is beyond words. She cannot be defined in mere words that the English Language has to offer."

"You remember Stephanie from CBC? She looks like her. Actually, even better than her I must say, ha ha ha."

Jemima could not stop herself, and quickly jumped into the conversation, "Really, oh gosh, Steph is the cynosure of all eyes. She is a class apart. And we thought you were falling in love with her all this while and, hence, we were wondering why you did not take up the same assignment as hers."

"Yeah, Steph is a gem, and I respect her and like her, too. Noosh is slightly aware of the intensity of my feeling towards her. It has only grown more after she left for Afghanistan."

While she moved to her home land, Kabir moved on to pursue journalism. He wanted to come to Afghanistan, under any circumstances. She wanted to work with a U.S NGO, then take up the cause of women. This NGO was also a lot about eradicating illicit opium trade. For her, philanthropy was the motive. She had let go of her other so called better opportunities.

While they studied together during their graduation, Kabir did ask her out a few times in Russia. She refused as she wanted to focus on her studies then. And now, Kabir just wanted to revive all the moments and time spent with her during his days in engineering college. Kabir wanted to come to Afghanistan, under any circumstances. He did, finally, but the opportunity had not come to him that easily. He knew, that now it would be easier to marry Noosh for he lived here too.

"Nooshistan." Nikita shouted out loud and all started laughing.

"You got that perfectly fine," said Kabir.

"It's all in the name hon."

"I love her name. What does her name mean Kabir? I believe, the names here have a meaning associated with it," Jemima asked.

"I told you before, she is a bundle of joy, and that's what her name signifies. I call her Noosh, her complete name is Nooshafarin. It is so appropriate, so lively and so very pleasant. Her eyes reflect beauty, and she is beauty personified."

"And, Kabir, you said you will tell us about her in time, or when we meet her we would know, and now you don't stop." Nikita said.

"Oh, I did not notice that, I was deeply engrossed."

Quickly realizing the shift, Nikita asked, "Why don't we get her along on our assignment?"

"Yeah, you got these two musketeers here, and then Noosh, and then maybe, we can find some hunks for ourselves, let this be rechristened as some family tours and travels." Jemima said laughingly.

"Not a bad idea, Jemima. Let it be The Khorasan Tours and Travels."

"Wow, you got this one right. And, yes, it is all in the name." Kabir chuckled.

Salem and Meer had dozed off, by now. They had no clue about the day's proceedings. They knew, when the mini truck stopped jolting, they would be on duty. For now, sonorous songs, near perfect weather setting, a lively crew and an enthusiastic driver at the wheel were the perfect combination for a siesta.

The day was just beginning to unfold. They were driving from Jalalabad to Herat. A recce had been performed by Kabir already. The local guide was to be picked up from a village on the way, per original plan. But now, they dropped the idea. Their transport vehicle was too crowded.

"It is 10 A.M guys, time to swing into action." It sounded like a wakeup call from Nikita.

Kabir had taken more than a few dozen picture shots in his revamped camera, thanks to Salem and his owner.

These look perfect. "Oh My God. Look at this one, wow, and this too. I just cannot believe it," Jemima could not stop praising.

While Jemima was lost in her thoughts, and Nikita was busy preparing the day's schedule looking at the stretch, Kabir kept his clicks on. He knew how to take those flawless shots. He had represented his college in the photography fests as a leader, and had never stood second in photography.

One of his shots taken at the famous Hotel Taj Palace in Bombay, was published on the Times front page describing the urban side of the nation.

He would always focus and capture the positive aspects of the subject in his pictures. To all, he was gifted. To his professor in college, he was gifted. To his parents, he was the best gift himself.

Kabir looked at Nikita, "This is all yours, please begin to write when you get time. Let me know if you find any to be re shot; we can always come back here again."

"Really, Kabir. I won't mind though, yet it seems to be no point, returning here. Why would we want to come back to Jalalabad? Does Noosh live here? Tell us please. We need a convincing reason."

"Guys, come on, I was just being sarcastic. Thanks, Niks, for your banters, though."

Salem whispered in Meer's ears, "Let us wake up before we are thrown out in the hills."

With a hint of guilt, Meer looked at Nikita with respect, as they were now aware that she was the team leader., "Do we offer you chips, or coke?"

Kabir, handed over a water bottle to them, "Sirs, May I offer you some water, so you can wash your eyes and know that you are here to help us, please?"

With a stern tough look and a hidden smile, he jumped out of the Jeep, raking up some dust.

Nikita dusted off her plain white tee shirt.

"Wow, we have done hundred miles in two and a half hours, terrific! And it has been uneventful."

Their summers were really warm and arid but worth it. Kabul was slightly better than Jalalabad in the summers. The winters would have snow in most parts of this central Asian nation. None of these members would stop talking at any point. They loved to talk. It kept them going.

"Kabir, Are you the tallest man in India?" Nikita asked, with added humor, "I have read and heard from many that most men are short and medium, and you are way over six feet, with Mr. Amitabh Bachchan as an exception."

"I have seen movies too, and, yeah, he is tall but then, you seem to be equal or taller."

"Before I answer that for you, you know Mr. Bachchan is a super star in India. Do you know people queue up in front of his house at a particular time just to catch a glimpse of him? His last movie that I saw was *Deewar*. What a splendid performance, that was. In fact, Mr. Shashi Kapoor's too."

"Aha, I saw him in Shoola."

"Haha, it is *Sholay*."

Salem remembered some dialogues from *Sholay*, and began to act. He became Jai, and asked Meer to play Veeru. In all this, Jemima was *Basanti,* but she was driving and not riding a horse cart.

Kabir was automatically Gabbar, and the entire unit was ready. A few powerful scenes from the movie were enacted. And, it ended with Jemima shouting, *Chal dhanno, in kutho khe semne math naakna.*

"Wow, guys, this was an amazing off beat performance, with only mild pronunciation mistakes."

The day, so far, had consisted of nice sporty events. And, it had been progressing real well. The crew seemed to be tolerant if not too fond of each other. Salem and Meer too did not feel left out. They were bonding well.

Jemima looked at Kabir, "Do you not feel uncomfortable to be led by women?"

Kabir, with a pause and controlled statement, "Why do I feel you have asked this before?"

"You mean like a déjà vu?"

"Yes, exactly."

"And, then, what would you have said?"

"I would still say the same what I said in déjà vu. I am least uncomfortable. I am happy to be led by you girls."

The women were definitely intelligent, and had a good command on the subject. It was all about merit. According to him, there was no correlation with gender. "Now, when I think about it, I realize we have such tremendous gender diversity in journalism. Look around, that CBC woman, our crew, and there are many more."

Both of them got emotional and hugged Kabir. "We are proud of you. Does every Indian male think like this?"

"Yes, in many areas it holds true, not overall though, and the biggest example is of our country being led by a woman prime minister, Indira Gandhi. India is progressing. We have a long way to go, but it is evolving."

"My mother wanted to teach in a school, but my father did not allow her. I hope it soon happens when no woman has to seek permission to work," said Salem.

"Oh, we are so sorry to hear that. Hope things change soon."

Suddenly, Jemima realized how one of her peers, Mary, wanted to start an NGO with a women's forum out there in India. It sparked a nice discussion as Jemima mentioned her name to the group.

"Oh, yes, how she is doing?" Nikita asked.

"She is fine; might join us in winters. We are unsure at this point, though."

"That's wonderful."

"Wow, we are going to be the all-girls crew very soon."

It was interesting to note that amidst all the discussion, the boys were in complete participation too. Salem asked Kabir, "Saab, can you teach me photography? You are gifted."

"Ha-ha," Kabir looked back instantly, Et tu Salem? "Of course, now that you are with us, we will teach you photography, journalism and a few writing tips. You'll have it all."

"Saab, I am serious. Please do so. Perhaps, that is the reason why we had to meet you."

"Saab, please teach us everything that you said, and I promise I shall teach you all non-vegetarian Mughlai dishes." Meer joined in.

While these guys were busy talking, Jemima and Niks were busy looking at the pictures that Kabir had taken.

"This guy is a gem, Jems. Look at this picture. Look at the way, the sky is kissing the mountains, and see this one. Did you even realize we had a horse race in between?"

"Oh, wow, these are huge stallions."

"Look at these men, what are they doing?"

"That's the mini sports arena on the way, and these men are playing Buzkashi."

"Yes, this is an age old traditional Afghani sports."

"I love your camera. Who recommended this to you?" shouted Nikita, as she had walked quite a distance from the Jeep and the men.

"Can't hear you, Niks, be loud."

"Camera…"

"What is with the camera?"

"Whoops, coming to you."

"Come fast, I might run away."

"Hahaha," laughed Nikita, leaving the camera with Jemima as she ran towards him.

Meer said to Salem in whispers, "I am telling you, Kabir saab likes her. Look at the way he is waiting for her."

"No, he likes someone else, he mentioned on the way; maybe, he is fond of Nikita madam, just casually."

"And, do you also remember he mentioned to us about that girl. What was her name?"

"I don't remember. But he said she meant Joy or something."

"Yes, exactly. Now, can you pass on the *garam masala* and *elaichi* to me please?" And they moved towards the stove.

By this time, Nikita arrived, "Yes Kabir, I am here, and thanks for not running away," she said with a hint of naughtiness in her smile.

"Whoops, I hurt my foot I guess, sharp pebbles."

Kabir immediately got some water and cleaned it.Salem had provided a first aid box by now, and a bandage was applied. Jemima was far from all this, and kept gazing at the beautiful stretch of land on the opposite side. And, Salem returned to Meer looking to prepare a nice brunch. They both pulled out the stove and started preparing Afghani chicken.

"Thanks Kabir," said Nikita.

"My pleasure."

"Come, let us go to that lakeside." While they walked, Kabir asked what she had been asking.

Nikita immediately changed the topic, and said she wanted to know if she looked beautiful.

"What? I thought you said camera."

"Of course! I meant do I look beautiful enough to be captured by your camera?"

"*Mashallah*, you are a very beautiful woman. Glad you asked. I would love to take your pictures."

While he said that, he reminisced about Noosh.

"What are you thinking Mr. Lover?"

"Ha-ha, no, no, I am not thinking of her. I was just thinking about the plan to take your pictures and paint your portrait too."

"Really, Kabir? And you did not think of Ms. Joy during this time. I know Photography is your strength and you don't need to go in silence to think of it."

Salem and Meer spoke at the same time. "See, her name is Joy."

"Yeah, you got it. Something just happened to me, and I thought of her."

"Okay, tell me more about her, please."

"Certainly, in time."

"This place is smelling of good food, what an aroma! Guys, this is much better than how it was when you guys had served me food in the hotel."

"What are you cooking?"

"We are preparing special Afghani chicken and Pulao. And, yes, Saab, we got new spices yesterday. We selected these in the bazaar."

Brunch was served on a rug as they sat down in typical afghan *dastarkhan* style. Food was good. Nobody was a guest. They all enjoyed the delectable chicken and pulao.

Nikita said in a humble tone, "Guys, you need to teach me this recipe. This is the best meal I have ever had in my entire life, that I can think of."

"They have decided to teach me the same. You join me while they make us chefs, and I make them photographers. By the way, Niks, can you pull out the map and hand it over to me? We have a 700 mile stretch to cover on this A77 highway. We have done 110 now, and are 40 miles from Kabul. We need to cover Bamyan and Herat in the coming months."

"There are many lakes, as I see on the map."

"It ought to be a breath-taking landscape."

Kabir took the wheels from Jemima now, and they sped away on the stretch of broken roads.

Chapter 4

"Kaal kare so aaj kar, aaj kare so ub
Pal main pralaya hoyegi, bahuri karoge kub."
"Finish your work today, all that you had left for tomorrow
Finish today's work now, for if the moment is lost, when will it
be done."

FINALLY THE CREW REACHED KABUL.

"Look at the beautiful valley."

"This is so beautiful; look at those cluster of white houses."

"Are those Hindu Kush Mountains, in the backdrop?"

"Yes. Just so that you know, even one of the Vedas in India, I believe it is Rig Veda, has mentioned that Kabul is a vision of paradise set in the mountains."

"That sounds very interesting."

"And, 'Kabir Veda' stated that paradise resides in Noosh's eyes... you know what I mean," laughed Nikita.

Within minutes of entering the town, they arrived at the huge Intercontinental hotel. This hotel was nestled at the foot of the Hindu Kush Mountains, with a breath taking view of the city.

The hotel staff was very warm and welcoming. Intercontinental was a very busy place, and it appeared that all of its one hundred and fifty only plus rooms were occupied.

The guests were welcomed with offerings of a glass of fresh juice or *Thhandai* and a piece of *Burfi*.

The hotel interiors reminded Kabir of the partial Victorian and Mughal Style décor. The architecture of this luxurious building was par excellent. The recent rating of this property had shot up after they had added more luxuries for their guests, an indoor hot water pool to mention amongst a few.

"No, no, we don't need porters. We are happy to carry our stuff," said Kabir.

"Oh, Salem, you are also here," said one of the staff members.

"*Arey waah*, Babu, so good to see you. What do you do here in Kabul?"

"I work for the hotel as a driver. I take tourists to the local gardens, museums, lakes and also farther west to Herat and Mazar i Sharif in the east; I prefer driving long distance. It fetches good tips. And, you know once, I even crossed into Iran, ha ha ha, lot of things to talk about."

There were plenty of foreign guests and many beautiful women by the concierge.

Nikita examined the lobby, in detail, and called it The Persian Kingdom.

"Intercontinental in London is nowhere close to this."

The lady at the reception desk, Nafisa arrived, "Sir, we have only reservations for three of you. But I believe you needed rooms for five?"

"No, don't worry about us, we are staying with Babu. He is our old friend. He has offered his staff quarters to us," said Salem.

"Oh, okay. Thank you for letting me know," said Nafisa.

Kabir tried to probe it further with Salem, "Are you sure, else we can check the occupancy, book rooms for you, if not here, then somewhere else?"

"No Saab, we are fine. We are meeting our friend after a long time. Maybe he will teach us to drive."

"Ha-ha, you want to learn it all guys. But we won't let you drive. Our *basanti* won't like it."

"Where is our luggage?"

"Well, sir, we had it moved it to your rooms. Hope you have a pleasant stay with us.

"Ma'am, Ms Nikita, there is a message for you from Ms Monica; please call her back."

It was a pleasant evening as they all went to their rooms on the 5th floor, adjacent to each other.

It was May 20th. No disappointments thus far, they had been having a great time. These people were doing exactly what they wanted to do in life. They were not following their parents' dreams or what society dictated.

Kabir had saved most of his salary to meet any unforeseen circumstances out here. Some of the money put into this assignment was from his pocket, as he would always want to expand the scope of the coverage.

Nikita, on the other hand, wanted to do a lot of shopping. She had heard of beautiful rugs, spices, dry fruits and scarves that were available in Afghanistan, and she wanted to purchase them. Her list was fondly prepared in consultation with her family.

Jemima was a cut above the rest. She wanted to explore the Hindu Kush, and wanted to look for some herbs like madwort, which she had heard of when her mother was undergoing a treatment for Asthma. And, yes, she wanted to stay away from weed. No opium. While her job would definitely hold her accountable for visiting these places, her purpose was a tad different from the rest of them. She was a historian by heart. She wanted to visit the places that were etched in history. Those revolutions. Those wars. The Buddha Statues. All of this was on her mind. She knew this land had a huge significance, and she never knew when she would come next. All the while, she was preparing her own notes on the way, and none included any shopping items, except the herbs.

This was a different world for most of the crew. Less for Kabir though. But, the others were amazed. It appeared, if given a chance they would never want to return to their home countries.

Kabir looked at the calendar to confirm the date, and pulled out his pocket diary that carried some details. He was away from the rest of the crew.

==========

KABIR WENT STRAIGHT TO HIS room.

"Room 505 is open for you, Sir," The porter handed over the keys to Kabir.

As Kabir sat on the couch, inside his room, and grabbed tea, he received a call at the hotel number.

A man's husky voice came through the line, "Are you all set?"

"Back in Russia, when the professor introduced me to you, you were never this prompt. I am very impressed Leonid."

"Yeah, we better be very prompt, else it upsets the higher ups in the agency."

"But, how do you know I am putting up in this room; they just allocated it, and it was never pre-decided, as far as I know."

"We have our people there."

"Oh, okay, so where do we meet?"

"Why don't you pick up today's newspaper and find the digit which is encircled. And, not talk about it over the phone."

"Well, on the 3rd page, do you see an advertisement? See a box there?"

"Yes."

"Pick the 3rd number that is the room number."

"Okay, now go to the last page. That is the hotel name."

So, it was room number 505, Hotel Kabul. This is where Leonid was staying.

"Okay, when do we meet? And where?" Kabir asked.

"You shall receive a call from Yuri in your room, and the taxi will take you to my hotel."

"Oh, so Yuri is my driver, is he?"

"No, you will know him in sometime. Yuri is the operator here in the Kabul faction. You won't know much about him. You just focus on our meeting for now."

He remembered what he was told by his professor, everyone here is safe for now except the rulers and the opponents. That implied even the President Sardar Mohammad Daud could be ousted anytime, even though he'd been ruling since 1973. Kabir was supposed to secretly join this team, or as they called it 'The Directorate' at his professor's behest. He knew it. He trusted him. Wherever Kabir stood today, he owed it to Professor Sizov. It was now known that Kabir always wanted to come to Afghanistan for Noosh. While on the one hand, his profession of journalism was of utmost priority to him, yet he wanted to leave no stone unturned to get to his first love. Professor had paved a path for Kabir to get him this opportunity, however it had come with some baggage.

It was primarily through Sizov that Kabir was introduced to the concerns of Afghanistan and how the Soviets viewed their friendly neighbor. He was told by his professor to come here and be instrumental in saving many lives here and also the socio economic fabric. People were divided into factions. The only way it seemed possible was to be a part of the Soviet intelligence network, Chekas, a well-known Russian secret services. It had spread its wings here over the past few years. The Directorate was deep rooted. Representatives were part of the KGB and the Russian embassy in Kabul was referred to as the 'Residency'. Both had secret agents employed. Kabir did not know a lot about the functioning of the KGB in Afghanistan, except for what he was trained on for four weeks. He did know that he would learn a lot more on the ground, through participation. Invariably, he would also add to the overall cause.

There was a lot going on in his head, and he began to believe that his life would take a great leap forward, and so would his personal experiences. The only conflict was his profession. He was employed by the Americans, and to work with the Soviets might create some conflict. Regarding this, he was assured by Sizov that it would be kept highly confidential, for he should not forget that he was an illegal spy. Everything that happened in the agency was part of secret services.

As these thoughts dawned upon him, he began to read the newspaper. The news did carry some stuff about the disturbances within the current regime. Nothing had remained consistent so far here. Everybody seemed to be wanting to rule here, and a very few wanted to change things for the good, per Kabir's wisdom that he had gained from his professor.

This country is used to being governed by rulers, and not any party. I believe I can help to an extent here, thought Kabir.

This was a moment of peace for Kabir. He still had a few hours before Yuri called him up. He traced his thoughts. Then, he began to sip his favorite Brooke Bond tea.

Kabir talked to his family once a week and, today, certainly was not a day for a phone call. Everything seemed to be changing so rapidly. So were his thoughts. All were random. He took out his cigar that he had bought from Crawford market in Bombay. Then he closed his eyes and disappeared into his own reverie.

==========

He recollected his conversation with his professor that happened a few months ago.

Professor Sizov was the chief advisor in the Russian Secret Services. He had been associated with them for over four decades now. His role was not limited within the USSR, however, owing to his old association due to him being partly educated in the U.S, he enjoyed a thorough International presence too. He could be seen participating in international seminars advocating world peace. Even within KGB, he played a pivotal role owing to his global affiliations.

Much like some in the Directorate, the professor held a different profession to keep his secret role hidden from the normal public. He taught journalism to the students in the University.

Kabir was his favorite student in the college. It was during the early part of January, in the year 1977, in his college in the University of Moscow. That was his last semester.

"Kabir, for the first time, you are late for my class. Are you all right?" asked Professor Sizov with some anxiety.

"Sir, you are such a great man. For you to ask me, even in the first instance, actually puts me on a pedestal."

The Professor waited for the students to go out as his class was headed for a recess, pulled out his cigar, and walked out with him to the garden. Rolling his pocket watch up, that had CCCP and hammer and sickle with a red star engraved on it, looked at the time and, with eyes straight into Kabir's, "Can I ask you something, son?"

"Sir, you are such a great man for you to seek my permission when I am your student, embarrasses me."

"Now that you have called me a great man twice, you must know that great men are wise and cynical. They are perceived to have a vision and knowledge about everything, usually. As my student, I feel you think the same about me too," Professor chuckled.

Kabir smiled.

Professor put his arms around Kabir, and walked with him in the garden.

> *Be motivated like the Falcon, Hunt gloriously*
> *Be magnificent as the Leopard, Fight to win*
> *Spend less time with Nightingales and peacocks*
> *One is all talk, the other is only colour.*
>
> *~Rumi*

Professor looked at Kabir, and smiled. "Son, I have some excellent information for you."

"Really Professor, please tell me."

"Yes, certainly. Hope you still want to go to Afghanistan?"

"Of course, Professor. You know everything. You know the reason too."

"Yeah, I know it so well, yet thought to ask, hope it is still all about Noosh."

"Very much, Professor."

"Tell me, why did you not go after finishing your engineering, when you both studied together?"

"Professor, I don't think I ever told you that engineering was something that my father wanted me to pursue, and I always wanted to be a Journo. So, I decided to finish it per my father's wish and then do Journalism."

"That is a smart move, and you know that is why I am so fond of you. Your priorities are set right."

"Thanks Professor. So tell me what is the good news you were referring to?"

"Well, I know you were disappointed when you were not offered a placement in Afghanistan. Ever since I have been thinking of how to place you there."

"I shall be indebted to you, please let me know now, what is the plan and how to go about it?"

"Kabir, I have a purpose cut out for you. We need to take care of the socio economic status in Afghanistan. I want you to work towards saving Marxism-Leninism in our friendly neighborhood. You need to join the Agency, The Chekas, to be precise. I shall have everything planned well for you."

Kabir was speechless. He sat down in the corner of a garden bench. And then, he immediately tried to hold himself back, "Sir, why would you want that? Are you connected to the KGB?"

"I advise them on anything that pertains to the betterment of society and especially our friends," Professor maintained a brief point of view. Now he wanted to give Kabir his time. So he did not interrupt his thoughts. He waited for him to say something. Then, he walked a little closer to him and, as he leaned towards the iron bench, Kabir moved backwards.

The principles of Marx were ambiguous to Kabir even during his college studies. It was an ideology that Kabir did not necessarily subscribe to.

The Professor wanted to ensure that he had been clear enough to convince Kabir. To him, Kabir appeared to be the best fit overall.

"This is almost frozen, son. How did you manage to sit on it this for so long?" Professor asked.

"I don't feel a thing."

"Since you are in a numb state of mind, how can you feel it?"

"No, I am not numb; I am just not sure what you just asked. I thought you were placing me in the field of my choice."

"So, what are you thinking?"

"This is not an easy thing for me to do. To spread communism and be in the agency, which would mean this would be done as some agent. It isn't possible. I see it as a fight against the people of Afghanistan in a way."

"There is no fight at all. Okay, tell me what is your purpose in life? Do you really want to be like all the others; feel over confident of your achievements; serve people the news, and then feel you know it all?"

The Professor began to breathe heavily as he was getting ready to engage his disciple. He redefined the purpose of Marxism to Kabir in terms of development and not endangering anyone.

"Bringing facts before people, and participating in the cause, have different meanings. You must find your purpose now. I know you would make a great journalist. However, I also know that you would make a better strategist and operative."

His lecture was unstoppable. He wanted to make sure that Kabir understood the larger perspective. He saw Kabir as someone who held the potential, natural demographic advantages, understanding of the region and above all, proximity to him in all positive sense.

It was not clear, yet, whether the professor had decided to take Kabir on with this current understanding, or if there was something else coming his way.

"Kabir, I would have never insisted had I not seen that mettle in you. You are more favorable for other reasons too. You know the languages spoken; you will easily mix with the people and, hence, the *Dushmen* will not doubt you."

He continued to check Kabir's expression while he spoke. His motive seemed positive.

"The color of your skin will help you stay free of any probable trouble that someone else may land in. And, all of this would only be required in the extreme conditions; for the most part, you would play the role of a strategist and work on key programs and initiatives. There is absolutely no fight, I assure you. You will not be involved in any. Take my word for it. It is only going to benefit the neighbors. You shall be my illegal resident out there."

Kabir was quiet. Professor continued in his husky, low, yet very powerful tone.

"You need to travel across the country and work on the objectives set for you. For this, I have something to share with you that shall pep you up."

He was getting a little agitated, as this was the first time he could remember Kabir staying unresponsive for so long.

"Now, do you mind getting up and showing some respect to your professor?

I am your teacher, you must always know that. Should you have an iota of doubt, you are free to continue what you want to do—take pictures, write articles, and sell magazines, newspapers. whoaaaaa."

Kabir was getting incited to an extent, as he knew the professor would only mean good. "I know what you meant professor. All this while, as I sat on this bench, did you observe what I was doing?"

"No." was the blunt answer.

"I was looking at Lenin's statue. I was thinking."

"Come here," Professor said. "This camera is yours now. It is the best of the breed. Send your application tomorrow to The Daily Times. They need an ace photographer and a journalist. I dialed a couple of influential people yesterday. They are waiting for your application."

"Are you serious, Professor?"

"Yes, I don't mince words, and you know it. I saved the best for the last. And, let me remind you. If you do not like what I have asked you to do, you may choose otherwise. You would still continue to work and fulfill your passion for journalism. But, remember, if you ever get caught doing information gathering, you will have no diplomatic immunity."

Kabir was eager to know more about this part. Professor continued to explain in detail.

"Since you are going to be a journalist working for an American company, I cannot recruit you directly in the agency as my man. Unless you want to join me directly and stop dreaming of your Journo dream? You tell me?"

"No professor, I want to be a Journo first."

"Well, I knew it. Therefore, you will only work undercover when required. You must know that, in Afghanistan, the only way we can be successful is by operating secretly. Do note that there are many other countries who have their vested interest in the region and, hence, I want to strengthen our position there."

Kabir looked at the professor with 'I am brought in' expression, and asked him, "Professor, how long have you been associated with The Chekas? Much is said in closed circles about the infamous covert operations that they are into."

By now, the daylight was gone and evening graced the moment.

"I know I can trust you now. Let me tell you before I answer that. Do not trust anyone except the person who commands you in the unit. Now, coming to your question, do you see that tree out there?"

"Yes, I do."

"What do you see ahead of it?"

"I see many things."

"Name a few, please."

"I see houses, lamp posts, statue, a post office", then Kabir narrowed his eyes, "I can also see a train", looks farther away, "I also see a t...t...track and yes Professor, a million stars too."

"What about you Professor? What do you see?"

"Well, Kabir anywhere I look, I see universe. I just see the Universe."

"You mean, I need to widen my perspective. I understand that."

"Yes, and, then, it does not matter whether I have been with them since ten months or ten years. It has always been my utmost loyalty that matters."

In those days, such actions were absolutely normal. Kabir did seek some answers on his job with an American firm when he would also be supporting the Russians.

Professor clarified that there were no issues with it. They exchanged mutual favors, as and when required. While the secret activities and show of military supremacy continued, yet such deals happened all the time. Moreover, he said he was only his medium or a facilitator to help him grow in life.

In the end, Professor was able to persuade Kabir. The reason why Kabir arrived in the country a week before his fellow colleagues was at the behest of the professor who, in his conversation, had asked him to get familiarized with the country by himself as that would help him later. Kabir had followed his advice so far.

==========

KABIR REMEMBERED EVERY WORD THAT PROFESSOR spoke with him. Inside the hotel, in his room, as he began to lift himself up from the chair, he suddenly remembered the wrought iron bench yet again. "Oh, what a child I was."

He opened his wooden cupboard. Then, he pulled out an old piece of paper, folded in countless creases, and took out some crystals. Now bring me luck. He placed them in a corner, and chanted. Show me Noosh. Show me Peace. Show me Noosh. Show me peace, and then he returned to his chair.

I did not realize my cigar, Whoops. I've burnt it till the end. Let me grab the butt. He puffed away on it.

Chapter 5

"Chalti chakki dekh kar, Diya Kabira roye
Dui Paatan ke beech main, sabit bacha na koye."
"Looking at the grinding stones, Kabira laments
In the duel of wheels, nothing stays intact."

EVENING SET IN WITH a leisurely pace. The clock struck six.

The telephone rang in Jemima's room. "Hello there. How is it going for you?" It was Kabir on the other side.

"Hello Kabir. I tried calling your room after the check in, your phone was engaged."

"Oh, okay, my parents had called," Kabir lied.

"So we are all set for tomorrow, right?"

"Yes, with a slight change. We leave at 8 now instead of 9."

"Any reason for the change, Kabir?"

"Yes, that shall help us cover more during the day."

"Okay, great. And what time do we meet for dinner tonight?"

"How does 9 pm sound?"

Jemima did not want to push anything with Kabir, as she could sense he was preoccupied. So she said yes in affirmation.

She put the phone down and looked closely at the itinerary. I am super excited. Tomorrow is the city walls and Moghul Gardens of Kabul, then it is Bamiyan Valley and Band-e Amir Lakes. And, it will be terrific to visit the beautiful Panjshir Valley and then Herat, and how could I forget Niks' shopping. This is going to be simply adventurous.

Suddenly, she was reminded of her brief conversation with Kabir over the phone earlier.

She wondered why he had sounded so pre-occupied. Then, she decided to forget it for now and sort it out with him the next day. For now, she decided to check on Nikita. 'Hope she is not dining with the Americans staying in this hotel' she smiled her way out of her room and began knocking at her door.

Nikita opened the door, carrying The Kabul Times in her folded hands. "Did you see the food sections page?"

Jemima, looked at her in surprise, "Are you sure you want to look at the newspaper to order food?"

"Oh, come on, how could you miss it? This is so exotic here. There is a grand food festival in the hotel tomorrow. Look at the spread, baby. Can we shift our plan by a day? Let us not miss it. We are anyway not returning to our homeland any sooner." Nikita coaxed Jemima

"Why don't you go to Kabir's room and let him know?" Jemima said.

"Okay, let me call him up," she went to the phone and dialed his room.

She reached his voice mail. After the beep, she left him a message. "He must be not around. Jems, I will speak with him when he is around. By the way, I have this handsome hunk as my neighbor. He looks American to me."

"Is he the reason you want to stay back tomorrow? Come on Nikita, tell me the truth."

"Yes and No, Jems."

"I got it. Let us then stay back here. Niks, have you seen these guys Salem and Meer?"

"No, they must be with Babu, learning how to drive."

"And, is that your gut feeling?"

"No, remember these guys were talking about some plans. Hence I assumed."

"I believe they must be chilling in Babu's room. They have never seen a hotel like this before. We can let the concierge know about our plan, so they can pass the message to these folks."

"Certainly, that's a good idea."

Then, they began to discuss their plans in detail.

==========

Kabir had silently and secretly left his room to meet Yuri outside the hotel.

It was 6:45 pm. Kabir felt a mild summer breeze caress his skin as he stepped outside the rear doors of the hotel.

A black Toyota arrived, and slid to a stop in front of Kabir. Inside, on the back seat, was a man whose demeanor and height matched Kabir's; his long legs seemed to disappear beneath the front seat of the car. His sharp focused eyes landed on Kabir, and his small mouth greeted him with a big hello.

Yuri wore a crisp white shirt. His Silk tie dropped from the sharp middle of the collars, like a perfect arrow in the bow. The Italian summer black jacket must have been the most expensive outfit on him. He completed this appearance with a black hat. None of what he wore looked inexpensive. And everything fitted him to perfection.

Kabir complimented him on his outfit.

"Well, this is Italian made. They call it a suit. My brother lives there, and works for the underworld, Mafioso," said Yuri with pride, "I had gone to meet him after I retired from my services at the artillery. I needed his help then."

"Really, this sounds big."

Yuri continued with great interest, "It was his influence and connections that got me a place in the residency and, later, with the Intelligence in USSR. I even went to Czechoslovakia. We have a lot of work there. We keep meddling in the affairs of other countries," he laughed it off with his hands up in the air.

Kabir realized Yuri was no ordinary man. He kept thinking as to why Yuri would come in person to fetch him. He thought that it could be the Professor effect and, hence, he wanted to warm him up and make him feel welcomed. Kabir wanted to give the best impression possible and, hence, he did not appear very inquisitive about these trivialities, though he had a plethora of queries striking his active mind.

Yuri remained silent, and then asked, "Aren't you wondering why I am not wearing a red cap?"

"I am sure there are times when you don't want to be noticed." Kabir responded.

"I am impressed. Just so that you know further, we have been here for a long time. We have played a major role in helping Afghans work towards united party politics. We have built tunnels for them. We bring them materials. They drink beverages as we get it for them. They get it all from us. They get millions of Roubles too.

We want their development. And, we want them to follow communism. That is our aim. We are their friends."

Kabir had grasped the intention earlier, on a few occasions when Professor and he spoke on the subject. "I had a similar discussion with the professor, earlier this year." One other thing that would come out was how subtly their development and communism agenda was merged.

Patiently listening to their conversation was the Pushto driver. While he was the driver, he also was part of the Russian information services. He waited for instructions from Yuri, as to when to drive off.

"Okay," sighed Yuri, "Let us drive down to Leonid's hotel. He is Nur. Has been with us for last thirty years. He will be your driver from tomorrow, for the rest of your stay here."

"Where are you from, Nur?"

Nur remained quiet. There was no response, and Kabir did not insist either.

"So, will he be my driver for all purposes?"

"Yes, till you are here in Afghanistan. Let me clarify, he shall be your driver for driving purposes," laughed Yuri.

"It appears to me, you want me to be here forever. And you are Leonid's confidante. He shared that with me."

Yuri hinted to reserve his crucial discussion points for later.

"Well, if destiny wants it, you might have a palace here, and a hefty bank account. Nur might be forever in charge of your duty, who knows."

"Well, I would want to take someone from here to Bombay, you know."

"Are you in love?"

"Yes."

"Is she the reason that stopped you from going to Switzerland?"

"She lives here, and also professor wanted to pick me for Afghanistan."

Yuri felt that he was getting personal and, therefore, he corrected himself and now meant business.

"That is great, so how did this induction with the Directorate happen?"

Kabir too wanted to switch over to another discussion point, "I have been given a lot of freedom by Professor Sizov. If I do not like it, I can exit anytime." Kabir responded and tried to gauge his position with Yuri.

"Yes, that is correct. We know that. But why do you talk about exiting even before joining formally?"

Kabir responded, "Cmdr. Yuri, I want to fix things, and do it the right away. Tell me what my job is. Oh, I know Leonid needs to tell me that."

The conversation continued for a few minutes before the car arrived at the hotel. The *durban* opened the door.

"Did you just give him some currency?" asked Yuri.

"Yes, I did. I was always taught to tip these folks."

"Okay, now onwards, you are not supposed to socialize to this extent with anyone except the ones you are being asked to. Nobody should remember you. When you do such acts of generosity, people tend to remember you forever."

"Isn't Nur anyway supposed to remember me forever? Leave it. Tell me who shall train me on these aspects? Would it be naïve to ask this, right away?"

There was no response for a minute and Kabir wondered why he was rude.

He entered the lobby thinking about his role in the organization.

"There are some Do's and Don'ts that you shall receive soon from the Chief. We call it literature, and it is utmost confidential." Yuri informed Kabir.

"I feel important, suddenly. I feel like a King. Aha, the savior."

"We are aware that you are in a profession which is all about stories and glam."

"No, you are wrong. I am in a profession which is all about facts. You may consider them stories. There is no glam, certainly."

"How difficult would it be for you to absorb all of this and refrain from sharing in any form?"

"Do you not have some sort of psychometric test? Some test paper? So you can confirm if I am the right candidate. Also, to set the record straight, I am here to help and not seek any favors."

Kabir appeared candid and fearless. At least, he was trying his best to give that impression; inside he was slightly nervous.

"You are already part of the close circle. This was more of a small talk. Remember, we would always be watching you, just kidding."

"You never asked me anything about my family, my interests, and my soviet affinity? Are you guys usually this odd?"

"Do not mind, and please do not feel offended if I tell you that we have all that information about you."

"Okay, I am certain of that. First of all, I am pleased that for the first time, you were polite. I love this place. For my own reasons," suddenly, Kabir stopped as he knew he might just get carried away. Moreover, Yuri was nonchalant too.

Kabir was fascinated by the other side, or so called less known. In this case, it was all unknown to him thus far. He had no clue how it was going to be from an execution standpoint. He wanted to wait for his meeting with Leonid so that the purpose is well defined, in addition to the overview that Professor had given.

Yuri and Kabir reached the 5th floor now. The lift stopped with a rumble that could be heard. "Aha, this is Honeywell. Made in U.S.A."

"Yeah, they have done some construction here."

Yuri opened the door. Kabir looked puzzled.

"Why wouldn't the chief open it from inside?"

"Come, take a seat," said Yuri as he reached out to the minibar. He evaded the question. The suite was big, and from the appearance it made, there were two or three rooms.

"What do you prefer?" asked Yuri.

"You still haven't answered my question. And, now, please do not tell me that asking questions is part of your Don'ts category under your ordinance or literature."

"Haha you are a smart man. Professor certainly made the right choice." Yuri was leaving no room for him not to feel confident about his abilities, so he continued to extol him. But he also made sure to tell Kabir his flaws, telling him that he was very impatient and childlike at times.

Kabir registered it in his head. He was unsure of how he could work on it.

"Okay, Kabir, you shall get all your answers. Tell me what you want, else I will offer you Vodka.

If you want to help yourself, please feel free. However I am aware, in Bombay, you prefer to be hosted when you are a guest. Right?"

Kabir smiled and said, "Well not just in Bombay, it holds true nationwide. Considering, I spent about six years in Moscow, it is understandable how these things do not matter to me anymore."

Yuri wanted to be escaped for some time and told Kabir that he will be back in a while, and let Leonid know of his arrival. Kabir stretched his body and extended his arms towards the bar. He decided to pick a beer instead. He began to enjoy the Bee-thoven in the background, and, drawing the curtains aside, he could not resist appreciating the beautiful night view outside the hotel. The corner palatial suite seemed to have been specially carved out for Leonid.

In about fifteen minutes, he saw this slightly healthy man appearing from inside.

"You are not Leonid, are you? Ummm, well, where is Yuri? You look somewhat different than when we met briefly with the professor. Yes, it was dark, so maybe I don't remember your image much."

"You still talk so much. Did Yuri describe me any differently? I have just gained a couple of extra pounds, that is all."

Through a precision eye, Leonid appeared about an inch shorter to Yuri. He seemed to weigh a few extra pounds over Yuri. Donning a Russian cap, smart beard and a long mustache, he looked no less than Marlon Brando or some other real Mafioso.

If anything fell short in his persona, his lit up original Cuban Cigar, Red crossed Cufflink, and white dial Omega wrist watch made up for it.

While looking into Kabir's glaring eyes, he turned on the television.

"Do you watch news?"

"Yes, I do. What else do you expect from a Journo? I see lot of news and, that apart, I also tune in to some local Persian music shows that they show in between, and, yes, I am extremely fond of Mr. Amitabh Bachchan's movies. We watch it all the time on the recorder."

By this time, Kabir was so engrossed that he did not even talk about Yuri, nor did he ask him anything. Leonid had that charisma. There was a deep defining voice that kept guiding Kabir. He seemed to be in awe of Leonid. At least, that was the impression being formed. There was still a doubt whether Kabir thought in the same direction.

"Chief, you are a good speaker. You talk well. You look influential too. You must be raking in the rubles. You must have amassed a huge lot of Golden Rubles in your bank account, by now."

"What do you want to hear Kabir? I am like any other Government employee who is doing service to humanity. The money goes in the pockets of the party rulers here. They take money from Americans and Soviets. At times, it is even hard to know whose side they are on.

It is utter chaos. This is why you and I are here. People like us find the rats and moles. I do understand, this is not what you wanted to do. I also understand you want to do a lot. And, you believe in us.

You must know I have served the artillery before. I found out about hundreds of traitors, while serving there and I got this job. This is a tougher job, indeed."

"You look very tough on the outside, Chief. I am also impressed with your command over English. My professor would mix Russian when he would converse."

"Your Professor must be not drinking Vodka, like I do."

"Ha-ha," laughed Kabir.

Leonid mentioned how any development done by Americans and Chinese in the region was a big threat to the socio economic fabric of the nation. According to him, it was a threat that needed to be curtailed. The only way was to strengthen their own presence, and by means of secret operations, they would bring success. It sounded simple, but was not.

He appeared firm. However, it wasn't sure if Kabir had placed all his faith in him yet.

By this time, Leonid mentioned further about his relationship with Sizov. He had married his daughter. Kabir also had some unconfirmed report about Leonid from Andropov that, at some point, Leonid had charges of fraud placed on him. Professor had bailed him out of the situation, and now Leonid was serving his second chance, his only chance. There was no way for Kabir to confirm that with him so early in their acquaintance, but that did continue to play on his mind. Also, Leonid did not mention to him much about his past. One other revelation that Professor never told Kabir was about his daughter being married to Leonid. Maybe, he did not find it relevant, or forgot to mention if. If there was any other reason, Kabir was not aware of it.

"You mind if I get another beer?"

"By all means, the bar is yours to savor. These are the perks that come with the job. We feed people Vodka and their choice of drinks, so they do not complain about wages." He kept walking smartly inside the room, and, then, after a couple of minutes, he made his way to the cupboard. He pulled out a well-drawn and detailed sketch of a human face.

"This is how you will look like on the days of operation."

Then, taking out another sketch he said,

"And, this is mine. This is how I look like on some days."

Kabir, with a little surprise looks at the sketch, "But this is how you look like anyway? What is so different?"

"I thought you would react at yours. That means, you liked your disguise."

"Yes, I do. This is quite a bit of makeup and makeover."

"I like the fact that you raise the right questions at the right time. You still know you will get all the other answers, anyway. I also like the fact that we are good at disguising ourselves."

Kabir understood it all by now. He quickly gulped the second beer. Without wasting any further time, he immediately got up and walked towards the window. Without facing Leonid, he asked how he did it, "You are just not recognizable, Yuri. I mean, Chief."

"Don't fumble. You need to do this on some occasions, and I will guide you," Leonid briefed him, as he stood behind his back. He continued with much assertiveness now. He spoke about the disturbance in the President circuit and the national political party. "There could be a coup. If this continued there won't be much peace, and that is the role of an operative, to find out moles in the system and weed them out, as I said earlier."

Soon, Kabir was told that his code name would be Yogi. Leonid handed him a gun, and said, "This is the latest expensive equipment that we procured from Italy. Keep it with you at all times. Take this briefcase. This has all that you need. And you may address me as Yuri."

Before Kabir could ask why he would need a gun, Yuri told him that it was for self-defense.

"And, yes, your friends want you to stay back tomorrow. You must listen to them. Spend some time around the city. When you step out of the hotel, leave your bag on the mirror table. And, yes, gun with you at all times."

Kabir knew such operations and intelligence was beyond his comprehension at this point, however, in times to come, he would gain a significant hold and would only use it for good purposes. To him, covert meant it could be a positive conversion too.

These guys are very powerful. Not sure how many people like me they have planted all across the country and, maybe, in many others, Kabir thought in his head.

As he stepped out, Yuri said to him, "Well, Nur shall drop you back. He will be there waiting for you. One more thing, Kabir, next time we meet, leave your camera behind. You will only carry your gun. Another key thing, you need to take out a packet from this and push it inside room no 507. You need to do this at sharp 9:48 pm tonight. That is your neighbor. He is your American neighbor, Mr. Jonathan."

"Okay, Chief. I shall do the needful. Hope I am all set now. It has been my pleasure to see you in person. May I ask you something? How does Dedov look like?" He knew he had asked this before, but he had not received a convincing answer.

"You'd be surprised to know he looks like me. And, I am not Dedov, in case you think so."

"Okay, it is good to have that information. At some point, I would like to meet him."

"Before you leave, I must assure you, if you are good, he would like to meet you. Now you take care and must have a good rest. Oh, one more thing, before any next step or plans, you must read the book inside the briefcase. It has just a few points for you. And, this is a secret. Good night."

"Goodnight, Chief."

Leonid was code named Yuri, just like Kabir was Yogi.

Kabir gained knowledge that Yuri and Professor Sizov appeared to be close to each other. He also knew by now that there was actually a point when Yuri almost defected to London, however, it was Sizov who came to his rescue. Yuri was not somebody that could be trusted. He was under the scanner. Hence, it was more important for him to change his perception in the Secret Agency circle. He was on the job. He seemed to be thinking of using Kabir for his own gains.

Kabir staggered his way out of the hotel. A light film of dust had settled on the car as Nur waited for him outside the building.

The light from the street lamp fell brightly on the layer of dust and highlighted it. Kabir subconsciously swiped his finger on the car and confirmed the presence of dust.

On seeing this, Nur immediately jumped into the action. He took a piece of neat cloth and cleaned the side of the car that Kabir sat was sitting in.

Kabir apparently seemed relaxed from the initial expressions he gave to Nur. After getting inside the car, he closed his eyes and tried to catch up on a short nap.

"Saab, do I play some nice Hindi music for you? I have this from the super hit movie of Bachchan Saab."

"Yes," came an instant reply.

Nice soulful music from *Abhiman* played in the background. Kabir kept humming along slowly. This was his old time tactic to beat his inner stress. More often he has been quite successful at that.

Meet na mila re man ka....

Meet na.....

Nur kept talking in between, and then kept mum when he failed to get any response from his new boss. Kabir was actually extremely tired today.

He clarified to Kabir as to why he did not talk much before Yuri, and that came across as part of the instructions provided to him.

Kabir carried mixed feelings. Now was his solo time to think-Gun? Disguise? Conflict? It did not exactly match with Professor's version, though it was not too different, either. He wanted to give it time and thought for now, it offered a good learning opportunity for him.

All his conversation, so far, with Sizov and Leonid were around helping the Afghans. It was not about launching any covert operations yet. But, then, why would Leonid talk about western influence? Did it mean that Russia wanted to rule here? It was more about establishing communism. Such thoughts were normal for anyone who was perceived to be taking a new role in the new dynamics.

As he woke up after a disturbed nap, he felt he had some clarity. He knew if there is something really secretive that even he did not know, he held the power to bring it out before the world. The only dilemma was the trust that was placed in him now. Hence, he believed what he was doing was correct.

He had not compromised with his professional or personal integrity. The two aspects should not be mixed together. One was a professional responsibility, and the other was a duty that he needed to fulfill like a brave man. And, he never considered their Russian rebels, his enemies.

His friends were primarily from the west and also from Moscow. The crew he worked with was all western. The students he befriended in college were mostly Russians. All this was fairly complicated. Professor had used contacts in the west to place Kabir in the media agency here.

The links between the professor and the Americans only meant that he had a tight rope to walk on. He was too new to the subject. Or, maybe, such international 'Chanakya' style matters might stay in his head to keep him curious for a long time.

Time will tell what he unravelled during the course of his journey. For now, he was on the mission. Rather two missions. Or one and a half. Other half being secretive. Or maybe one. Yes, it was that ambiguous.

He took the road less travelled. He trusted the Professor and was guided by his instinct at every step he took. He looked at this watch as he reached the hotel. It was 9:40 p.m already. He rushed to the room and slipped the envelope beneath the door.

Then he reached his room, and introspected deeply. He thought that the political situation of this country was least supportive of the development here. The conditions were not very ripe, and how he as an individual could contribute in any possible way, maybe the time will tell. For now he kept himself grounded and balanced.

Chapter 6

"Chinta aisi dakini, kat kaleja khaye
Vaid bechara kya kare, kahan tak dawa lagaye"
"Worry is the bandit that eats into one's heart
What can the doctor do, what can the medicines offer?"

AS THE MORNING HOURS SEEPED in, the days ahead predictably appeared to bring about many changes, and new developments as the mission of this American employed crew had an illegal resident in it.

The doorbell rang on Kabir's room, as he swiftly got up from his teak bed in his corset. He wrapped the bed cover around his waist, flowing down till his knees as he half opened the door.

To his surprise, Nikita and Jemima had showed up. He immediately closed the door. They both giggled.

"Kabir, we just saw your face and nothing else. And yes, you look dapper in this white wrap around," said Nikita.

Kabir looked embarrassed. "I wasn't expecting you guys, thought it was the newspaper man."

He wore his clothes quickly, opened the door and, before he could speak, Nikita began to talk, "Don't worry, we are not coming inside. We had gone down for breakfast, called your room and, when there was no response, wanted to make sure you were all right, and so we come here personally. Last night too, you did not pick up our calls. We were worried. We got more worried when someone in the lobby mentioned about something weird happening on the 5th floor last night. And hence, we wanted to talk to you."

"Weird, what do you mean?" questioned Kabir.

"We did not delve into it, as we were more worried for you. Were you tired and asleep? You did not pick up our call."

Kabir remained intensely quiet.

Before Nikita could complete her statement, Kabir asked her if cops had come to the hotel? "Did you notice anything? Did you find anything untoward, yourself?"

He knew, if Nikita felt so and did not delve, that does not mean he can let it go. He felt this might be linked to room 507, where Jonathan stayed and eventually have some connection with the Russians.

Blood rushed into his head. He got uneasy. He did not know where to begin. He turned back to Nikita, and told her to meet at 10 a.m in the lobby. He wanted to buy time, so he could investigate from his end from his end in the interim.

Nikita observed the sudden changes in Kabir, but preferred to keep silent. Jemima was a shadow away from her, and could not hear the conversation. Upon seeing her turn back with a questioning expression, Jemima could not resist asking, "What happened? What did Kabir say?"

She changed her posture at once, "No, nothing, Jems. He seemed tired. He needs some time. I was slightly upset as I saw our local plan for the day seemed hindered. He shall meet us at 10."

"And, breakfast?"

"He will have it in his room. Let us plan the day ahead during our breakfast. So we are ready when Kabir is."

"That sounds great, Niks."

==========

In the room, it was time for Kabir to open the briefcase that Yuri had handed to him. There was an envelope. He cut it open without a thought. In Russian, there was a card that read as 'Thank you'. A mere glance at the items revealed the nature of the work that might be involved in the future, for it included material for disguise too. It also included a Semi-automatic Barrett 72 in a holster. In the side pouch of the briefcase, there was an expensive looking pen, a notepad and some device, which he did not quite recognize.

The letter welcomed Kabir to the agency. It was duly signed by Dedov, and directed Kabir to keep an eye on his neighbor, Jonathan.

It appeared slightly abrupt to him. Even though he was young and fearless, it did bother him to some extent. The intent in the letter was twofold. One was to welcome him, and second was to test him, to see if he could solve the neighbor mystery. And, it quite successfully seemed to be achieving the purpose. Kabir did not return the gun or the suitcase, and had followed all the steps so far.

The other material in the briefcase must have significance at some point. And, I have to retain it with me now, grumbled Kabir.

As he walked downstairs, he kept thinking randomly about the direction in which he was headed. He wanted to meet Yuri one more time, for some reassurance.

His resolve was unshaken though. He knew he would be here and do things rightly. He was yet to find out what actually happened on the floor.

Before he did that, he called the Professor and spoke with him briefly. Professor guided him to meet Yuri, and also mentioned that per direction, he must find out more about the neighbor. Professor also added that Yuri was very sharp and there must be some positive intent behind his motive. He was told of his meeting with Dedov and him next month. This calmed his frayed nerves.

As he reached the lobby area, he asked for Salem. Nur showed up in no time, "*Saab,* you need me?"

"How do you know I am here, Nur?"

"I was supposed to report here at 9:30, Saab. Is all okay?"

Kabir attempted to hide his terrible state of mind.

"So, I came here to let you know that he has returned to Russia. He is strengthening the directorate. He wants to leave no stone unturned."

"Is that why he sent you here?"

"*Saab*, you can confide in me. I know a lot here. I find you a good man. I have been a close aide of Yuri. Most of the operatives here are ferried by me. Come with me. As Nur spoke, Kabir had his hands around his shoulders and walked along."

Kabir asked Nur if he knew Dedov, to which Nur mentioned he drove him just once. Kabir had begun to trust Nur.

"Are you aware of what happened here last night?"

"Yes, I do, to some extent."

"Nur, I found out about my so called neighbor, and wanted to convey to Yuri. The neighbor is no American. He is a Russian."

"Great, you achieved the purpose then. Last night there was a little fire in the hallway. That created chaos, nothing else."

Yuri had a plan. He wanted to create an environment for Kabir, where he would lose focus and, hence, it would matter how he acted upon directions in a tough situation. While it did create some confusion, yet Kabir figured out from the Hotel register, that he was a Russian. The way he signed in the register was not an American handwriting. It was Russian style.

Kabir was successful in his task.

This man, so called Jonathan had left the place. He was merely planted there temporarily.

"Do not worry, *Saab*. This is one of his tactics to surprise a new comer. That letter you mentioned, this so called frivolous act, is his own way to show you how he runs covert operations. He, in a way, wanted to induct you into his team."

"Yes, I mean, one after the other. First, the disguise and, now, this. Well, he tried it all with me," Kabir suddenly stopped talking, as he did not want to speak everything in his mind.

"He was testing you."

I was anyway fully trained in all this, but this man was way too sharp, Kabir said to himself.

Before Nur could respond, Kabir nodded his head "Hell, yes. He has been quite successful."

Kabir, without any further utterance, returned to his room. This time, he took the elevator. As instructed by Yuri, he put the gun around his waist. Then he pulled it towards his back. It was tucked under his shirt. The thought of how he would roam like this openly struck him, and he took the gun off his belt. Instead, he put it in the holster, and placed it firmly inside the briefcase. He did think of returning this metal piece, yet again, however, he was not a coward per his own account. So, he firmly believed, he would confront it all.

He decided to plan his day under a nice hot shower. This one seemed to be lasting forever.

Yet again, his stress buster for now would be none other than Kishore Kumar from Mr. Bachchan's movie. There have been quite a few stress buster moments for Kabir in the past few days.

> *Kabhi Kabhi Mere dil me, Khayal aata hai*
> *Kabhi Kabhi Mere dil me, Khayal aata hai*
> *Ke Jaise Tujhko Banaya gaya hai mere liye*
> *Tu ase pehle sitaron main bas rahi thee kahin*

....

He dressed himself in formals and chose to wear very crisply ironed steel grey trousers with pleats, staid blue shirt, a Zodiac tie, and kept a golden nib old style Sheaffer pen in his shirt pocket.

Most of his clothes were brought in Russia. Some were still saved from his Bombay collection. The tinsel town offered some of the best clothing lines. It supplied textiles across India and to almost all other parts of the world. A part of wardrobe, that was picked in Russia, was made in India. Mostly in Bombay, as one would have thought.

Without wasting any more time, he slipped into his hand made shoes.. His father had gifted it to him, and mentioned this was made with very fine leather in a place in India called Kanpur, and the sole was assembled in Agra. Both these places were known for leather and good shoes.

A horse shoe symbol was engraved on the soles of the shoes. It was a symbol for good luck.

Spending a brief minute in front of the mirror, he pulled out the map and focussed deep on the highlighted areas. Then he marked about a few odd places on the map. Thereafter, he put a date on each of those. The marks were from the memory he carried while at the hotel, when Yuri pulled the drawer out. There was this atlas that had similar markings.

He picked up the briefcase, stepped out taking big strides, and went downstairs.

Kabir always had this habit of altering his routes and timings of doing any repeat tasks. He would keep any observer or a spy guessing. He was one half, himself, now.

As he looked at his watch, it was still 9:20, and that gave him time to observe things around. He did not follow the obvious, that was, sticking to 10 a.m. as he had committed to Nikita.

Being early is no offense, Kabir thought in his head. He used this time to familiarize himself with the hotel and the staff too.

==========

Chapter 7

"Mala pherat jug bhaya, phira na man ka pher
Kar ka man ka dar de, man ka manka pher."
"Eons have passed whirling rosary, yet mind remains restless
Give up the beads of rosary, and rotate the beads of mind."

THE LOBBY WAS FILLED with people. It had a very characteristic chandelier, more visible now, than when these folks had arrived. The view outside the lobby was panoramic, and there were two doors, one in the front and the other in the back of the hotel. A beautiful, finely hand crafted blue and crimson Persian rug donned the length of the floor.

The artefacts were the best one could imagine. Most of the clocks were handmade, that is, the ones that weren't were either USA or USSR labelled. In the lobby were small plants, like bonsai, of almonds and pomegranates. It seemed that Japanese also influenced the multi ethnic and multinational culture here. The seats were upholstered in satin and velvet. All of them were occupied. It was a busy hotel.

This country had extremes. The cities were overcrowded, while the terrains and national highways were mostly desolate. While Kabul was a big city, more populous than Jalalabad, it also became evident that this city was more advanced, too.

Locals and tourists had all thronged the place. Europeans, Americans, and people from many other countries came around as tourists. Russians were here like their second home, or rather their own home. Despite this being home for the communists, the need for covert ops and driving one's own agenda was very vital to the sustainability of their existence and the spread of communism. So, this was a known factor now. Not a secret anymore.

Nobody knew who were here for business; who were tourists, or if they were spies. It definitely was frequented by folks from the Agency all the time.

One of the key characteristics of Kabir was his urge for writing details down to the wire. He had a big notepad to use, provided in the briefcase, although he had a choice over whether to use that or one of his own.

Being an engineer by qualification, and an artist in his head, he would write and draw features with ease. That was clearly explained by the hotel lobby map that he drew while standing. While he spent a good thirty minutes engaged in his own work, he also used the time to find out further about Jonathan from the hotel staff. They feigned ignorance.

Within a few minutes, Nikita showed up, emerging from the breakfast hall. Her lemon grass smelling body lotion travelled before she did, now it was mixed with the smell of coffee.

"It is nothing like Kabul inside. This is all so western, Kabir," said Nikita.

"Yes, you and I are responsible for it."

"Guess what, I left my stomach half empty. I want to try some real Afghani food. I have been told we have a special invitation from the Minister in Kabul for lunch today. Also, we have a dinner invite for tomorrow from the American Embassy here, which will include folks from Britain too.

They mentioned, it is a point here for this invitation as a stretch of courtesy for any western media who is here on official tour. Their emissaries were extremely apologetic for the miscommunication and, hence, the delay," added Jemima.

"But, isn't this an invasion on our privacy?" said Nikita childishly.

"Come on," Jumped in Jemima. "It is a special invite to us. They must have missed it. Let us follow the courtesy extended to us. I see no reason for us to doubt them. Let us oblige."

Kabir wanted to stay away from any controversy. He only suspected the timing. Nonetheless, he liked the idea.

"Yes, of course, Jemima. We must. We will. And, you both smell of more coffee than all of Brazil put together. Looks like you have been having coffee all morning."

"Whoops, is it? Anyway, is there anyone else on the list or just us," asked Nikita.

"Usually, they have a list with them ready; I believe there would be more. It is a good opportunity for us to interact with more people. And, also know the more influential people here."

"Customs, Rituals?"

"May be we can carry wine."

"No, I don't think that is a good idea"

"Oh no, I was talking about the dinner at the embassy."

"Still, no. Let us pick a rug or a craft item."

"Don't they have those in plenty here?"

"Hey Kabir, why don't you give away your camera?"

Haha, they laughed.

"And, none of you told me earlier about the camera that you are carrying."

"Well, we all were given cameras by our boss, Kabir. You knew it. Only you figured the one you have, your personal camera is better than the one we got here."

"But, I like Leica more."

"My preference still would be Minolta."

"See, I was gifted a top end Nikon, and that's it. We would use this. Yours would be secondary, or to be used as a parallel. Whichever has more meaningful stuff we shall use, okay?"

"Hang on, I am missing something? Where the heck is my camera?"

Kabir suddenly realized that his camera was not on him. He did not remember if it was in the room. He had certainly carried it into his room.

He suddenly left them, "Folks, I shall be right back."

Nikita wondered, and looked at Jemima, "Didn't you observe a weird state of mind exhibited by Kabir? He does not seem to be himself."

"Yes, he looks baffled. He is certainly not himself. Without any presumption, let us confront him. He cannot hide anything. His expressions reveal it all."

While they were talking, Samir and Meer showed up.

"*Salaam,* Madamji. How have you been? We had a great time with Babu. Hope you enjoyed your evening."

"*Salaam* to you both. Yes, we had a relaxed evening. All of us had, in fact."

"But, we saw Kabir sir, leaving with someone last evening. He was with a foreigner like you."

"You mean, he was with a woman? Are you serious, guys?"

"No, no we did not mean that. He was with a man, driven by a local."

"This is giving me a severe migraine now," said Nikita.

"Let us not forget my palpitations," responded Jemima.

"Please say something so I feel better, Jems."

Salem and Meer began to feel that something had gone horribly wrong, and it probably wasn't a great idea to share the news about Kabir.

They tried to improve the situation. "It is possible that he wants to give you a surprise, and so he went out to plan something. Maybe you will find out about it later."

"Not possible. Knowing Kabir as much by now, he is not that candid. He keeps a distance. And, none of us is Noosh here, either."

"Well, the only better thing I can tell you, Niks, is that we need to confront him right away. If it is a surprise, he would reveal it, and it is okay. If, no, then we need to know what he is hiding from us. Unless he is some goddamn spy to snoop on both of us or anyone else, that we are oblivious to. And, yes, we are nobody from that standpoint. Oh hell, I cannot think straight. I need some fresh air." Jemima walked out of the lobby and stood near the smoking bay.

Nikita went aside to grab some coffee.

Salem looked at Meer in angst, "It seems we have bitterly messed up. May be Kabir *saab* is a spy."

"I knew it from day one. If you have observed him carefully, his tall height, his deep eyes, camera, his clothes all resemble those villains from Bond movies. And, don't you remember the other day, the way he addressed us as innocent people? Did you notice that smile behind it?"

"Hahaha. But I feel he resembles James Bond, more than anybody else. He is a hero. He cannot be a villain."

"Okay, if you insist. Now we need to save him an embarrassment from these women. If we leave Nikita madam's sight, she might come chasing us."

"Okay, why don't you go up to Kabir *saab's* room, Salem? I am here to keep guard."

While Salem was going up, Kabir came down from the other staircase, route altered, yet again.

"Whoops," shouted Meer.

"What happened kid? He immediately looked at his fly. This is shut, too."

"No, nothing. Saab, Salaam. Please come here."

"I need to quickly share something important with you." said Meer in a hurry.

Nikita came around.

"Hey, Kabir." Without a minute getting wasted, she held his hand and took him out of the lobby, to where Jemima stood, watching the view.

Kabir walked with floated steps.

"Kabir, you know what really happened on the 5th floor, don't you?" asked Jemima.

"That is why you kept being inquisitive. You are hiding something you know." added Nikita to the flurry of questions.

"That is why you were his neighbor. Weren't you?"

"Who is the man you had gone with?"

The flurry of questions, required a decent explanation for the ladies to be calm.

"Oh, my God. How'd you know all this? How'd you know that I killed that man?"

"What?? You killed that man for real? You mean there was a murder?"

"Yes, how'd you know that the man I left with was the plotter and they had come to kill you guys? I saved your life. I told them you are in room 507 and he blindly shot at the room."

"Oh, my God, but why?"

"And, you believe this?" he said.

"What? So what is the truth?"

Kabir was certainly trying to dodge the question.

"Ladies, I had planned a surprise for you. So, I had gone out. And, yes, I know some people here already. Do not forget, I arrived here before you both. Now, can we plan our days ahead, since there is a lot to be done? And, yes, you guys should be sorry for the commotion."

"So, what was that 5th floor incident all about?"

"No, nothing, somebody was smoking in the aisle, and the carpet caught fire; that is all."

"We are extremely sorry for doubting you. Shall we?" as Jemima asked both of them to proceed inside the lobby area.

Suddenly, the lobby turned vacant.

"Wow, hard to believe. They have all disappeared in 60 seconds."

"Yeah, either we spent more time outside, and did not realize. Or this is something else."

The guy at the reception, hearing them, came forward, "Sir, there were three groups here, so the buses came for the day tour. Hence, they all left."

"Oh, okay, thanks for clarifying."

Salem and Meer showed up. "*Saab,* I am glad Salem met you while you were coming down. I was nervous when I saw you coming from the other side."

"That is history guys. What else do you know?"

"We know nothing more than that Saab. Babu mentioned he knows Nur. He has connections with those James Bond kind of people here. Also, I believe, with ministers and all. Nur is usually spotted with foreigners or ministers. So, when we saw you going with James Bond, driven by Nur, we almost knew you are some big man. And, these two girls are just to help you achieve your goals. Trust us, *Saab,* last night all three of us only talked about you."

"Okay, man. Thanks for sharing with me. Give me thirty minutes. I shall come back, and then we are driving to the city, before heading for lunch at Minister Shah's house."

"Okay, *Saab*. Would you prefer Babu as your driver, or Nur will take us now?"

"I am not sure at this point. Let me speak with Nur."

Kabir realized there was a definite atmosphere of mistrust here. He did not want to carry this guilt, for he was not a spy and he wanted to come clean.

"May I have you aside, please?" Kabir said politely to both the ladies.

"I want to confide in both of you. I also want to let you know that I cannot carry this guilt of being unfaithful. I am not a spy. I cannot be one. I cannot cheat you. I cannot cheat anyone. At least I want to clear it up from my head," Kabir, in a very short span of time, gave all the details about his activities with the Russians to them. But, he made sure to only give the bare minimum of facts required to ease their fears. He did not tell them about his upcoming meeting with Dedov, or his training in Russia, or that fact that he now had a gun of his own. It was more about the meeting that had already taken place.

"What's next, Kabir? It seems you are caught between fire and hell. We have many further questions, however, at this point, we want to help you. We are your friends, your peers, your buddies here in this land. Who else we got? It is just us. So stay assured. Tell us what you think." Jemima said with reassurance.

"Further to what I said, let me tell you, I am not taking part in any covert operations. I was blinded. Rather I was forced to be blindfolded. When you are in that state, and somebody asks you to run till the finishing line, you want to feel competitive against yourself. You don't want to let yourself down, as you believe you owe it to yourself," clarified Kabir. It was his moment to fight back with his conscience.

He also mentioned that he trusted his professor, but he found Yuri untrustworthy.

"In this case, it was like a deed I owed to myself. Well, It helped me to come to Afghanistan too; I won't deny that. Overall, I saw it as a positive challenge. I wanted to tread the path of wisdom and glory. I was made to believe it was a task, and I needed to finish it. Moreover, I need to finish it with my eyes closed. That is what covert was supposed to be. If I open my eyes, then I might see things that would hinder my run. Things that would hinder my intent. I saw it, and understood it all when I was shown this sketch. It was confirmed further, when I saw this map from the atlas in the chest of the drawer, that Yuri pulled out. It had these cities marked. I understood this was dangerous. But, if they found me as a perfect recruit, I found a perfect opportunity in this. And, the bottom-line is, I will work towards development, only, no matter what."

The ladies were awestruck as they heard him spell out the events.

"I can withdraw if I want to. I was told that I can pull myself out, anytime. I was so much in awe of them that I thought, no matter how hard I try, I have landed myself in a cage. A cage that has no public view around you. You are caught."

Kabir began to feel lighter and better. He was more committed towards the cause of humanity and he stood by it.

"So, to answer you Jemima, life goes on normal for us. And, yes, with one big change. We definitely need to cover the cities that were marked in the atlas; I need to ensure now that I am more observant, and so should you all. We need to make sure we do our duty and fulfill our responsibility. And, yes, this remains amongst us now. Let them protect communism. We need to protect the humanity here. That is above all."

They knew, in the name of Communism, it was all about Imperialism, the control.

Jemima stood up and began to applaud, followed by Nikita. They both got emotional, and hugged Kabir with greater comfort.

Nikita was the first one to speak, "I am slightly choked, but I can tell you Kabir, you are an excellent human being. You deserve another hug from me," she held him tightly and did not leave him till Jemima came around and hugged them both. The quick second hug was followed by more.

Salem and Meer had left them in private.

All three held their hands firmly. Their relationship emerged stronger now.

"And, Kabir, in these testing times, when hands are held so strongly, they never fall apart. You must know this."

"Yes, I do, and I believe it."

Nikita asked him to be cautious now. The ladies suggested him to confront Dedov and the Professor, and let them know that he wishes to exit it.

Kabir heard them.

Melodious sufi music played in the background. Kabir could immediately grasp the lyrics, and the singer and started humming. Both the ladies enjoyed it and called it soulful.

"I am glad, the hotel plays nice music," said Nikita.

They readied now for lunch. Nur sat in a corner of the hotel. That was the drivers' designated waiting area.

Nur walked towards Kabir. "Saab, I just wanted to let you know, you are on your own now. I overheard a part of your conversation.

Do not worry at all. I will not be with you. I will be at your behest when you need me. I won't share a thing with Yuri."

Breathing a sigh of relief, Kabir instantly grabbed Nur's shoulder. "I hope this is not some other trick. How could you leave me so easily?"

"Nobody trusts anybody here. You think Yuri trusts us? He only plans to use you, that's how I look at it," said Nur.

What Nur said to him got him thinking.

Babu had arrived by now.

==========

Chapter 8

"Dosh paraye dekhi kari, chala hasant hasant
Apne yaad na aavayi, jinka aadi na anth."
"We laugh when we see shortcoming in others
But we forget our own long list that is endless."

IN THE TOWN OF HERAT, the same day, the much talked about development activities were in progress. This town was well funded by the westerns, especially the Americans.

The afternoon was sultry and dry. The sun had almost moved away from mid-sky towards the white clouds, filtering through it and creating a prism like haze. It was primarily white and blue. Temperature was around 39 degree Celsius. There were hutments. There were some buildings under construction. It appeared that rail track construction work was about to begin.

One could see boulders and heavy machineries placed around the area. Some of the local kids were busy picking the sand and bricks to play with, and could be seen just running away. The contractor and his men could be seen hurling local abuses at them.

Suddenly, a Ford Mustang Cobra arrived on the scene. It was covered in dust. There were kids running alongside the car. Some were trying to race, some were trying to touch and falling on the way.

The car stopped at the door steps of an old building. It was a two floor, Moghul style building. Front of the structure was carved in stone. A few sparrows were flying across. And, some were sitting inside a carved niche.

Two young women came running outside, and stopped right in front of the rear door of this Ford's robust Mustang model.

One of them tried to open the door; immediately, the driver intervened, "If you don't know how to open them, then why do you keep trying it every day?"

The driver, Jafer, though a very polite man, seemed to be getting frustrated with the daily attempts made by these women.

One of the women turned back, and said, "Why don't you first clean your car?"

"Don't you know I drive through areas that has all mud and no roads?"

A beautiful, petite, young Persian emerged out of the car, wearing a smart *salwar kurta*, head covered with a deep embroidered Persian styled scarf. She had deep shining brown eyes, and they were glowing. She wore a nicely beaded *mala*. It had some precious stones adding to her personality.

"Hello Noosh, good to see you again. You look beautiful as ever. This is a very lovely scarf."

As the conversation continued, Jafar drove off the car to the cleaner.

Noosh waved at him, "Take care Jafar uncle." Jafer was like a brother to her father.

Inside the palatial building was a lobby. The lobby had a chandelier similar to the one in the Hotel in Kabul. The building was segregated basis the activity that was being performed.

Sparrows were seen on the top of this office building. The hall was covered with iron rods on the top. During rains, the water poured inside the building into a specially built receptacle.

From some far end, hawkers could be heard selling fruits and dry fruits.

It was lunch time now. *Dastarkhan* was being prepared. The *Khansama* had yet again prepared delicacies.

"Uncle, today, you need to let me know the recipe for this special *pulao* and *mutton korma,* and even this sweet *phirni*."

What followed was the dictation of the recipe and Noosh scribbled it down quickly in her notepad.

The recipe dictation continued until Noosh had all the information that she needed. "Thanks Khansama Uncle," She expressed her gratitude to the self appointed chef.

A fellow member of the group asked Noosh, "Today is day three of our self-defense class. Shall we do some revision steps?"

"Okay," and the women gathered in that room began to warm up for the practice.

Noosh, along with her American counterpart, Lisa had been operating an NGO from the hotel premises for quite some time now. The Russians were unaware of most of what happened here. For this reason, they wanted to spread out to regions like these where most of the work was funded by America. Most of the positions were filled here, except for that of the project head. This particular vacancy had only been rolled out in closed circles, so far.

Noosh was staying in the hotel in Herat, though she had her house here, only a mile away. It was part of the appointment that she could not have stayed with relatives, and was supposed to be staying in the same hotel as Lisa. She had no option, and hence abided by it.

Outside, in the room next to the lobby hall area, were about a few women who were studying and preparing for some exams. They all knew English, Persian and Afghan. A couple of them could converse in German too, and Russian, with much ease.

The discussion among the members turned to Noosh, "Is Noosh not appearing slightly upset today?"

"Yes, exactly, I noticed that too."

"Shall we ask her why she is upset?"

"No, I believe we can give her some time and check with her in the evening."

"She seemed perfectly fine after meeting *Khansama*. Maybe, she was hungry."

"Oh, now I remember; I believe she was infuriated after Jafer spoke to you rudely."

"Yes, possible, nonetheless we can check. But, definitely, it was not the hunger."

Small talk continued.

Noosh and Lisa Dwyer were deep in conversation.

"Hello, Noosh. I know you must be very frustrated. I have told the government to send the funds sooner. This time, Bill seems to have goofed up."

"I tried looking into the finances. There is a huge gap. Against 75000 USD, we received 45000 USD. We still do not know where the money is going. Some say, it is with the ministers. They want to use it for some operations," Lisa said on the disappearance of a part of the funds. They definitely needed a project head and direct money allocation.

Noosh was about to say something, but was cut short by Lisa as she was beginning to take charge.

"Others say, it is still with the Government and there are some clerical errors. I have no idea. At times, I feel, they do not value what we are doing."

"Oh, my God!," shouted Noosh.

"What happened?"

Noosh pointed a shaking finger outside, and Lisa joined her to look outside the window. Jafer had been shot at and the police from the nearby check-post had run to the scene. The police-post was adjacent to the highway, and was always very busy. A man was killed in broad daylight and, within minutes, the place was deserted except for the cops. The contractor, the laborers, the children had all disappeared.

Noosh was gasping in a state of shock. Jafar was dead, murdered under the bright sun, now surrounded by people.

The ladies had encountered a murder, for the first time in their life. It was gruesome. She was clueless. He was like family. She was disconsolate.

The inspector looked around for any possible clues, and continued to talk to Lisa.

"Yes, we can tell you that the way he has been killed suggests some foreign hand. This is my view for now. We shall tell you more when we have more information," said the inspector.

"Tell Noosh Madam the same. Control her. She is howling," the Inspector continued, as he left the spot for his investigation. The body was taken away for post-mortem.

Lisa had never seen Noosh like this before. Never so inconsolable Never so agitated.

Jafer had always been there for these ladies. He was working for the purpose. About a couple of years ago, when Noosh had visited Herat during her summer break from Moscow, Jafer and his family had taken care of her. At that time, Noosh's father was in Kabul working with the ministry.

Jafer was extremely close to the Americans. He usually drove them to wherever they wanted to go... Being a local, the place was well known to him.

There was chaos all over the place.

A couple of hours later, the contractors showed up. The scene was back to normal.

The activities for the day began to wrap up much before the defined time.

Lisa and Noosh headed for the hotel they were staying in.

They were transported in another local taxi.

"We need to go and meet his family, as soon as we can."

"Yes."

"Do we go to the hotel first?"

"No, we must go to the police first."

"Oh, okay. Let us do that."

One of the local boys came running out of nowhere and stopped their car midway.

"Madamji, please do not go to Jafer's place. There are locals going mad."

"Do not worry; we will go with the cops," said Lisa.

"I am a local here, so I will take care," said Noosh. Finally, they decided to go to the Hotel first.

The ladies reached their Hotel in Herat. They sat down for a discussion, but Noosh was still not able to come out of her distress.

This was crucial for them, for they suspected their lives might be endangered, too.

"Okay, let me call up the embassy. I still believe this is a bigger conspiracy. Things have not been looking fine, over the last few days. There have been severe money issues. And, now, this murder has taken place."

During their discussion, Lisa shared with Noosh some information about three crew members from a media agency arriving in Herat. The investors were the same as their NGO, so the interest was common. This news puzzled Noosh. She noted one of them was Kabir, and there was Jemima also in the group. Jemima and Lisa had worked on an assignment together at some point. She also mentioned the minister's lunch invite to these people. It came as a rude shock to her that they were not even informed of any such gathering, leave alone an invitation courtesy.

"You mentioned to me, some time back, about this man called Kabir."

"Lisa, can we talk about it later?"

"Okay, but we must. I am trying to build a context here. He arrived here a few weeks ago. He is close to the Soviets. All that is happening here has only begun in the last few weeks. The interesting part is that it is speculated that Russian reference landed him a job in an American agency."

"What are you talking about? He and I studied together. He is a brilliant man. Yes, he was the best student in the class. He would solve all math puzzles fast. Once, he made a tunnel system that was unimaginable. That was just one of the many things that won many a teacher's heart. Then, he switched his stream to Journalism, and became Professor's favorite, as I heard from many of my friends. He wanted to marry me. But I refused, as I wanted to come here, and he wanted to go to the U.S. That is all I know." Noosh defended Kabir.

Noosh finished a half-liter water bottle while stating these hard facts. "I still do not know why he would want to come here."

"That is exactly what I am telling you. I had some information on him from the U.S embassy," said Lisa and sneezed.

"Bless you."

"There was some mention of an operation. I am forgetting the word. Once I recollect, I will let you know."

After their discussion, they headed to the police station.

A cop escorted them inside.

"Madamji, we just received a call from the US embassy. They want to ensure you are safe. We are placing one guard with you 24/7 now," cop said.

"No, we don't want that," Lisa said.

"Yes, we want to be free. We are safe," added Noosh.

"I am sorry, but that is an order from the higher ups," the cop replied in an assertive tone.

"Oh, Gosh. This is insane."

While they went to the police station with an intent to discuss the incident in detail, it ended up as an extra security cover for them.

They were strictly asked to avoid going to Jafer's house, and returned to the hotel with no significant development.

During the course of their discussion earlier, Lisa had asked Noosh why she had decided to join the Americans despite studying in Moscow. She explained how her father had worked towards the welfare of the nation in the ministry, but he was made a scapegoat when a certain money fraud happened. This appeared to be the same case that Yuri was a significant part of.

There was a lot of internal politics. It was seething. There were cracks within the system. Many were engulfed in the same. To ensure the safety of their workers, Americans tried their best to work through their own internal network. The same was now being extended to Noosh and Lisa.

Noosh had reserved a part of her discussion to be dealt with on Kabir's arrival.

==========

Around the same time during the day in Kabul, at the Minister's place, the function had begun. Minister Shah was the close confidante of the President. He enjoyed a great relationship with the Soviets. It was upon the request placed by the agency, that the entire arrangement for the get together today was made.

"So, how are you finding your stay here?" enquired Minister Shah.

"It is wonderful. I simply love the hospitality here. I truly appreciate your invite," replied Kabir.

"It is our pleasure," Minister Shah responded politely. "Let us go to the best room in the palace."

Kabir was amazed to see how well it was built.

"Yes, this is our treasure. We built this with a lot of pride. Some of the artefacts here are from your country. We love what people in Bombay and Hyderabad do. Remarkable. Not to mention, how big a fan I am of Mr. Amitabh Bachchan. Also, of Mr. Raj Kapoor."

"Yes, sir. The entire nation is," beamed Kabir with a glow on his face.

"I just got some information of certain killings that took place in Herat." said Shah. "I must tell you, the perpetrators are Americans. They are behind all this. We need to stop it. Did Yuri speak to you about Project Skylight?"

"No, he did not speak much about it. He just gave it a brief mention."

The information that the minister carried was that Skylight was solely aimed at exposing financial trails whereas, in reality, it was also designed to get closer to the American network and gain access to the classified and confidential American intelligence information.

Minister Shah handed out a document containing several confidential details. It included names of the people responsible for Afghan's success and those who could be trusted.

This list of people mentioned in the document could not be suspected. The country was divided on views and, hence, it became crucial to have the support of people like Kabir, who could send positive message out to the world while being in close Soviet proximity and, now, his too.

It wasn't certain if the list had the hand of people like Yuri. It could only be assumed they might know as his name did feature in the same.

"These people belong to one of the national political parties. They are always willing to take the nation to the next level. We have a good alliance with the other parties too. Together we are working towards building this country. We have amassed a huge support from the Soviets. Financial as well as strategic."

The minister had a slightly different point of view on communism, though, for the large part, he shared the common view. It could also been driven by the money he received from them in the name of development.

"You shall be guided further."

Kabir knew there was nothing new in what he was hearing, so he nodded.

Shah continued.

"And, how about your dinner plans at the embassy tomorrow? Just be aware of Captain Mike; he is very shrewd. I won't be surprised if he is the one behind the killings in the Western region," Minister remarked unexpectedly.

Kabir was lost. He was caught unawares. He had no clue what the minister was talking about. Minister was very blunt and candid. Kabir maintained a balanced tone.

"Which killings, sir?"

"Many. We will talk in detail."

"Sure, Minister Sir. If you permit, may I take your leave for now?"

"Of course, please enjoy the rest of the day. Do read the document in detail."

He got the required intelligence. He only wondered how the minister did not know of his unwillingness in any of these projects; in any of these covert operations.

I don't know why. I can always figure that out, Kabir thought. "Hi Niks, Hello Jemima! Hope you guys did not miss me too much."

"Come on Kabir. It seems you are a star guest here."

"We have been enjoying the courtesies here. Food is the best I had in years."

Good music was playing in the background. From Beethoven's symphony to Kishore Kumar's songs and Mohammed Rafi's *nagme,* all kinds of music livened up the atmosphere.

Kabir was soulfully lost in the music. He was listening to these songs after a very long time. The minister's personal assistance, Razak, took centre stage with the mike and began to address the gathering.

"Ladies and Gentlemen, thank you so much for being our lovely guests for lunch. Hope you enjoyed the pleasantries." Razak said.

"We wish to welcome our visitors from Russia here, Mr Nokowic, Mr Rostov and our guests on mission here, the beautiful ladies Ms. Nikita Pina and Ms Jemima Miller; and the lovely man, Mr. Kabir. Also, with them are their personal assistants, Mr. Salem and Mr. Meer.

Also, would like to thank our generous Minister Shah and all our leaders here.

In this moment of happiness, I do not want to miss an important announcement. Some of our nationals have been killed in western Afghanistan. In all confidence on behalf of the nation, I assure you we shall leave no stone unturned to find out the culprits behind this. We are all committed to each and every one of us.

We would like to thank our Russian partners for offering relentless support.

A while ago, we got some information of the killing of Jafar. He was the brother of our very close aide- Nur. He was doing some brilliant work, out there. We are saddened by this loss.

We must extend all our support to the family. I have instructed our administration to look into this with a fine tooth comb and share the report with us within 48 hours.

Thanks, again."

There were handshakes now. Some people showed concern. Some spoke about minister's travel plans to Moscow.

There were also some discussions on strengthening the representatives and also the residency, much of the discussion focusing on operation Skylight.

Kabir was assigned the task to read the document, but he also thought this was the right time to go to Herat.

He was stunned and shocked at the news of Nur's brother. It also took him a while to figure out the extremes, with one brother on the Soviet side, and the other in the American team.

Kabir and the crew spent some additional time here after the lunch had finished.

After he had read the letter that contained details of operation Skylight, and as the evening began to draw in, a very careful and pragmatic Kabir decided to meet the minister. This one resulted in a fast paced conversation between the two.

Kabir: "I read it."

Minister: "That was quick."

Kabir: "I disagree."

Minister: "I knew it."

Kabir: "To use funds for relief purposes for your gains is not right."

Minister: "It is our money. Did Sizov not give you any briefing?"

Kabir: "How do we strengthen the use of funds, then?"

Minister: "Exactly why I need you."

Kabir: "Not to steal funds, please."

Minister: "If I may reiterate, it is about our own funds?"

Kabir: "Let me look into it and help assess."

Minister: "Meet Jamal. He will guide you upon return in a month's time. It is our land, and hence we need to control things here."

Kabir: "Leave the rest to me. Thank you."

Minister: "I am glad you understand. Thank you."

What made Kabir's position strong before the minister was the outcome of his journalism education in Russia; his intellect; employment in an American agency; proximity to the Soviets, yet working with the Americans and his strong relationships with the locals. He could yet be trusted. More than anything, his closeness to Sizov and trust in each other could not be taken for granted.

Kabir knew further engagement in the discussion might be a deterrent. This was good. He had an opportunity. He could help. He also knew the mention of Noosh meant trouble for him if Minister found out she had studied with him. Even If he already knew about it, Kabir knew it was best to be silent.

"Kabir, please note one more thing before you leave. Noosh's father was a minister with the President. She is very strong headed. But, she is working with the Americans. You are close to Soviets more. Take care of yourself and your friends."

Kabir left. He knew he was being softly warned.

Nikita and Jemima followed, and all three erupted in talks.

"Oh, the food was awesome."

"Yes, we had only gone for food."

"But, they did not invite us just for food."

"Yes, we could see that."

"Is this going to happen tomorrow during the dinner, as well?"

"Knowing Americans and British well, they are direct. More direct. I assume it is going to be wine and dine."

"For now, let us meet Nur and offer our condolences."

Upon reaching at the hotel reception, Kabir asked the front desk executive, "Did you see Nur around"?

"Yes, Sir, he was looking for you. He left this note for you."

Kabir tore open the envelope. A very quickly written note read as below.

Dear Kabir Saab,

I am extremely saddened with the state of affairs in our region. I have always been loyal to 'The Representatives' and 'The Residents' alike.

My brother has been killed. It seems to be a foreign hand. I do not know. I trust you. Once you find out, let me know. I know the police is looking into this. They will look at it with a different eye, since they are aware I am closer to the Russians. The police out there do not like Russians.

I know the minister, himself, has asked for a fair probe. I seem to only trust you. Just to let you know further, my brother was working with funded money.

That money belonged to Americans. But he did not do anyone harm. That could be the reason of his killing. It could be anyone here.

I hope you found this letter sealed. And, I know you are aware as to how to find that.

I am leaving immediately for Herat. Meet you there.

Yours truly,

NUR 'Jack'

He immediately checked the seal to find it intact. It was now revealed that Nur was code named Jack. In time, Kabir would want to find out more on this.

So far as Jafer was concerned, he knew the best would be to reach Herat and find out more from his end. For now, he believed he had made a good impression before the minister, while not forgetting what Nur had mentioned to him. Nobody trusts anybody here.

This letter had shaken him to a vast inexplicable degree. Many a time, it did hit his mind to share with the western media, his employer primarily, on the state of affairs in the country. He avoided it as he was not in a position yet to take any side. This cannot be a one sided story; even the Americans must be engaged in some or the other secret plans, Kabir thought.

Once he got hold of something, he would find the right contact to share the information with, and that would be his biggest win. To share just the news upfront with the media was ruled out.

His faith was shaken, and it looked like it would only deteriorate further.

Chapter 9

"Tinka kabahu na nindiye, Jo pawan tar hoye
Kabahu udi aankhin pade, toh peer ghaneri hoye"
"One should not even abuse a blade of grass under one's feet
For it strikes one's eye, then it causes immense pain."

"On MAY 27th, MORNING 0700 HOURS, we leave for Herat," Kabir announced to his colleagues. "And that leaves us with 2 more days in Kabul."

As one would expect, the next day's newspaper carried many news, and it appeared the judgement was passed. The news media was run by the political loyalists. It carried the news that there was a western nation hand in the crimes.

They will print what they want people to read. This is not right. How do they know without any fair investigation; that this has the hand of rebels? Why is the Afghan media a mouth piece of Russia and so biased? Kabir thought.

This was well discussed within the crew. It was hard for them to derive any conclusion yet. The interesting part was how one was blaming the other. This was the beginning for Kabir to get inducted in the country. He was no more a beginner. He felt responsible.

Jemima and Nikita were warned to be extra cautious during the embassy dinner that day. They decided not to talk about the discussion with the minister, fearing it might have some serious outcome. The rats could be anywhere. They had to be as far away from this as possible, and operate only secretly. Hence, it should all sound as a very normal customary meeting.

Kabir had started taking some subtle decisions for the team, and it was well respected too. This included the discussion agenda, travel plan, team expansion plans, and the strategy to deal with the ministry and their office likewise.

Understanding the crucial situation, Nikita even offered him some guidance. She mentioned how her father could be of great help, and he could be well trusted as well. Kabir mentioned that he would let her know at the right time. Political circles in London or the U.S was not something he believed would play much of a role at this stage. Nonetheless, he made a note of it.

That day, Kabir spent much time with the hotel staff and local shop owners. Not everything was as perfect as it appeared. He was even cautioned to be on alert when he reached Herat. Situation could be different from what it appeared in Kabul. The capital city was the resident of many landlords and rich business men, however Herat and its nearby areas had the farmers and small time artisans etc. He prepared some notes and a schedule that would come handy in Herat. Nikita, although the official team lead found it completely okay.

Kabir seemed to have transformed vastly over the last two weeks. He was near perfect in his approach. His conduct, tone, body language combined with wit, earned him a greater network in a short time span.

Towards the evening, the group was all set to head out for the dinner.

Upon arrival at the dinner hosted jointly by the British and American Embassies, they received a grand welcome. This dinner was planned by the chief secretary in the Embassy, Michael Dean.

"It is nice to see that the tradition continues here," Kabir told Jemima.

"Oh, yes, Americans do not like to see another America when they travel outside."

"And Indians look for Indian food every once in a while, no matter where they travel. Haha," laughed Kabir.

"Well, even Americans look for Indian food."

"What you are eating is all akin to Indian. In fact, you get most of this in India. I still miss the Pulao we had in Jalalabad."

While the crew walked in towards the corner of the lobby, Michael arrived.

"Hello Nikita, Hello Jemima, Hello, Kabir. Welcome and thanks for being our lovely guests tonight."

"Hello Mr. Mike. How are you?"

"I am as good as you are, Kabir."

"We wanted to make sure we do not repeat what you ate yesterday."

"Oh, you know what we ate yesterday?"

"Yes, of course. We sent our men to discuss the menu and ensure it wasn't poisoned," laughed Mike.

"You seem to have an excellent sense of humour Mr. Mike."

"Yes, my mom says I was born with that. My wife shares similar thoughts, which happens rarely though."

"Haha," laughed Kabir.

"You are an intelligent man."

"Oh, thank you. But I consider you far more intelligent. I am still learning."

"Only an intelligent man finds me in that category. I have been blessed with humor and intelligence. Much like your professor," guffawed Mike at his own remark.

"What about professor?"

"Well, he is definitely a good man He is on good terms with the global diaspora; we regard him with high respect. He is one of those who would never cross the line."

Michael had high praises for the professor. It was through Michael that he had influenced the placement of Kabir here. It was apparent they shared a bond. Kabir did find it awkward, but he exercised restraint.

"You know why he picked you?"

"Why?"

"He saw a reflection of himself in you."

"How often did you speak with him?"

"See, I told you. You are an intelligent man. I just shared some thoughts about your favorite man, and here you are coming straight to the point."

Michael came across as a good man, composed and not stiff, at all. He appeared trustworthy. Kabir seemed way too reserved now.

Mike could gather Kabir's feelings from his bizarre expression, so he began to soothe him, "Look, Kabir, he wanted to take care of you. He saw you as his son, too. I know because he made those references on occasions with me.

He is a definite Soviet Loyal."

"Then, why would you like him?"

"He would tell me on my face that he is a loyal, yet he meant no harm. He would confide in me about the lady he fell in love with. We had more of a personal connect. There was nothing official about it."

"How did you meet him?"

"Just like any other Russian could meet an American. I became fond of him when he wrote this beautiful book called 'The Captives'. It had details of soviet invasion in the early century. He is a fearless genius. All his participation in any operation was to kill the enemy in the front; take a bullet to save his friends, and treat his foes with respect. He never stopped smiling, even during the tough times. He is an inspiration. Some of the people in my circle hate me, for my fondness of him.

Professor had played a mediator role in resolving the conflicts between Romania and Czechoslovakia, too."

"How do you keep the loyalties intact?"

"What is that? You need to be loyal to yourself. Integrity is of prime value. I am the right judge of human beings. I am honest with those I like, and dishonest to the core with those who I want to eat up. This is why the minister hates me. Not because I am an American. It does not matter to him. You may be from anywhere in the world. If you offer him gold, he will be your servant and behave like one, too."

"So, you want to eat him up?"

"No, no, not him. There are quite a few in his own network who would chew him up. He does not realize it."

"Oh, how much I miss my professor. I wish he were part of this conversation."

"Yes. Kabir, do you mind if I ask you something?"

"Sure Sir."

"Come, let us step outside."

"Here," (Mike offered him a tissue). "In every practical way, you landed here to do the most practical thing of being a journalist. You wanted to meet Noosh. She belongs here.

Everything started moving for you in that direction. You had strong reasons to come here. Now you have an additional motive, which is to help this country further.

In every practical way, you did not slip on any grounds of morality or integrity. So far, you score 10 on 10.

You would start losing marks when you get to know that you were going to support the people who killed Nur's brother. Now that takes away the practical aspect, and moves you to the phenomenal aspect. You are on the verge of executing the phenomenon. That phenomenon is a disaster that cannot be recovered. They have profiled you. They might have bugged you too. Kid, you know nothing. Just take pictures. Write nicely. Do not endanger your life or the life of the innocent citizens here, and keep me posted on whatever you find further.

I would love to see you and Noosh together some day. I pray for your goodness. Noosh's father served in the ministry, and is known to me. He is a good man, on our side. If you need anything, you can always send me a telegram, letter, or call up the embassy.

I head back to Washington tomorrow. There is some investigation we need to do for the funds displacement; the amount is paltry, yet there could be a mole. We need to discover that. Whatever you find, I need to be aware.

And, yes, I have my men who shall help you to find out the perpetrators behind the killing game up there in Western Afghanistan. We are very strong there. It was very unlikely to happen. My wishes are with you."

Michael gave Kabir enough reasons to trust him strongly. It was only getting stronger. Kabir seemed to have found his local connection. Kabir and Michael discussed at length on how things should be approached from future perspective. If Kabir were to find any more information, he would inform Michael. In return, Michael would provide all the help that Kabir needed for his tasks.

He even mentioned the security cover provided to Noosh and Lisa in Herat. Kabir listened to him patiently.

"But, why would you do this for me?"

"Professor, Noosh, her father, are these not good enough reasons? More than anything else, I need someone who understands it all, and you are the chosen one." Michael realized Kabir was on his side now. He asked to be excused, with a firm handshake.

Kabir could only be seen feeling more than comfortable. He did get emotional, too. He did miss his professor.

"Kabir, you look so rattled. Your eyes are swollen," asked Nikita in a state of shock.

"Yes, Niks, and say I cried too."

"Oh, my goodness, let me get you some water; you are in a bad state. Oh no, Jemima, listen, can you take care of my sweetheart?"

"Kabir, what happened to your eyes; did you just cry?"

"Oh no, don't ask him too many questions, Jemima. He seems to have had a glass extra."

"Ladies, come on. Can't I have my moment?"

Nikita held Jemima as Kabir walked to the restroom.

Michael was seen leaving the place.

Kabir looked at the mirror. He started blabbering. I need to do what I deem is right. I do not know who to trust more. I shall do what is right. And, yes, I will not deviate from my values. I miss you mom. I miss you dad. I miss you Noosh.. I love you.

I am coming.

I miss you Professor. I trust myself. I trust you...., He carried on in this manner, then he jerked himself upright and washed his face.

Was my drink spiked? Hell, my father always said, drink in the company of people you trust. No, no..I think I had a glass extra....

Oh, dear Lord. Oh, the lord of Khorasan."

A few things had gained a greater clarity in the last couple of days. The minister wanted to gain more control over financial matters. The public announcement regarding the perpetrators behind Jafer's killing seemed farcical. On the other hand, Michael had discussed it personally with Kabir, so he retained genuine interest. As a true journalist in the know-how of so much so soon, Kabir had to find the real culprit and also look into the financial matters within his own capacity. It was a great day for him, for he had established a true connection with Michael. His worry about sharing the information was alleviated. Michael was his go to person. The perspective added a new dimension.

As the folks got back to the hotel, Nikita called up her boss. She spoke briefly, and discussed a few things on the pre scheduled call. She spoke good things about Kabir, as the seniors in U.S wanted to know the situation on the ground. It was more or less decided that Kabir shall assume bigger responsibilities in the region. His engineering background was suitable for the project head role in Herat. This transition would not be tough, as the media group, as well as the company running projects, had common board and investors, and they would agree with the decision.

For now, Nikita did not talk about her conversation with anyone.

Chapter 10

"Kabira soota kya kare, koore kaaj niwaar
Jis panthu tu chaalna, soyee path samwaar."
"Arise from slumber O Kabir, divest yourself of the rubbish deeds,
Be focused and illumine the path that you were meant to tread."

THE MUCH AWAITED DAY HAD arrived. The crew was all set for their trip to Herat.

The morning was very pleasant. There was a sense of relief in the air. "Sense of a relief for most of us. Do we not feel free? Let us celebrate our freedom. We are the global citizens, yes," shouted Nikita.

"Kabir, by the way, you looked very funny last night. I believe some ghost gripped you. Ghost of Mr. Mike. Captain Mike. The Mike," she added.

She began to imitate Kabir and Mike.

"And you guys were following me," said Kabir

"No, we just passed by you both a, few times, and the best was, when Mike said, come Kabir, let us step outside."

"You guys find it funny, huh. I was so conscious and alert. You know these guys in the agency cannot be trusted at all, except the Professor."

Yet again, the crew cautioned him to watch his steps and actions and focus on the job at hand. Overall, they were able to cover a good part in their scribe. It covered the country and its conditions in good detail, from whatever they could understand. The submission would take a few more weeks, and Herat would play a major role.

"And, guys, guess what, who did I miss after that extra drink?" asked Kabir

"Noosh, of course."

"And you both."

"Really. We are honored Mr. Kabir."

"May I ask you something personal?"

"Feel free."

"Why do you never use your last name?"

"Oh, there is a reason behind it. Kabir was a great poet. Philosopher. Thinker. And, he was found by his parents."

"So, were you found by your parents?"

"No, that is not the case."

"Then, you are a poet, philosopher?"

"It means a warrior. The name has significance; do you really need a last name to support it further?"

"That is nice. It is very rare for anyone to do so. I don't mind doing that. Imagine, if the world over, there is only your name. Hey, that is very interesting; how about our pets? I had a Whippet breed, and we all know pets just have their first name. Imagine a pet, imagine my dog named as Simba Shepherd or Simba Whippet, funny."

"Yeah, it seems, Niks, you are going to revolutionize this."

"Kabir, I am thinking to drop my last name, too."

"Me too," quipped Jemima.

"How about your would be husbands? Won't they object?"

"Revolutionize. Right? That's what you just said, so who is going to seek their permission anyway?"

"Yes, I trust you ladies."

"Kabir, you are a big influence on us."

"Salem, Meer, why are you guys so quiet today?"

"Oh, they seem to have slept off."

"Babu, *sambhal kar chalao gadi bhaiya,*" said Kabir.

E"Babu, Please drive the car carefully, brother."

"Ji Sir, sorry, jhapki lag gayi…"

E"Sure Sir, Sorry, I caught a nap."

"Arey toh utaro aur mooh dholo."

E "Then, please get down and wash your face."

"Niks, pass on the bottle please."

Babu washed his face. Kabir took charge at the wheel.

"Sir, now I am fine."

"You know Babu, there is much more fun in sleeping after washing your face; I have tried it. You will feel better."

"Ouch," shouted Nikita.

"Whoops, this terrain."

"The country needs you Kabir. You need to build roads and tunnels and tracks here."

"Hey, Babu, wake up now."

"*Ji,* Sir."

Kabir pulled out his notepad and began to draw the details of the area.

"Get off, Kabir, and build it now; you are such a show off."

"No, no I am just so much into it; maybe, some day, when we finish our assignments."

"Assignments?"

"Yeah, finish the work for the magazine and construct roads, tunnel, and contribute towards infra too. I am glad I did engineering; being here on the ground makes me realize there is so much to do."

A few maps, typewriter, ink pens, Cameras, easels, ropes, knives, shopping bags, gun, small gas cylinders, cooking utensils formed a quarter of Toyota truck. All of this was neatly packed in jute bags, except the gun.

"This is a huge country."

"Yes, this is the Heart of Asia."

After two days of traveling, they reached Herat. It was stopped at one of the check posts. Babu reached for his ID card.

"What is this Babu?"

"Wait sir."

The cop looked at it, and lets them go without a question.

"Do we not show a driving license or jeep registration here?"

He showed the ID card that had minister's signature. Babu had served as minister's personal driver for quite some time.

"You are the biggest man in our group, Babu."

Babu giggled.

They were not too far from the Hotel.

==========

In the hotel in Herat, Noosh rushed out of her room, she waited patiently for Lisa in the lobby.

"What happened, Noosh? Why do you look flummoxed?" asked Lisa.

"I have some news for you," said Noosh with a near pale expression.

"What?"

"I received a call."

"From?"

"The police station."

"So?" Lisa wondered.

"Kabir has arrived in town."

"Yeah, so? He anyway had to. Didn't we know? Are you nervous?"

"No, no hang on; oh, hell. I cannot think straight, Lisa. How the hell, sorry, they are here definitely to botch up the case of Jafer, you were right."

"Now I have my doubts, Noosh." said Lisa. The tables seemed to have turned as Lisa defended Kabir.

"Then, why would they enter using the minister's name. They have other ways to prove their identity."

"It does not matter, Noosh; you are over reacting. The Journos have free passage anyway, so you need not think much about this," said Lisa.

Upon hearing a positive version from Lisa, she retracted her line of argument.

"I know Kabir. He is a good man, and he is determined too. You never know, he might be playing to the gallery. The minister in Kabul planned a get together, and they discussed some operation, you said."

"But, that is not certain, and we are supposed to confront him; calm your nerves."

"And?"

"Let us not be judgmental here; it is very complicated, anyway."

"Okay. I hear you." said Noosh.

"He is staying in our hotel. I received this letter from Michael's office, in the morning. It was sent by Kabir via his office," said Lisa.

Noosh was only surprised as to why she had not revealed this yet. However Lisa clarified that she did not give her a chance to speak at all.

Then Lisa added further. "The letter says that we all have things to fix here; be prepared. See you. Isn't that nice; if he were to hide, why would he want to be here with us?"

"I hope so. It is just that the memories of the recent incident, and how my father suffered at the hands of ministers and the Soviets, have only made me doubt all these things."

"You are mixing it all, Noosh. Do note, there is no Soviet hand in his travel or their stay arrangements. It is all done by the office, and further by American Embassy."

"Okay, I will calm down. I don't mean that Kabir is involved directly. Maybe, he is being used, that is all." said Noosh.

At the end of it, things appeared simpler and fine as they were discussed and clarified at length.

==========

One the other hand, the Daily Times crew had made it to Herat safely.

"Guys, finally we have arrived," said Kabir.

Kabir and Nikita continued their conversation in detail.

"Kabir, you have taken some real good pictures"

"Niks, you have taken some excellent notes, too."

"Our book shall contain pictures, photographs, food, and then we can take it to rest of the world."

"Yeah, and politics too."

"And now, anyway, our roles and goals will increase manifold."

"Yes, especially after all of us have been told to work closely with the NGOs and the related organizations."

"Not sure how Noosh and her friends are going to take it."

"Have they not been informed yet?"

"I was told, not yet. But, considering Michael, the news of our induction would have travelled."

"Lisa will know about it tomorrow. She will share it with Noosh."

While Kabir had informed them of the travel plan to Herat, it was not confirmed if the news of the changed roles would have been shared. Also, for last few days, while they were on the road, they were not connected to their office headquarters either. It was presumed things would have been shared.

"Kabir, how do you feel?" asked Nikita.

"Finally, you landed up where you wanted, with who you wanted," said Jemima, looking at Kabir and then shifting towards Nikita.

"Girls, There is a right time and a right place for everything. Maybe, it is about to begin for me, now."

"Who on this earth would have imagined that a journalist who studied in Moscow would fall in love with a Persian; get handpicked by a Russian professor for Soviet duties, but he would work for Americans and then influence all of us. Wow, wow! Hats off mister," laughed Jemima.

"Yeah, yeah, Mr. Mike's influence," added Nikita.

"Now, who will bell the cat?" asked Kabir. He was hinting at the announcement of the role changes that Nikita told them about. He wanted to check as to who will make the announcement.

"The cat?" asked Nikita.

"Sorry, the lioness." said Kabir.

"Hahahaha, Lisa will."

"Tomorrow, Monica will call up Lisa, and that will be the starting point.

She will bell Lisa, that will ring her bells, and then Lisa will, if she has the guts, she will do it, else, I am willing to do so from my end, if that do's not break the protocol," said Kabir.

"The protocol? Per protocol, Nikita was supposed to spend thirty minutes with Mr. Mike.

Per protocol, you are supposed to almost act like her assistant, Kabir," said Jemima jokingly.

"Anything for you, my love," said Nikita.

"What, you love Kabir?" said Jemima with a wink.

"Yes, from day one."

The atmosphere had lightened now.

Jemima complemented Kabir on his network, and told him that she was amazed as to how he was aware of what Monica might discuss.

They all checked into their respective rooms in the hotel. This hotel had been built by the Americans, and most of the meetings regarding the western regions took place here.

It had an American Diner and a Punjabi dhaba style restaurant, pearls shop, couple of rugs stores, you name it, they had it.

Kabir looked at his itinerary, and figured out how soon he would be facing Dedov and also meet Professor. Here, there were chances of him meeting up with more members of the organization in the office of The Directorate. He had accounted for some time to also meet up with his friends Andropov, and some more who were fairly well connected.

Kabir wanted to keep himself reserved for the evening. He decided to meet Noosh, only in a next couple of days, so that it does not make him appear too fast and create a wrong impression. He was conscious now, and hence exercised control.

Chapter 11

"Pothi padi padi jag mua, Pandit bhaya na koi
Dhai Aakhar prem ka, padhe so pandit hoye."
"Reading books, everyone died, no one became wise
One who reads the word of love, only becomes wise."

BREAKFAST IN THE HOTEL WAS SERVED FROM 7.00 am to 10.00 am. However, on the day after the arrival of the team from Kabul, breakfast was served until 11.00 am, upon Noosh's request. She had gone to bed late the previous night, and wanted to sleep in. She hated breakfasting in her room and so, asked that they keep it open an hour longer. Everybody in the staff knew Noosh personally, and had no problems acceding to her request.

Scene at the breakfast table was a treat to watch out for this crew.

Salem and Meer, along with Babu, were put in the staff quarters. They were the first ones to arrive at the breakfast table.

"Do you know, Salem, yesterday Niki madam told Kabir saab that she loves him.?"

"See, I have been telling Meer from day one, she loves him."

"No, you always said Kabir saab loves her."

"Shhh, talk slow, they can hear us."

"No, no, they are far."

"Babu, it is ill manners to talk behind someone so loud," said Kabir softly.

"Oh, sorry saab, we never talk bad about you. We are simply gossiping."

"What are they talking? And what is this ill manners about talking loudly. I thought talking behind somebody's back is ill manners," said Nikita.

"I don't want to control them; now they can talk, so we don't hear. Otherwise, they would have contained so much inside." replied Kabir, with a straight face.

"It is nice to see we are all back to American breakfast." said Nikita.

"They knew we would want it now." said Jemima.

"Kabir, you like it too, don't you?" asked Nikita.

"Being an Indian, having toast, fruit juice, corn flakes, and egg is considered normal. We don't have pancakes and waffles and, usually, sausages are considered a treat. When you score good marks in class, in India your mom promises you *aloo parantha* for breakfast, and you might have picked a thing or two from your class, especially when you are studying in a boarding, you end up asking for sausages, chocolate shakes et. el."

"That sounds very interesting."

Then, he began to randomly talk about Indian cities; he was getting flashes of the cities in his head, from his memory and the times he spent there. It was natural for someone who was away from his country for so long, and the interest shown by his friends only instigated him to tell more.

"Yeah, and my favorite places are Bombay, Calcutta, Patna, Madras, Delhi, Lucknow Dehradun and Hyderabad."

"Really, that is quite a number. So, tell us more about India." And, the random talk at the breakfast table went on. After the nice get-together over breakfast, Kabir informed the crew about the day ahead of them. Nikita and Jemima decided to work on finishing the writing on the basis of the pictures, scribes, details that they had accumulated over all those worthy weeks spent in traveling. For now, the work responsibilities were also divided. Informally, Nikita had told him that he should now work on the project plan, details of which shall follow officially. He could not thank his father enough for forcing him into engineering. Also, his role elevation was now getting possible due to his American association.

He stepped out now. As planned and discussed, Kabir had drawn out a roadmap. He did not waste any time. He mustered the resources in Herat. His local contact was on the job. This is something that Kabir had envisaged during his tour earlier. He stepped out across the river, and viewed the places that were marked. He put in a few details as he looked at the smudged horizon. His intention was to now work on the plan that he genuinely set himself up for- the development and the related construction.

He calculated the material requirement to build passage across the torn up roads. He was also accompanied by Singh, the hotel manager. Singh assured him further of any local requirement that might arise apart from the ones he already had.

Using the labor at hand, he volunteered to do the worksite analysis. Through the day, he figured out the potential hazards and the special requirement for using the cranes and hoists underground.

The work day also included highlighting the open positions for competent people; for drinking water inspections, and the associated equipment.

Site control procedures were in place. Training requirements were laid out. Everything, from explosives to mechanical equipment, illumination, communication methodology, personal protection gears, ground support of shafts and fire prevention controls were detailed out at a higher level. In coming days, this was supposed to be broken at procedural level.

Kabir had to ensure to take the development tasks to the next level. He was filling the open position of the Project lead for the same activity that Noosh and Lisa were working towards.

His role in the annual edition was more or less over. It appeared so far that the executive team in the U.S had realized it, and he was entrusted to continue with the same. He worked on his prelim report to be submitted to the Headquarters sooner.

He could well finish his work on time, as it began to rain later in the day. He returned thanking the entire team, and assuring them of greater employment opportunity in days to come. Kabir was on the job.

==========

Next day, there was some humidity in the air, after the rains from the previous evening. It was misty. A perfect day to stay indoors. It also gave Kabir some moments of privacy.

He was looking forward to his meeting with Noosh. She wanted Kabir to take the first step to meet him.

Kabir had found out that late breakfast thing for her, today too, so he knew he could stay here till she arrives.

Not many people would be around then. Not many people were anyway around at that hour. Not many people. Maybe, just the bell boys, receptionists, and just the two of them. And, yes, wonderful Mr. Singh too.

Not to forget, Babu. He was very fond of spending his mornings near the small fountain.

There was a small fountain inside, which had some historical significance.

Kabir looked at the water and babu, and murmured,

"Dear water, you are pure magic; you can be a river, or can be a soothing fountain; you give me life and can take it too. I think of love when I look at you, for you are soon going to soothe my senses when I meet her now."

Noosh spotted Kabir staring at the fountain. Her face was a study of shifting expressions. When you really do not know how to react and, at the same time, want to react heavily. Maybe, over react.

Kabir did not notice Noosh's arrival, he was looking at the fountain.

What perfect timing. We can have a late breakfast. Kabir and I. Just us. I am certain, he is not going to let go off me easily today and, maybe, in many days to come. Okay, Noosh brace yourself. Do not fall apart. In a million towns, couple of hundred nations, and so many women, why did you have to choose me and this city for your story, Kabir? Noosh thought in bewilderment.

"Hello, Noosh. Greetings." He had waited for this moment, all these years. He did not want to hold himself back any further. His greetings had a zillion smiles hidden, as he appeared composed. Only his heart knew what he was going through.

"Hello Kabir," came a soft reply with a wide grin.

Kabir was not prepared on what to say next, so, before Noosh could ask, he clarified his purpose, in the most articulate way, fitting it abruptly to strike a long lasting conversation.

"Before you ask me why I am here, well, I came for the epic." Kabir was in his natural self now.

"Epic?"

"Yes, epic."

The conversation seemed to have started on a good interesting note.

"Really, and I always believed, in fact, the world over it is known, that great epics were only written in India."

"India does not have you, Noosh. And I am not talking about history."

"Aha, and you so well know of my professional commitments."

"You think, I do not have those. Since when do professional commitments stop couples from being together?"

"No, no Kabir, you do not realize the sensitivity here. Aren't you seeing for yourself, what is going on here?"

"Are you able to control anything?"

"I am doing what I can; if I do not, things can only worsen."

"I dream of marrying you, Noosh, I ask you—Marry me, for we can win over anything under one roof. I also know, you cannot pull it off alone."

"I am a self-made woman, Kabir. Also, how shall we survive unsettled? There are no resources yet."

"Well, so far as the resources go, that was not part of the dream. And, as much as I know your father worked in the ministry. You have all the influence."

"Despite, I mean I just never misused my father's position, and you might not know Kabir. The minister treated him badly, when he uncovered some bitter truths. Father was framed."

"Yes, I do have an idea. I met some Russians in Jalalabad and in Kabul. Not the entire story, just the preface, maybe."

On hearing this, Noosh mentioned the discussion she and Lisa had had about their doubts regarding his activities. Kabir had an opportunity to clarify his position, and clear any misunderstanding. Noosh seemed comforted with his explanation.

"Well, do not mind, Noosh. There is so much more that could have been done, together."

"Are you really sure you want to marry me?"

"Why, what makes you doubt me? I have been waiting for last six years, and came here for you; epics are never etched in doubt."

"I said, since you are only criticizing me."

"Do you not know that well-wishers criticize, and they do it in person, and for the good?"

"Oh, thanks so much Kabir for not humiliating me in public."

"Humiliate? Did I? Are you not extra strong headed?"

"See, I knew this. In just a few minutes of our conversation, you get on a hot plate."

"Hot plate? But I …I ..I am talking calmly, Noosh. I am composed, trust me."

"No, but you are the one to use strong words like capable and questioned my capability."

"I never used that word, and when did I even question your capability; you got me all wrong here."

"Oh, Kabir, come on; that is what is implied, isn't it? Anyway, if we get under one roof, we will probably kill each other."

"No, you might think of killing me; it is not my endeavor, and, yes, I would gladly accept death by your hands. It would be an honor."

"Now, you are accusing me and trying to gain some sort of sympathy, if not love."

"That is the third strong word of the day, so far, Noosh, back in college you would average at five a day."

"Oh, come on; gain some senses Kabir."

"Who wants to? I want to lose my senses in you, for you."

"How poetic and romantic, mister; try more and remember, poets and romanticists do not build the nation, they write books and people read, and, then, when people are sad, they get sadder, and so on and so forth."

"But they build people; artists build people; my father always used to tell me, no matter what profession you choose, retain one art; women fall for artists, so artists build people and people build the nation. I love your Bedil, what an amazing poet, what a great *fankaar* he was."

"And, I love Mirza Ghalib."

"In last six years, it is the first time you have confessed that we have something in common."

"Hmmmm." Noosh nodded.

Now Kabir recited.

"Hazaron khwahishein aisi....ki har khwahish par dum nikle...

Bahut nikle mere armaan lekin phir bhee kam nikle..."

"Thousands of desires, each worth dying for

Many of them I have realized, yet I yearn for more."

"Kabir, it sounds so beautiful, so mesmerizing, can you sing also? I have heard you have Mr. Jagjit Singh in India who sings Mirza Ghalib's Ghazals."

"Yes, he is good, young and good ghazal singer."

"By the way, Kabir, it is a repeat; do not take offense to it, however, you only have this *shayari*, each time."

"It is always situation based, Noosh, and, each time, when I begin things with you, one situation that arises is this, well, yes each time you must appreciate that I am always consistent and stable in my expression of love."

"Yeah, and look at how we started talking of building the nation and ended up discussing love."

"Nation is built when you are in love with your lover.

When you are not, you only destruct or obstruct."

"I am really impressed Kabir, sir. Look in no way did I mean to hurt you with my words; it was not deliberate; I did not mean a thing. I apologize."

"Great, so are we reconciling?"

"Yes, we are."

"That is not a bad start, ahem."

"Yes, not a bad start. But, I am not ready to marry you Kabir, not yet."

"That isn't a bad next step, either."

"Next step? Which one?"

"Well, you do not marry after reconciliation, you only get to know each other more with a different perspective."

"What do you want to know about me Kabir? You always had my friends, and you always tried a lot to know it all, what else?"

Just one last thing, now and for the rest of my life. I would not want to know anything else."

"What is that?" Noosh wondered.

"Is your heart placed towards the right side of you?"

"Shut up!" said Noosh as she began to look around.

Much of Kabir's wish seemed to be falling in place. He was more motivated, confident and positive than ever before. Added to all this professional ambitions, his personal life might soon start soaring too. He had confided in his parents, about his lady. They were happy and excited for their only son. During the course of the day, Lisa and Kabir also got introduced to each other.

==========

In Moscow.

The Russian government operated from one of the oldest buildings standing high in the center of Moscow. It had close to twenty four spacious rooms, and these rooms were equipped with the latest technology. It was not the center of nuclear control but, nevertheless, it was the hub of covert activities.

One of the rooms was dedicated to the KGB senior leadership. The Chief of operations, Dedov was in a pensive mood.

Dedov, very well dressed, wearing a red glossy tie, white shirt, and grey suit, called his commander Glostinov to his office.

"We have been extremely saddened with the death of our commander Sergei." said Dedov.

"Yeah, losing a heavy weight, untimely is certain bad news for us, Sir. Knowing that he always helped us in times of need, was very close to Sizov and, considering the connect he built with the Americans, it is further more unfortunate. On many occasions, he bridged that gap and helped clear any ambiguity. Do you remember the meeting in Czechoslovakia last year?" responded Glostinov.

"Yes, I do. He played a pivotal role. He helped figure out the rats and moles, on several occasions."

"Yes. And also helped us in controlling American ambitions. He would have been a treasure, especially for the western region now, knowing we are weaker there."

"Have we profiled this man, Kabir? Hope he is on the radar."

"Yes, Sir. Yuri and his close aide Mozowic have been taking care of that. You need not worry. Kabir is in Herat."

"Okay. Were you able to find out who was behind Jafer's killing. I want you to be involved and update me further."

"I am assuming the rebels were behind Jafer's killing sir. A day before he was killed, there was some altercation between him and a group of locals. It seemed there was some personal animosity. Something to do with American funds."

"And, they are pointing fingers at us?"

"We have controlled the press. The minister was prompt."

"The rulers run the media there. They are in power." Dedov was furious. "I would like to find out the 'rat' here. I am not convinced that this was to do with the Americans or the rebels. Logical, isn't it? If the Americans are funding, why would they kill for their own money? Rebels join them, and they have a good system of exchange. This appears fishy to me commander."

"Okay, chief. Let me ask the Embassy. Our residents in the embassy in Kabul are powerful owing to their direct connect with the ministry. It could be a diversionary tactic, to get the world to look at us with suspicion, so they can continue with their secret ops and all other activities, in the name of development."

"If need be, rope in the representatives from the agency here, not the embassy. We might need other level of our secret services here. This is big."

"At your behest, Sir."

Kabir's meeting was discussed further. Dedov asserted that he needed to meet him sooner now. The message was already sent to Kabir. He also wasn't sure about why Kabir was cozying up to Michael. It appeared to him similar to what Sizov did. In the meantime, Professor also joined the meeting, and they both discussed the state of affairs.

Dedov was a little suspicious of Yuri. He feared Yuri's hand in the killing and misplacing of funds in the western region. Professor assured him that this time, he would not support Yuri, who was missing from the scene. According to the information available, he was in Czechoslovakia, purpose unknown.

==========

In Kabul, at Minister's office.

After the President's palace, the minister's office was probably the best construction in town. This building had enough space for luxuries, for the people too.

The minister had the information that his deputy minister Ramez had a hand in Jafer's murder. He summoned him for a confrontation, visibly angry at this news.

"What are you up to? You killed his brother for money? What on earth were you thinking? We always have resources for money. You know this is going to be big. I never thought someone in my party could even think of this. For once, the opposition could do it. Not us. This will cause unrest, and people will lose faith in me." The minister was clearly agitated and very direct.

"I did it for us, Sir. He was feeding on American money." replied Ramez with no self-defense in this case.

"So, did he steal your money? Even if he did, you do not kill people. Your act is detestable."

"Sir, I understand, and that was not the intent, it was bad timing. It just happened in a fit. We wanted some funds, and we knew he could help us with the same. However, he refused. So, he had some altercation with the locals there."

"Do the soviets know?"

"The chiefs don't. But some do. In fact, one of them helped hatch the plan."

"So, we have scoundrels across the lines. We do not know who is playing what game. It is so not acceptable. So who else was involved?"

"It was someone from Yuri's office who met me about the plan. There is trouble, sir. So far as the money is concerned, I do not know where it has gone. I was assured we will get it, however, the secret agent has likely fled the scene now. I used our agent 'Dar' in Herat to get this done."

The Deputy thought it was best to confide and share everything. He defended himself, stating he would have told the Minister at some point. He knew that he could be executed for this mistake. However, the minister was in a state of dilemma. He did not want this news to get out, for the reason that people might suspect him as well. Also, considering the fact that he had very proudly announced, he would find the real people behind the crime.

The minister feared the situation would offer a lot of discomfort to him later. It would become a serious perception issue globally, for it had American funds involved.

Suddenly, a letter arrived.

"Why don't you just leave the room now, and ensure this is taken care of? I do not want any issues. We have some folks from the representatives coming over for a meeting, in the next few days. They will raise this pertinent question.

I can assume, they would have initiated an investigation into this. The letter seems to be indicating the same."

"What is the point, sir? Even their men are involved in this," said Ramez, who looked very upset.

"If my men were not involved, I would have risen from my chair; booked my first flight to Moscow, and given them my stern message.

Sadly, you and your interests are going to ruin us."

"Do not worry, sir. Things shall be swept under the carpet."

"I worry. I worry a lot. And despite all this, you don't even know where the money has gone. And, look at me, I made a fool of myself; operation Skylight was planned to find out all about these financial frauds and related issues, not knowing the canons would all aim at me."

Minister lost his cool, and asked him to watch out for Kabir. He was worried if Kabir got to know, he might spill the beans and share it widely with the western media. In this case, the directorate won't even come to his rescue.

He had no reason to trust his own subordinate any further. However, taking any action against the minister would only turn the tables around, and would not benefit his own political career.

"This is your last chance; any further mistake, and I will not mind throwing you out," remarked Minister Shah.

"I assure you," said Ramez nervously.

"What assurance are we talking about, Mr. Ramez?

Do you not know what happened, about a couple of years ago? Remember? That girl Nooshafarina's father?"

"Yes, he was Shir," murmured Mr. Ramez.

"He found out something similar and informed the Americans and Germans about it, and we could not do anything except sacking him. Ethically, we should not have, however, we just wanted to defend ourselves at that time. Yuri was involved again.

It is people like you, who bring a bad name to the nation, to our society. I want everything to be clean. I never believed, and never shall, in killing anybody. You must know that. This is our country, and we better take care of it, and not kill people; they can be on any side, killing can always be avoided."

Saying this on a firm note, Minister Shah left the room with a stern look on his face.

==========

In Moscow.

There was a seeming shift in the strategy. Dedov enquired about Kabir's acceptance for the meeting at an earlier date. He was told that the message through their key aide would be passed on.

"I want to see Yuri in my office; along with Kabir; this coming week," Dedov informed Glostinov.

"Why so sudden, sir?"

"We are going to Kabul, in a few days, as planned some time back, and need to redraw our strategy. Need to recruit more people and change the way we do currently; we also need to have a counter intelligence for China and America. Then, there is a rising threat from Pakistan. We need to have discussions around the borders, too. Also, take a note, I want to ensure, the right word goes out in the media about us."

"Okay, sir will do."

Dedov asked Professor to be around when Kabir arrived. Professor had called on Kabir to find out the ground situation. He planned to involve him in some covert operations from his end. He was thinking to involve Kabir in recruiting more people and also participate in operations to stall American lead development activities. Since Kabir was an illegal resident, nobody would doubt him.

==========

Chapter 12

"Pehle shabd pehchaniye, pichhe keeje mol
Paarkhi parkhe rattan ko, shabd ka mol na tol."
"First, understand the words spoken, then evaluate those
The Goldsmith tests the purity of Gold, words are neither
valued nor have a weight."

IN HERAT, THE INVESTIGATIONS WERE IN FULL SWING. Contrary to Minister's belief, the investigating officer was unbiased and uninfluenced. He shared a good relationship with Noosh's father.

To ensure sound probe, the inspector along with his cops arrived at the hotel for the pre-scheduled discussion.

Babu sat near the fountain, waiting for Salem and Meer.

"Did you hear a gun shot?" asked Inspector Jamaal.

"No, we heard a bomb explosion," replied Lisa, laughing.

Kabir intervened, "Lisa, please be serious. This is not funny. Did you not read the newspaper filled with the news? This episode of murder, money fraud seems to be becoming a matter of pride for a few nations."

Inspector felt good after Kabir's support, "Thank you, mister. What is your name? I forgot."

"My name is Kabir."

"And?"

"What else; I mean, what and?"

"What is your full name, I mean, last name, Mister Kabir."

"Is it necessary, Inspector Saab, to have a last name?"

"His name is Kabir trickster," responded Nikita with a big smile.

"Oh, so you are an Anglo? I have not seen you here before."

"Yes, he is Anglo Persian," answered Nikita.

Kabir smiled, and pulled her aside, "Thanks, Nikita, I just discovered that."

"Oh, very nice…then you must be aware of the great poet, Bedil."

"Yeah."

"Jamaal *saab, hazaron khwaishein aisi,*" continued Noosh, hiding her laughter beneath her hand, folded around her mouth.

"Okay, I got it; now, ladies and sir, here are a few pertinent views, as we are nearing the end of the probe.

The prima facie report indicated that he was killed in front of the building at a point blank range. It was a perfect shot.

This was an unlicensed one; I mean, from some unlicensed pistol, and the gun seems to have been made in Italy… they make good guns…class…this one is a class apart. We know that Russians have supplied plenty of these guns to their agents here..

We are not drawing any conclusion here, however, Noosh's father knows me well, and he knows I can solve cases; all I need from you is, if you get any information, do not publish in America simply because you are working for them; come to me first."

The inspector spoke non-stop.

"Do you think, he was disturbed?" asked Inspector as he looked at Noosh.

"Well, we all were. We were supposed to receive some funds, but some of it went missing. We couldn't figure out what happened, and we informed the NGO about it; they are investigating too," replied Noosh.

"So, you believe this is a finance related murder," asked Inspector.

"That you need to figure out," said Jemima

"May I ask you something, Inspector?" asked Kabir.

"Yes, you may."

"Are you not being approached by the minister? I mean, I know why would you admit, yet you know there is that curious thing in your head, that feeling of getting it out of your system."

"You are accusing me, Mr. Trickster. I know your approach goes as far as West, yet I must tell you this is absolutely absurd and baseless."

"Then, why were we let inside freely, not that we are not allowed to, however, instead of asking for the relevant papers, the check post officer let us cross; we showed him a minister signed ID, that's all."

"Oh, so you have been scrutinizing me? Anyway, that has nothing to do with this case. It is considered very normal here; it is to do with the status and stature."

"Exactly, stature is what does it all; it leads to corruption."

"Do you even know what you are talking about? He is a man of great repute, and commands huge respect from the population… we will not tolerate anything that is said against him."

"And, Ms. Noosh, why don't you enlighten this man further?"

"Kabir, we know him; he has worked with my father, on one occasion. Inspector will be fair in his probe."

"And, just so that you know, we know what privileges you guys enjoy; the passports that you all carry. I mean, you are foreigners, and some of you have U.S, U.K and Indian passports. You can move here without any hindrance. So do not lecture me on status and stature please," said the Inspector in anger.

"Okay, officer, please carry on…I apologize for any hasty accusation."

Without even pausing to take a breath, the inspector continued, "Let me share with you further. We might be ready with the sketch of the accomplices. There are some eye witnesses. Trouble is, during cross examination, they had difference of answers. We might be able to ascertain something, by the end of the day.

And, yes, next time, we will call you to our station. We came here to talk to you because of the status," Inspector said sarcastically.

"Sure, Officer; we are around, whenever you need us."

"Okay, and please do not leave the city. You need to be around."

The inspector walked out of the hotel. While he was leaving, Babu and his friends sat frozen by the fountain. They looked very scared.

Babu came running to Kabir, "Sir, I know all this happened because of me."

"What, Babu? You killed Jafer?"

"No, no, sir, don't scare me further. I mean, I showed the ID to the inspector and it caused you a great deal of humiliation today."

"Babu, you must remember one thing always in life."

"What, sir?"

"That, when you fumble, do not spit out while talking."

Nikita bursted into laughter, and Jemima and the folks at the reception started laughing along. Kabir maintained a straight face, looking deep into Babu's eyes. Babu was trembling with fear.

"Sir, sorry again, I will take care," Babu started stepping back to the fountain.

Kabir started laughing as he saw Babu retracing his steps towards the fountain and shouted at Babu, "Hey Babu, relax."

"Okay, sir; okay, sir."

Kabir looked at everyone, "Guys, it has been a very tiring day, and we have a long one again tomorrow, I suggest we do our own thing now. As for me, I would like to catch up on my sleep."

"And, listen, Babu," he shouted again. "Philosophically speaking, you are never wrong till the other person bashes you black and blue, so you are safe."

"Wow, Kabir, quite philosophical," said Noosh.

"I am glad, Noosh; at least, you find my philosophy better than my *shayari*," he responded with a wink; then, they all bid goodbye for the day and retired to their rooms in the hotel.

It was a huge surprise to Kabir that Noosh was staying in the room opposite to his. There were no reactions to this yet, both of them tried to put it under the rug and pretended they remained unaffected with the room arrangement. They behaved like normal, mature adults, and did not give this much importance.

Kabir opened his room and turned around, "Have a great rest of the evening, Noosh, and thank you."

"Well, I did you many favors today, I know, but which one is this for?"

"This is for choosing the room opposite mine," said Kabir.

"Really, man, you came after me. I have been here for a long time, and why did you irritate me? I mean, who does that."

"Only Kabir does that," he walked inside, with his hand saluting Noosh.

==========

Noosh stood still for a moment, smiling and looking at her door. She turned around, making sure Kabir had gone into his room. Then, she opened her door, walked inside slowly, biting her lower lip, and threw herself on the bed. She was deep in thought, and very tired as well, but the moment she thought of Kabir in the room opposite to hers, fatigue vanished in no time, and she felt lively again.

She got up, threw her shoe around, changed clothes in no more than a minute, washed her face and, before wiping it dry, she held the sink, bent down slightly and peered at her face closely in the mirror. Then, she thumped her left cheek and said gently, Noosh, Noosh, and she repeated this on her right cheek as well, a little harder this time. Her cheeks turned red, very red. Then, she returned to her bed, jumped on it, lay down and began to sing in a soft voice,

hazaron khwahishein aisee ki har khwaishh pe dum nikle....

Am I nervous? Okay. All set, Noosh all set, she murmured and soon fell asleep.

==========

Inside his room, Kabir was all charged up from the excitement of having the perfect neighbor. After letting out a loud 'wooooo-hoooooo', he turned his attention to his work. Pulling out his diary from the briefcase, he made notes about the day. Then, he picked up his gun to clean it. Suddenly, a very crucial thought struck him just in time.

He looked at the gun, it was Italian made Barrett 72. The gun discussion that took place at length with the inspector in the lobby, somehow, settled in his head, and hence he could immediately draw a parallel. He distinctly remembered Yuri telling him that most of the guns here were unlicensed as they were given unofficially to spies and agents all the time and, at times, locals too. This had made Kabir aware of the entire nexus; Yuri had more or less meant that he ran this trade. So, somewhere, Kabir began to feel and correlate that Yuri had some linkage with this murder.

Kabir wanted to expose this with whatever evidence he had at hand. To begin with, he thought to share it with Michael. Also, he decided to share it with Professor as well, as he would be meeting him soon.

He knew what he wanted to do next, but he definitely wanted to discuss it with Noosh before taking action.

Next morning, Kabir, Nikita, Jemima and Lisa arrived at 8 am to the breakfast table.

Singh came to greet Kabir, and covertly informed him about a message from Moscow, confirming the early meeting schedule.

"Sir, I request you all to proceed towards Mayfair Ballroom. Today, the breakfast is being served there," Singh announced.

"I find that room very classy," said Nikita

"Yes, I remember, this is the same room that Kabir also has in mind for his wedding reception," laughed Jemima.

"Where is she today?" asked Nikita

"Must be on the way; I called her room, no one answered," said Jemima

"Is it not slightly odd?" said Nikita.

"Yeah, I would think so," said Jemima, confirming to Nikita.

"Hey Singh," Kabir shouted.

Singh came running. "Yes Sir."

"Can you quickly call at Ms. Noosh's room, number 301?"

"But, sir, madamji left in the morning."

"Where did she go?" Kabir was surprised hearing this.

"No clue, sir, but she seemed to be in a rush."

"That is why Babu is not near the fountain today."

"Yes, sir, he drove her out."

"Well, she could have told any of us at least," Kabir wondered.

"Maybe, sir, she did not want to bother you. I just heard her calling Babu and telling him it is very important as she left."

"Well, I do not think she would be planning to go very far. She knows the car did not have much fuel left. It would only drive ten kilometers within the city, and that is the entire area of the city, too. So, she must be in the city.

And when did she leave?" Kabir continued with his questions.

"At 7 am, Sir."

"Exactly 7 or before?"

"May be 6:30, Sir; I am not sure. Let me check with the *Durbaan*."

As he gets back, "Sir, it was around 6:15 in the morning."

"Oh, okay. I know where she is, and who has she gone to meet up with."

Kabir hinted that he was aware where she would be.

Chapter 13

"Padha suna seekha sabhi, miti na sanshay shool
Kahe Kabir kaso kahu, ye sab dukh ka mool."
"One may read, listen and learn it all, yet remain confused
Kabir is in pain to explain that confusion is the root cause of
all sorrows."

A MILE AWAY FROM THE HOTEL, THERE was a cluster of houses. Some were single storied; some two storied and, still, others had one or two rooms on the first floor. A lot of these houses ran shops on the ground floor, in the front half of the building. It was bustling with activity. In one of those houses, Noosh's father resided. Adjacent to the house, Babu had parked the official car. Some children from the street could be seen drawing birds and unknown animals on the window panes, and the others who were left with no space there, tried to cover the windscreen and the rear glass.

A few old men tried to chase them away.

"Hey, boys, Go do some work; it is a holiday, we know; help your poor parents, and don't spoil the car. This must belong to someone wealthy; they will not like it." Nobody cared, and the activities continued.

In the ground floor of a nicely built dwelling, there could be heard a series of conversations, that were between a father and a daughter.

Noosh could be seen holding her father's hand, and weeping continuously. Shir was emotional, too, on seeing his daughter. Her work kept her busy, so they were not able to meet on daily basis.

"Noosh, I miss your mother today," said Shir.

"I miss her all the time, dad," said Noosh, wiping her tears.

"If she were alive, she would be very proud of you."

"I hope I am making you proud, too, dad."

"Yes, indeed, you are doing us all proud. You are doing great work. One day, I am very certain you shall be rewarded for your deeds."

"Only if I wanted to get something in return. There is no fun in doing something with the aim to be recognized in mind."

"You have gone on your mother."

"If mom were alive, she would have been the minister today."

"The ministry is a maze, daughter. I have served there."

"Is there something you want to tell me dad?"

"This is the exact thing that happened, couple of years ago. I was the whistle-blower. They shunned me for the rest of my life."

"You mean, Jafer's killing is yet another hand of someone in the higher circle."

"I am not sure, just my doubts. I met up with the inspector last night. I told him to look deeper into this one. This cannot continue, and there is very less we could do, except mourn."

"I understand you, father. But, this time around, we can certainly do more."

"How long would you continue alone, Noosh. I am also turning old. I have a good man in my mind. You must get married now."

"Dad, I have told earlier, and I shall maintain the same."

"If you have anyone in your mind, please do not hesitate to tell me."

Nur was a silent spectator so far, as he finished sipping his morning tea. He was going through all the news in the day's paper, in much detail. Looking a little uncomfortable, he then stepped out of the room, went towards the car, and shouted Babu's name.

Babu was holding a tea glass with a biscuit as he kept staring at the kids doing wonders.

"Yes, Nur?"

"Here, take this money. The petrol pump must be open by now." Nur asked Babu to get the tank filled.

Shir came out and asked Nur to join them, "Nur, please come inside. You are part of our family. It is a huge loss, equally for us as well. Your guidance further means a lot." Nur lived adjacently in the joint family set up. He looked at Shir, then composed himself. It appeared he wanted to gather some courage and say a thing or two that might be awkward, but he said it.

"If you both do not mind, I have the best man in town in my head."

"How can a best man in town be in your head, Nur uncle?" Smiled Noosh. "He has to be in my head. Sorry, dad. I am liberal in my views here."

"So, shall I say his name?" asked Nur with excitement.

"By now, you should have shown his photo to dad, uncle."

"Ok, ok Nur *bhai*. Come out with it. How is it possible, you know and I do not know?"

"Okay, his name is Kabir."

The moment Noosh heard Kabir's name, she turned red, blushed and walked into the kitchen looking at the floor. "Okay, dad, do you want snacks with the tea, or just the biscuits?" She left both of them in the room alone to let them continue with the conversation.

"I have heard this name before. I believe, I heard this name from Noosh. I cannot recollect. Noosh *beta,* is this the same guy who studied in engineering class with you?" asked Shir.

Noosh came out of the kitchen, "Yes, father. He is the same man."

"Is he in the country?"

"*Bhaijaan*, he is very much here, and he is working very closely with us in the development of our country."

"I know you are very well connected with the Soviets. Is this your soviet connection, by any chance Nur bhai?"

"Yes, in a way, yes. And, he is a good man. I discovered his side, working with people who can be your enemy in a day; I have this knack of reading human behaviour. I have seen him very closely. He is very sharp, and witty, and is turning out be an asset to us.

I have seen the other side of his. He is a practical, and a very generous man, too." Nur pulled out Afghans from his pocket, "This is what he gave to him for the service I offered him. How many people do this in today's times. Tell me, Shir *bhai*."

"Is he from Jalalabad?"

"No, he is from India. I believe he is from Bombay. Same place where Mr. Amitabh Bachchan lives. Same place where money speaks. And yes, he is extremely well behaved and cultured." Nur was doing well at the task of pitching good things about Kabir.

"See, Nur *bhai*, I see that in your eyes. I can read that man in your shining eyes. I wish, one day, I could read that man in Noosh's eyes too.

I have always let my daughter take her independent decisions. Yes, when it comes to marriage, I believe, she would want us elders, to take that call. Yet, I would seek her opinion."

"This is perfectly fine Nur *bhai*."

Then, he added further, "Also, I am very certain of Yuri's hand in Jafer's killing. I do not have evidence, though."

"I also would like to believe you."

It was about 9:30 am now.

"Okay, dad, I must leave. I have an action packed day. You can always drop in the hotel or the old office building, whenever you wish. Also, sometime soon, we must renovate this place."

"You know, I am saving money for your wedding."

"Come on, dad, saving money is worthy, not when you do not spend it in the present day. Spend it on the renovation of the house. This is important. I shall get married at the right time."

Shir smiled as he put his hand on her head.

Khuda hafiz....

Babu parked the car, with the tank full. Noosh sat inside, and waved at her father, with tears in her eyes. As the car pulled to a stop outside the hotel main door, *Durbaan* opened the door and addressed Noosh on a low voice, "Madam, Kabir saab was looking for you."

"Oh, okay, thank you. I shall meet him."

Kabir showed up, the moment Noosh entered the hotel.

"Hello Kabir. Good Morning."

"Good Morning, Noosh. How is your father?"

"Oh, well, he is good. How'd you know I met him?"

"I know you. Remember, during college days, whenever he would come, it would always be in the morning."

"He still carried that belief and faith. If he is around and, as you know, he wants to start his day by looking at me," said Noosh.

"I know, you are his charm."

"Yes, and he continues to believe, daughters are the best thing that can happen to mankind."

"Is he a lucky father or, are you a lucky daughter or, maybe, both? I wish I had a sister!"

"You have two here with you, don't you?" Noosh bursted with laughter.

"You mean, Jemima and Nikita?"

"Yeah, yeah," replied Noosh.

"Haha, you really did not mean it, did you?"

"Your straight faced humor rubbed on me, I suppose."

"Perhaps, it is a good company to keep. Tell me more. What did you and your father discuss? I have something at my end that I wish to speak with you, too," said Kabir.

"I know, Kabir, whatever you are going to tell me," said Noosh.

"Do you know it, already?" Kabir seemed surprised.

"Yeah, I am a soothsayer. I am a foreteller. I have a crystal ball."

"Really? How well I know you. Now, come out with it."

"You have been promoted, right?"

Around the time, when Nikita spoke with Monica, some days ago, an urgent meeting had been held in New York. The affairs of Afghanistan were discussed in the leadership circles. Certain Government level appointments were made. At the same time, to have a stronger overall control, apart from the secret operations, the support of the NGOs, and the media was also garnered. Some big changes and decisions were discussed. It was believed that the situation in the country was turning out to be graver and, thus, the guidance and direction needed immediate changes. There was a far sightedness in the works. The new mission was aimed under Green Nation. The projects that were once held under various initiatives, were merged and took on a more strategic and developmental stage.

The report that Kabir submitted to the board impressed them thoroughly, and sealed his fate.

Kabir was made completely responsible for overseeing rail tracks, tunnels and hospital projects across the length and breadth of the country.

Kabir confirmed the news with a sheepish smile "Aha, that thing, yes. I got to know about it, just a couple of days ago. So, Lisa told you?"

"Yes, of course, who else will? Nikita will not open her mouth till gets a go ahead from you. She is so much into Kabir."

"Are you jealous of her? I mean, already; don't get offended now. I am kidding"

"Why'd I be jealous of any woman who is very close to you? No, no, I am not. I merely stated a fact."

"I never noticed that, Noosh. If you ask me, I shall keep a distance. She is just a good friend. Oh, now I know why you said that sister thing and all. You are jealous."

"Okay, if you think so."

"And Lisa is supposed to announce the details to the team today," said Kabir

"Yeah, I know, you need to act as if I did not tell you anything; I just could not stop myself. You appeared to be sharing something spectacular with me, so I just guessed it."

"Thanks Noosh."

"And one more thing- How do you remain so active, so non tireless, so committed to everything. You never give up on anything."

"And, the sun rises in the west and sets in the east." Kabir said with a cunning smile. "That is complete flattery. I remember those lines from Shakespeare, remember when Caesar mentioned 'that base spaniel fawning', when we enacted the drama in college."

"I think it was from Julius Caesar," said Noosh.

"Yeah, you are right, and I did not mean in the sense that Caesar noted."

"And, I do not need to flatter you," said Noosh.

"Why not, now that I am your boss?"

"Haha, go take a walk Kabir."

"You shift gears very fast, Noosh. You can be a great biker."

"You bet."

"By the way, I want to take you out for a bike ride, tomorrow, on the Royal Enfield. Singh has a Royal Enfield here. He will lend it to us".

"Well, I shall let you know."

"Do not demoralize me; please give me an answer now."

"Okay, yes; you need to be patient, Kabir."

"I am; who can be more patient than I?" he sighed, "Waiting for six long years."

"Yeah, that can be tested further," she smiled, "So, now tell me Kabir, what did you have to tell?"

Kabir wanted to confide in Noosh. Now he had a partner. He narrated the series of events to her, and clarified his own position. He shared the Russian angle with her in entirety.

This caught Noosh by surprise. She was astonished, yet, she maintained her stand and cautioned Kabir. She asked him to stay away from being double and this resident spy and all, as that would risk his life directly. "Take a position and forget Russia, please," she said with concern. "I had a hunch, you might have slipped into something like this."

Kabir understood the point.

"I have some evidence, on me. I am not sure; I am shooting in the dark here. I was given a gun by a soviet commander called Yuri, some time back, and it is a classy Italian made product. If the inspector is able to prove the guns were similar, at least we know who to be wary of. Currently the news in the media is all fabricated. This will clear the air, at least in our heads. Accordingly, I can take it up with the western allies."

"You are right, Kabir. Nur and father also said the same thing."

The ongoing mention of Noosh's father drifted Kabir's mind to the memory of his. He hadn't spoken to his father in quite some time. The last time when such a long break had occurred was when Kabir had newly joined the college in Moscow. Unlike many other children, when Kabir landed in a new situation, he usually did not speak with his family. Neither would his father be worried. They had raised to be fiercely independent. Moreover, his mother believed that too much interference would irk him and limit his chance of success. His parents' emotions usually resided inside, and were sparingly revealed when needed the most. Such was his warm, cordial and a very practical relationship with his parents.

Noosh looked at Kabir and tried to gage his expression. "Kabir, I would like to know more about your parents. Even back in college, I do not remember if they came over to meet you."

"Yes Noosh, that is correct. They wanted to come over for vacations, once, but I preferred to spend time with them in Bombay. And, that was it. That is the only grown up vacation I had with them. We did Bombay to Goa in dad's Ambassador car. It was fun. Then mom insisted that I stay longer, for her desire was to go to the Tirupathi temple, Ajmer Sharif Dargah and places of religious interest."

"So, you are a Hindu?"

He told her that he preferred to stay as Kabir, and just that. Kabir had a very open upbringing. His family was multi-ethnic, and aunts and uncles married people from different backgrounds. In his growing years, he had found it relatively easy to shed off his religious mask. He had practiced it all his life, and believed that it was simpler to live this way.

"I am an Indian Global Citizen, who wears patriotism and karma on his sleeve."

"And, that is why you are just Kabir."

"Yes, I prefer to stay that way, for the rest of my life. Religion wise, I have every religion in the clan, trust me. Hence, all the more reason for me not to be able to get very particular about one or two. I believe it is a matter of faith. I have mine; you have yours, and that defines us. And, that is okay."

"Do you believe?"

"I believe in God. I believe in the Almighty. I believe in my work. My values. My ethics. Never do anyone harm. Have a clear conscience. Be brutally honest. And, so on and so forth."

"But, yes, it is certainly good to know a lot more about you."

"Yeah, now you can write a book on me?" asked Kabir playfully.

"I do not write, but I read a lot," replied Noosh.

"What do you read?" asked Kabir.

"Well, I like Shakespeare, you know that. Then, my all-time favorite is Margaret Mitchell's Gone with the wind."

"So, one day, I will be your Romeo, you behave like my Juliet."

"Yes, I've won many awards for acting. I can always enact for you Kabir; now, can we discuss the plan ahead?"

"And I shall do for you, too." said Kabir.

My bounty is as boundless as the sea,
My love is as deep; the more I give to thee
The more I have, for both are infinite

Noosh reacted positively with a lovely smile.

"And, yes, a lot to plan, and do not forget the bike ride tomorrow," said Kabir.

"Okay, I shall remember."

Kabir, without losing focus, said to Noosh, "You must know they will not charge sheet any Soviet here; this will continue. Only, we need to be cautious," and, as he began to leave the place, he told her of his upcoming travel to Moscow in a couple of days.

Noosh and Kabir got into a minor argument at this point, as the former did not believe it was the right decision anymore. Nor did she believe there would be any benefit from Kabir's visit to Moscow. She knew it would only lead to more problems..

Kabir insisted that he had to confront the professor once again. He was able to convince her.

While he was leaving, Lisa arrived at the scene.

"Hello, guys, I was looking for you," said Lisa.

"Sure, what's the news?" asked Noosh.

"I need Nikita and Jemima, as well. There is some important announcement to be made."

"It is 10:30. They must be ready for the day. Let us wait for them here in the lobby."

"Okay, I see them coming. Guys, let us get together for a quick meeting. I am sorry; I did not inform you earlier. There is a lot going on, hence the slip up. I am here to announce to you all that, from this moment onwards, Kabir is going to lead the team. Received a letter from the bosses today. The note reads like this."

Dear Lisa,

We are aware of the hard work and diligence you and your team is displaying in central Asia. You have always done us proud. The noble work, the contribution and the selfless grit and determination does not go unnoticed.

We received some further information from Michael. We made relevant contacts, and have come to a conclusion. We would like to merge the efforts that Nikita and her team, and you and Noosh, have been putting.

The act of kindness shall benefit further from this unison. You shall now lead the overall administrative efforts that include the budgeting and financing.

So far, the work on journalism and news has yielded immense benefits for the projects too.

Keeping all factors in mind, Kabir shall lead the overall efforts of development and building strategies. Noosh, being an engineer by qualification, shall report to him. Lisa will have a dotted line reporting into Kabir. Nikita and Jemima will support you all till the end of the year.

Congratulations Lisa and Kabir in your new roles. We wish you all the best. All other specific details will be sent separately.

Best Regards,

Monica Douglas- Human Resources (The Daily Times)
Steven Richards- President (The Daily Times)

James Hamlisch- Asia Head (Green Nation)
CC: USA Embassy, Kabul.

There was a thunderous applause from everyone. This automatically led to cheers from the lovely hotel staff too.

Green Nation was growing at a rapid pace, owing to the work it was doing. It successfully ran three major programs: an NGO for women, then there was a unit that worked towards infrastructure and urban development, and the last one being dedicated towards education. Within infra and development, there were sub units that were all merged now, and Kabir was to take over the same.

Nikita and Jemima were slightly disappointed. Not because Kabir and Lisa got promoted. It was about their return at the end of the year. While it was still far away, they were not sure why weren't considered for a longer role than what they had been given.

Kabir observed the reaction of the crew, while Noosh and Lisa moved aside to a corner for a discussion. Within a few minutes, Singh appeared with a cake. He knew there was some big reason for the celebration. This brought a smile on the disappointed faces. It was supposed to be their favorite cake from the bakery.

"Nikita, sorry. This is not about your demotion and all."

"Kabir, I know that. This is about your promotion, and I am elated."

Jemima added, "Yes Kabir. The only piece we are trying to figure out is the expiration date of our assignment with this announcement, whereas it is silent in your case. Where are we going wrong? I mean no comparison, but still."

"Usually, the letters like this do not carry the explanation, and just the message and the intent. Maybe, they are looking at you for something else post that. Maybe something bigger and better than this," said Kabir.

"I can tell you Kabir, if ever there is something else that comes up, that requires to work together again, I shall be the first one to jump on the opportunity. I will grab it with both hands," said Nikita.

Noosh hugged Nikita and Jemima.

"Friendships that are built in hard times last forever. This is my utmost fortune moment. It means a lot to me, to all of us," said Lisa.

"The cake. Hey the cake," everybody shouted.

"Mr. Singh, we are extremely lucky to have you with us. You are so thoughtful. Do you always keep cakes in the reserve for any surprise or any occasion that comes up like this?" Kabir thanked Singh.

"This is the secret of hospitality industry, sir. We win hearts. We always try to win the hearts of our prestigious customers."

Kabir was pleasantly surprised at the speed of execution, not to mention the team name imprinted on the cake, too.

Just then, Inspector Jamaal turned up at the hotel.

"Kabir and Noosh, I would like to take a moment of your time."

"Certainly, Inspector."

"The news is that there is a Soviet hand in this. It is confirmed. The gun used was supplied by one of them. This news has stirred up trouble in higher circles. There is an atmosphere of uncertainty and loss of faith. Here is a blurred sketch of the suspect as he was seen from a distance."

"What does the minister have to say now?"

"Well, he is quiet on the subject. I believe some folks from Russia are meeting him soon. The news was that someone else, name not disclosed, was also traveling to Moscow to meet his boss.

"All of this has been happening way too fast. Definitely, there is a lot of shake up we can expect. And, there was a heated conversation, not heated, but the minister summoned the deputy and was very loud. Our internal sources have confirmed that."

"You and I cannot do much, if it is someone from the ministry; the political circles will most likely defend and, if it is Russian, the diplomatic immunity will save them. Yet from our end, we need to bring the truth in public domain and also share with the leadership. We never know how deep this connection goes."

"We truly appreciate the sense of duty you have displayed."

"I love my *vardi;* we call it *vardi,* uniform, and I can never betray it. I remember my oath, and I shall serve and support what is correct."

The inspector left the building.

Noosh, we were right. I see Yuri's hand here. But, he could not have done it alone. He must have conspired with Minister Ramez, as per my sources, and possibly it has minister's hand too."

Noosh looked worried, but did not say anything.

"I need to report this matter to Professor. He needs to know. I must let Michael know about this too," said Kabir.

Chapter 14

"Patta bola Vruksha se, suno Vruksha banraay
Ab ke bichhde na mile, door padenge jay."
"A leaf says to a tree, that it is going away forever
And there won't be any reunion, for it is off the tree now."

IT WAS THE MONTH OF JUNE. THE WEATHER WAS WARM, and Kabir was completely at home on this terrain. It was very different from what he had seen so far in his life, but he was enjoying every moment of his time there. He did not have any trouble adapting to the extreme climate of this country.

He gifted his persian love, a beautiful Persian Scarf and a *chador*. Noosh, at times, kept her head covered with it but, when on work, she did not like to do that. He filled up the Royal Enfield and, with her sitting behind him, set off for the day, fully intent on having fun with the woman of his dreams.

"Who would be as insane to take a beautiful woman out in the sun, on a day that is warm, and ride on a bike through these terrains?" said Kabir.

"So, why did you choose this Mr. Insane?"

"Well, Noosh, I wanted to be sure about my belief. I always rendered from my experience with you that you are beauty personified. No matter how the day is, or what time of the day is, or how rough these rides are, if it is you and me together, then nothing else matters."

Kabir had reached the lakeside. It was Qargi lake. He stopped the bike there.

"Kabir, I might sound monotonous now. You know how much I hate getting photographed," said Noosh, guessing that Kabir wanted to take photographs.

"Every time I try to surprise you, Noosh, you try your best to break it."

"You are mistaken, Kabir. You know I am a forecaster of sorts, don't you?"

"Then, let me tell you, I wanted you to take my pictures. There are many pictures in this camera, but not a single one has me in it. I had decided, long back, that I shall only get it photographed by you."

"Why do you sound so much a philanderer at times, rather many times?"

"When the girl in question is constant, it is called emotions, Noosh."

"It seems you had promised your parents that you shall go to India only when you are married to me. I see your conviction growing by leaps and bounds."

"This one is true. This is well predicted."

"Yes, of course."

"Okay, so your fondness for Mirza Ghalib must have grown by now, Noosh. Now that you have all the reasons."

"Let us go slow, Kabir. I am serious, let us go slow."

"But we are not going anywhere, the bike is parked."

"Oh Gosh, you and your humor!"

"I know that women like artists and, if humor is added as well, then it is lethal."

"Which women? I remember you mentioned the artist thing… but which women, and why do you regard me in the generic breed of women?"

"Well, in a conversation, we mention it this way, so as I know."

"Yeah, in a conversation you can also ask like this: Noosh, what do you like?"

"Sure. Noosh, what do you like? Well, I would rather know you by my observations rather than through questions."

"Is there any other way to know, Kabir?"

"Well, my belief is that time spent together and time spent like this does it all. To know a woman, you need not ask. To know you, I need not ask you questions."

"But, when I tell you something, you do not listen to me."

"Noosh, I listen to you when you look into my eyes, not when you talk."

"And, what do you see?"

"That I shall not disappoint my mother."

Noosh smiled as she threw pebbles in the lake. While doing that, water splashed onto Kabir's cheeks. Noticing this, Noosh immediately apologized, and rushed to wipe his face with her scarf. But then, in a moment, she stopped herself.

"Who would have known Noosh, you and I will be here one day? And just about a few miles from here, were the British who were killed till the last man. And the place now has you and me. I mean,

I would have imagined, but not so soon or here in this place, around these lakes; truly, you have a beautiful heart, I must say."

"Yes, Kabir, I remember my father used to share those stories with me. There is an old Indian connection with this soil."

"The Indian Army under the British came here to fight, and lost it like never before. Even the last soldier who set foot here was killed. Now, we have great friendly relations with this country."

"Certainly, see the way we have been bonding so well, so soon now."

The day had been spent extremely well together. They discovered many things about each other. They were at peace. A formidable partnership seemed to be in the making.

After they got back to their hotel, around early evening, Noosh gave Kabir an envelope. She asked him not to open it till she asked him to do so. This created a bit of anxiety in Kabir's mind, for he was not able to resist it. Although he knew it would be hard to stick to his word, he promised her that he would not open it.

Blushing slightly, she bid goodbye to Kabir and went to her room.

"Bye, and take care." said Kabir.

==========

When she reached her room, she repeated the activity of a few nights before. She fell on the bed, went to the washroom, and washed her face. But, today, there was a twist in the scene. After going to the bathroom, she did not go back to fall on the bed. Instead, she went to the mirror and did some mono-acting.

She looked in the mirror and called herself Juliet, and then began to talk to herself.

Noosh to Juliet – Hello, Juliet. How are you?

Juliet- Hello, Noosh…Noosh, right?

Yes, I am Noosh, and you are right.

What is Noosh? Is it a fruit?

What do you mean Juliet? It is my name! It means Joy

So I feel joyous, Noosh. It is so beautiful inside here.

Yeah, so you bet.

I love Kabir.

No, hello, what do you mean?

I mean, I love your Kabir.

How can two women love the same man? I love him.

Two woman can, but yes one woman cannot love two men, and vice versa.

Oh, that is all right then. You may love him. He loves me.

Yes, that is true Noosh. You win, I lose. Juliet loses to you.

From now, you are the Juliet, and I shall go away…

While talking, Noosh put her head into the sink, got up, beat her cheeks, and repeated, beat and repeated till it turned red. Eventually her face looked the way it did a couple of night ago. Essentially, she was following the ritual commonly portrayed in movies, the ritual called, 'Prince arriving on a white horse dreams' or the 'delirious state of mind of a woman in love'.

She composed herself, and looked up above. Thank you, God, for giving me this moment. It feels wonderful to feel special about yourself. Especially when someone as beautiful as Juliet lets you be her. Thank you, God, for making me feel like one. Even Shakespeare wouldn't have imagined that Juliet shall be born in the form of Noosh in Kabul. And, thank you for sending my Romeo.

Gradually, Noosh feel asleep while still in the process of thanking God for her good fortune.

==========

Finally, the day arrived when Kabir had to leave for Moscow. All the arrangements for Kabir's trip were made, and his flight was booked by the Russians.

That day, before taking off, he spent a great deal of time with Noosh, and carefully absorbed every word that she spoke. She cautioned him, and told him to be firm and stick to his stand. He needed to tell the Russians that he was not part of their Directorate any more. The discussion with Noosh kept Kabir balanced and well prepared.

Kabir took the flight and arrived in Moscow. He was supposed to meet the professor and Dedov at KGB headquarters. This was located in Lubyanka square. Kabir had seen this famous building, many times, however, he did not know that one day he would be visiting it too.

The building stood tall in the heart of Moscow. It was visible with a façade of yellow bricks. It had a clock centered in the uppermost band of the façade. In Soviet Russian jokes, it was referred to as the tallest building in Moscow, since Siberia could be seen from its basement. The design and architecture accentuated neo Renaissance detailing.

As he reached the main entrance door, the security let him in, as they had the prior information on Kabir. He was escorted to Sizov's office. His office was big to the point of being called a hall.

The wiring, gazettes, rotary phones, files crammed in the shelves, suggested that this was the hub of all activities.

In amazement, Kabir looked all around. Sizov asked him to relax and offered the chair.

Kabir was a little surprised, as he had not been aware that the Professsor was so deeply involved in government that he had his own office in the building.

He congratulated Kabir with a pat on his back, "Son, you are doing a good job, and you can do great. Only wish, you could have worked for us, rather than them."

Much to Kabir's surprise, as he had thought, Professor would initiate the conversation and make it straight to the point; he chose to remain quiet on the subject of killings and frauds and deteriorating human conditions in Afganistan.

"I am taken aback, Professor. You are not candid enough today," Kabir wanted to provoke the professor.

"So, you are judging me today, son, on what basis?" came an instant response.

Professor knew what was going in Kabir's head. Without actually naming Yuri, he stated, "Your catch has gone to Czechoslovakia".

Now the conversation began to open up. This meeting was way too different than the one that had happened earlier that year, with him, in the University grounds. Professor expressed his disappointment with Yuri, and mentioned how he had done something similar in the past.

"Money makes him go mad. I believe he has gone across to deposit the same. I gave him a second chance; he is my daughter's husband. I thought to give him another opportunity, as his work was flawless. He has made me look like a fool. Let us talk about next steps now."

The Professor moved on to the next topic. It looked like he didn't want to waste time talking about Yuri. He picked up a large map and spread it on the table. The map seemed familiar to Kabir. It was a map of Western Afghanistan. The exact map with markings was seen inside the hotel room of Yuri. Sizov valued time, and stuck to the point, "This is where our future lies. We need to fill open positions in this region."

He went on to the extent of telling Kabir that Yuri was supposed to hand over the plan to him, however, he might have feared that Kabir would take more control and, hence, there was a lack of will from Yuri's end.

Kabir looked for the right moment, when Sizov paused, grabbed the opportunity and shared his perspective, "Professor, I have spent a lot of time in the region now, and I can tell you, people out there, distrust and hate Russians."

"What about you; what do you think?"

"Of course, I do trust you, and I don't want to mislead you about my activities. I am directly involved in the development of the country as you had wanted it to be."

"With American money?"

"How does it matter?"

"Of course, it does! Why do you think they hate Russians? They see American money. So, whatever goes wrong, they suspect us. I want you to fix things. I want you to contribute now and recruit and strengthen our position. We need to hire several more. The perception in the global world will go negative if we don't act now."

"Not this time Professor. Not the way you want."

Kabir was better prepared, this time, and he said all with utmost honesty. Last time, when he had met the professor, he was clear from his perspective. He also remembered how well Noosh told him to stay firm, also the entire first-hand experience ruled Kabir's mind now.

Professor remained quiet for some time before launching his all-round verbal attack "You know they wanted to frame you, the Afghan minister was almost at it. They are good at framing the wrong guy."

He mentioned how the minister had tried to implicate him at one point, when it was revealed that Kabir had a similar gun to what was used in Jafer's murder. "Nobody would have trusted you, had that happened. They know how to distort facts and evidences. Do not forget you are a foreigner there."

Professor then told him that the investigation had been fair and just, due to his intervention.

At this point, Kabir could only thank him. Somehow, he found the discussion way too explicitly inclined towards Sizov's desires.

"Sorry, Professor, you need to pick somebody else this time. I cannot do this."

The only person that could influence Kabir was he himself.

He continued "Professor, the first time you told me about this, I was fascinated like a child. Yet, even then, I was only willing to attempt this in the name of development."

Strange, the thoughts that crossed his mind at one point when he was faced with a moral dilemma are now least impactful, Kabir thought. At one stage, he felt indebted to the professor, and now it did not seem to matter.

Professor, raising his eye brows, "Watch your back, Son. Do remember I would never mean any harm to you, ever. In this case too, it was more for you; well, yes it was mutual to an extent, however, more inclined to favour your growth. Anyway, it is up to you. Come, let us meet the exponent. You should not leave this place without meeting him, else it will be deemed disrespectful."

Professor took him down the passage, around the corner, and took the elevator to the third floor. Once they were out of the elevator, it was a few steps to the left, and then a turn to the right that took them straight into Chief's office. Dedov arose from the chair as Kabir extended to shake his hand with a firm greeting.

"So, what is the good news, Mr. Kabir?"

Kabir could not understand as to how to respond to Dedov. He looked at the professor.

"Well, Chief, Kabir has decided to be on their side?"

"If I may ask why, and did you not tell him the compensation, perks, diplomatic immunity, now that we are looking at a serious transition into a permanent position?"

"We could never get that far, Sir." Professor remained to the point.

Dedov looked extremely upset, and only tried to curtail his anger, "Then what are we doing in this room?" He turned around, signalling the meeting was over and they should leave.

Professor took him out, and said, "You take care, Son. Chief is upset, and I will take care of it."

He was escorted out by couple of security people.

Kabir left after spending little more than an hour in his supposedly last meeting with his teacher. He thought how well connected the professor was; he knew every small thing about what was happening in the neighborhood. He did not know who all were involved in the secret operations. Now that it was decided, he will be completely away from the agency; the little chance he had had of knowing anything about the covert operations was also diminished. That was okay with Kabir.

In the next few minutes, after a cold meeting, the man on the mission was out on the road as he walked a mile across the street to meet his old time friend, Andropov.

After Kabir left, Professor and Dedov had an unexpectedly heated argument. Dedov was already upset about the involvement of Yuri without his prior knowledge. Now, he had not even appeared for a meeting as scheduled. This added to Dedov's fury. Professor had thought Kabir would agree to take on the new, more powerful role and, hearing his refusal, Dedov burst out at Sizov. Dedov left no opportunity to yet again talk about how Sizov had saved Yuri earlier. This led to the argument.

"You are a misfit for the position now, professor."

Sizov remained quiet as he continued to listen to him.

"You are turning old, professor."

Sizov had known Dedov for many years, and he was aware, once Dedov calmed down, he would hear him out. After a moment, Sizov reminded Dedov of all the good work he had done in the past. Dedov mentioned that he was upset and, hence this burst of anger.

When things turned better after some time, they both discussed the key next steps and alternate plan to determine their success.

Sizov had great ideas as always, and Dedov wanted those to be acted upon.

On the other hand, Kabir was surprised to see a few other college mates as he met up with Andropov.

Andropov mentioned that the information he had on Yuri was that he was in Czechoslovaika. So, on that account, Sizov was correct. The network of his friends was well spread out in Airlines and Government offices.

Andropov did warn Kabir that officially, now, he was a Soviet traitor. He needed to be very cautious and guarded and, hence, he needed to even reach out to Michael to seek help.

Kabir did not want to leave any stone unturned and, therefore, a broad array of established connects were discussed. Many years ago, Andropov's father served imprisonment on account of false charges of treasury documents leakage. He was later acquitted, however, that left a scar.

Andropov grew up on this bitterness, and had decided to never support the ideologies of KGB. He would do anything in his personal capacity to derail or, at least, counter their operations whenever they get some information about the same.

The other college friends were part of the anti-communist group that was active since college days. They were all against any sort of Imperialism. During their movements in early days, they served imprisonment too, as they had protested Marxist principles on various occasions. So, they were all like-minded.

All these boys were risk takers. They had a thoroughly sorted out thought process. Kabir would have more access to information at this stage. At the end of the intensive discussions, it was decided that the communication exchange would be extremely crucial, and hence they would all stay in the loop. Also, Kabir needed to share more with Michael now to seek western blessings more deeply. Sharing with Michael would mean hideous designs of people like Yuri or the ones functioning at the behest of Dedov or pawns like Jonathan would get exposed.

In addition, this would throw away the fear that Kabir had earlier as a journalist. Rather than being seen directly in the thick of things, he would use Michael.

Before he left the country, he was handed extra camera batteries; his renewed passport, that was arranged with the connections in Indian Embassy in Moscow; a set of memory cards, and a few other relevant details that might aid Kabir in the future.

They wished him good luck for the marriage. Kabir left with a restored confidence that things might not look the same again. Either way, they were better equipped and prepared now. For anything else, he had Michael's support.

Chapter 15

"Paani kee tai paatla, Dhuan hee tai jheen
Pawana begi utawala, so dosat Kabira keenh."
"Kabir knows that his mind flows more easily than water
It is more obscure than smoke and it moves faster than wind."

KABIR MADE HIS MIND HIS BEST FRIEND, so he remained in control of his actions. When he reached Herat, he was extremely happy to see the development work had begun in the region. The plan that he had prepared was approved, and the work was in full swing. Heavy equipment and machineries could be seen thronging the town. A replica model was introduced in Kandahar and Panj-e-Sharif, so that all activities could happen simultaneously.

Noosh spent some time in Kandahar while Kabir divided his attention between Herat and other regions. Funds remained under control. Project Skylight was shelved. The project required more funds to be managed and, with the new strategy in place, Russians gave it up. Also, Russians treaded with utmost caution after their previous mistakes in the region. Americans were seen more active here.

Kabir hardly had any information on Soviet plans, whatever little he could gather was through, Andropov, who mentioned most of the activities were happening at a fairly higher level, and people like Yuri, were not even aware of the same. What he also highlighted was the fact that Yuri never returned from Czechoslovakia, so it was a possibility that he had sought refuge in that country, fearing his death. Kabir was not in the least surprised.

On the other hand, Nikita and Jemima were able to finish the remaining work on the annual edition. They all had worked very hard to reach the completion stage. Lisa led the effort quite well. It also included the relevant details of the country politics.

Time was flying, and things were changing at a steady pace. Activities continued in the right direction, and the crew travelled to many different places. Michael started meeting Kabir and his team more often. Some new people had joined the project too.

A lot of work under USAID and Green Nation team did not go unnoticed by the bosses in the U.S. It was a long term plan.

There was a great control on the opium dealers too. They were brought into the mainstream by being engaged in the construction work.

Summer went away, and winter arrived. Snow covered the ground, and most of the work had slowed down. The entire work related to concrete roads, and tunnel construction was halted.

In the month of November, a three month break was granted to the foreign team in Afghanistan. This included Kabir, Lisa and, the others who had participated in these development projects. It was also a time for more significant announcements. The hardest was the return of Nikita and Jemima as their assignment was finished end to end. They were supposed to leave within the next couple days, so it was very sad day for all of them.

"Oh, my God, I cannot believe how time flew," said Nikita.

"Yes, Niks, my boss." screamed Kabir.

"If I am ever granted an opportunity to be reborn, I would want you all in my life, over and over again," Nikita began to cry.

Noosh and the others could not control themselves either.

"We all need to drink endlessly, tonight," prompted Kabir.

Their friendship was formed to last forever.

Kabir ensured that all their travel arrangements were smooth, including Lisa who would spend an extended holiday in the US and return the next summer to continue her work.

On one hand, it took Kabir and Noosh some time to come to terms with the fact that their friends were going forever, and, on the other hand, another shock was awaiting him. Kabir had to immediately rush to India, as he was informed that his mother was to undergo a Kidney stone surgery. It was a fairly complicated operation. And, therefore, it was important for Kabir to be by her side. Noosh had no clue as to how to react to this situation. She knew Kabir had to be there and also she would feel very lonely.

Kabir and Noosh spent as much time together as possible, over the next few days before Kabir boarded his flight for Bombay. His return was scheduled for January next year. With heavy hearts and promises to keep in touch the couple parted at the airport in Herat.

==========

Kabir landed in India; he was right on time for his mother's surgery. He spoke to the doctors personally and ensured that he was present at the hospital during the procedure. His family and friends were very supportive too.

The surgery was successful. Life slowly began to turn back to normal. Kabir and Noosh began to write letters to each other. The letters included everything from their daily life details to the writings of Mirza Ghalib and Bedil.

Their love only grew with time, and this distance factor only fueled their desire for each other. It was almost an addiction.

One of the days, in his own available time, Kabir planned to get the photographs developed and also have the videos in tapes so that the entire family could watch together. He got duplicate copies for each of them. There were some unwanted videos as well. While he was deleting those, he came across a video that just made him sit up and take notice.

He watched that video many times over, trying to understand the context, and he was baffled. The video was from the day when his promotion was announced. He did not realize when the recording was left open.

To his utter surprise, there was a phone call that Singh, the Hotel manager, was attending and, immediately after that, he could be seen preparing the cake. Kabir watched that video very closely a few times only to ascertain his understanding.

How was it possible that a cake was prepared even before the promotion announcement was made? It was clearly visible in the video, and also from the sounds recorded; it could be discerned that the announcement of his promotion was made after the cake was prepared for the celebration.

This was definitely fishy. Who would he be talking to? This was a confidential matter. Only the closed groups would know. Also, everybody else who mattered was there at the scene. He did not want to just let it go. The only trouble was that Singh left his job, sometime after that day, and nobody knew where he had gone.

Nevertheless, it was a point on Kabir's agenda to look into this matter as soon as he returned to Herat.

Meanwhile, his mother had more or less recuperated. The discussion regarding Noosh was less, since she was still healing. Father and son exchanged some discussion points. He assured that he would return soon. On being asked about his assignment duration in Afghanistan, he only stated that it will still take him another couple of years, and then he shall be placed in India. At that time, he would look at settling down here for good. Parents had longed to hear this from Kabir.

As his time at home came towards an end, he was seen off by his family that also included his younger cousin, Akash who was very close to Kabir. In fact, most his time was spent either at home or with Akash. The younger one had joined the Indian Army, and was at home on short vacations.

Kabir arrived back in Herat on 20th January 1978. He was received at the airport by Babu and Noosh. Kabir and Noosh were ecstatic to be together again. Noosh had given him a surprise by going to the airport, and Kabir was thrilled about it.

Kabir had his agenda straight up in his head. He mentioned the strange video to Noosh, however, at this point, there was nothing that lead him to decide on the outcome of the video that he had seen.

They enquired from Salem and Meer, also, if they were aware of anything linked to this. It was important for Kabir to take the right steps in the right order. So, in his head, he had defined those very clearly.

First of all, he reached the hotel and checked with the Hotel Director about Singh. He also asked him to provide a photograph of Singh. So far, there was no issue at all. The problem arose when Kabir began to enquire about the call details that were made out and received around that time. Such an information required time, and there was an initial lack of support.

Kabir knew how to leverage his resources and contacts and, depending upon the level of work, he would exercise his option diligently. He roped in Inspector Jamaal to assist him with this task.

But, if there was some hand at a higher level, even within the hotel, this would not have been easy to nail down, in case there was a conspiracy involved at all.

Jamaal had to pull some strings to get on this case. He received all the details within a few days. Inspector was also keen in knowing about the act in progress.

There was a shock awaiting Kabir. The details showed much of the conversation took place between Moscow Agency office and American Embassy office.

Jamaal and Kabir had a series of meetings to find out the next steps. In course of time, it was established that Singh was in touch with someone in Dedov's office and also in the embassy. The doubt arose when the call record showed the same numbers featuring on multiple occasions.

The fingers were pointing at Singh's involvement with Yuri, considering the Moscow calls would have been made between him and Singh. What raised more concern was the American Embassy office. Entire details of Singh was procured. Jamaal was probing the case diligently.

"You would be shocked to know that the sketch matched Singh."

"What are you talking? You mean he killed Jafer?"

"Now I can connect the dots, Kabir."

"So Yuri got Singh to kill Jafer?"

"Yes, I can be sure on that now."

Jamaal alerted his counterparts and higher officials to look for this man. The records stated that he had never left the country. Jamaal even went to meet the Minister and waited for Michael to return to confront and find the mole in the Embassy.

His discussion with the minister yielded no results. The minister stated he had bigger things to look into. He wanted to avoid the discussion for all known reasons. He knew any cooperation would only mean discovery of the link to his minister Ramez.

In the course of time, Minister and the heads of the state had a tough time. The crimes in the country were on the rise. There was a section of the society which was not happy with the government at all. Those were the farmers, especially in Herat province. Their agrarian policies were discarded.

So far as these cases like financial frauds were concerned, they either were never highlighted or remained open. Hence, to expect any fair probe was futile. The government did not want any finger pointing and, therefore, stayed away from all the controversies.

Kabir met Michael and mentioned to him about the trouble in this region. He also discussed about Singh's connection with his office. Michael ignored it and told him to focus on his work. This irked Kabir. When he went into it further, Michael told him of severe internal concerns that this country was going through, and that he would not pay much heed to this one.

Kabir shared all the information he had on the case, as well as the documents related to the progress made and some other plans ahead.

He did not see any action from Professor against Yuri yet. Yuri was never brought back. Kabir was kept in the loop by Andropov on the developments. This did jolt him, and he decided to expose these happenings at the right time.

==========

On the personal front, Kabir and Noosh discussed about the future. They decided that they would tie the knot after completing all ongoing projects sometime next year.

Kabir and Nikita remained in touch with each other for professional reasons, apart from a normal friendly exchange of letters and notes.

As time went by, the situation in the country deteriorated. A few Ministers were overthrown from their positions. Afghan Army and rebels resorted to a bloody internal war.

Events that had started taking place in 1978 took a most gruesome turn in early 1979, and that led to the Herat Uprising. This led to a big loss. Many so called rebels and Army men lost their lives.

It was the reaction of the people to the policies that the Government had adopted. There was a total breakdown in law and order. The Afghan government requested Soviet intervention at this point. Kabir figured out that the Pakistan and Iran supplied arms to the rebels, and even America was involved in some covert operations. This did cause him some distress. He only thought he should not have shared so much information with Michael on the developmental projects. He confided his misgivings to Noosh, however, she asked him not to worry too much as a lot of this was governed at the national level. She comforted him and told him that from his end he had done the best he could. Though he could not still find out Singh's role in all this. Yet, whatever was within his means to try, he had tried his best on it.

Noosh mentioned all his achievements over the years, and what a significant role he had played in developing the infrastructure in Afghanistan. A lot of work had taken place in the country with the help of these philanthropic organizations. Kabir and his team had made a significant contribution to these tasks.

He had worked relentlessly over these couple of years and helped build tunnels, hospitals and schools etc. across the country. He furthered the plans and laid a three year strategy in place that would further connect the country through better road infrastructure and highways.

However, the political stuff going on in Afghanistan had substantial effects on the country.

As the year went by, Kabir planned to make another visit to India. He wanted to ensure things were all set in his hometown, before they moved to Bombay permanently. He wanted Noosh to travel along with him, however, it was decided otherwise. Noosh's father wanted to spend some time with her, as he knew she would be gone out of the country soon, forever. Kabir understood and empathized.

Finally, his travel plans were executed, and he travelled alone to Bombay. He was there for a three month well deserved break, from September to December. Initially, he had planned to return in January but, then, he was told that there would be an awards ceremony in the Christmas month, and his team would be honoured too for work done, so he returned in December.

He remembered the time that was spent in Afghanistan, and the friendships that were developed. This travel was a lot different from the previous one. His work assignment was nearing the end, and also his India project would be announced any soon now.

As Kabir arrived, there were Sens, Boxerwalas and most of the neighbours at home waiting for him. He was welcomed with warm sentiments and high voltage emotions. He was happy to notice that his mom had fully recovered now from the surgery.

"Kabir, you have lost so much weight," said Mrs. Prakash.

"Yes, mom, this time I had to travel a lot within the country. They assigned me multiple tasks."

"Don't worry. You are here for three months, now; I shall feed you well."

"What about Noosh? How how is she?" asked Mrs. Boxerwala.

"She is good, aunty."

"She must be very pretty; show us her pictures, Mr. Photographer."

"I left a few at home last time; didn't mom show it to you?"

The discussion continued. Meanwhile, Kabir's father also arrived, as he had stepped out regarding some new property in the vicinity.

Upon his arrival, discussion about the wedding took place. It was decided Kabir and Noosh would get married the Persian way in Kabul, and the folks from India would try to join them. If not, then the Indian wedding would take place, once they arrived in India after the Persian wedding. This would be done with full traditions. Everybody in the family and the close neighbourhood was enthralled with the idea.

The time was spent well. Kabir's parents were worried as they had heard of the recent turmoil in the country. He comforted them and told them that he would be moving to Kabul upon his return, and things were better in the capital.

Also, he shared a few more phone numbers, in case of emergency. He could not meet his cousin Akash this time around. He did not forget Babu, Salem, Nur and Meer either. He was very selective in choosing the gifts, though his mother had packed a lot of stuff from her end for the family too. Noosh had also sent many gifts with Kabir to her prospective in-laws.

The promise of returning in a couple of months was made. Everybody was excited and happy as they saw him off. He returned to Kabul on December 21st.

Noosh and Kabir spent the next day shopping for the awards and recognition night. Neither of them had the slightest of hint of how their life would turn upside down within a matter of hours. Nobody had.

****

Chapter 16

"Mann unmana na toliye, shabd ke mol na tol
Moorakh log na jansi, aapa khoya bol."
"When your mind is raged, do not react to words
For then the words have no meaning
The fools do not understand it
And lose the balance while talking."

IT WAS DECEMBER 24, 1979. THE EVENT ON THIS COLD WINTER evening was planned in same Hotel Intercontinental in Kabul. The entire symposium had a western style décor. Plenty of acknowledgements were to be announced that day. The event was not wide open for the public community. It was a well-planned, close knit affair. The invitees included Chancellors, State Heads, and Diplomats from Germany, U.S, Sweden and a few other nations.

Michael headed the course of the day.

There was slow instrumental music in the background, quite western. The aura matched everything that surrounded the place. The clothes that people wore, the overall ambience, everything lived up to the evening that day. It never appeared, looking at the gathering, that anything was amiss.

Lisa, Nikita, Jemima were all flown in. Almost everyone that evening was holding a glass of wine or some other alcoholic drink except for Noosh, who was holding a glass of coke. She never would drink alcohol, in a gathering. Only on couple of occasions in her life did she drink. The only last time she drank was when she had gone with Kabir for the Royal Enfield ride, and got back to the Hotel as Juliet.

Here, the big moment had arrived. The awards were announced. People applauded. Jemima, Nikita and Lisa were present and clapping joyously. They were here for only a couple of weeks, and had extended the trip more to spend some time with their friends rather than anything else.

The moment Noosh's name was announced, they all started cheering out loud. Next was Kabir, and all of them were awarded for their contribution. This included the efforts towards building roads in remote areas, working in the field of education and women empowerment, and also specific programs that Noosh had begun for the country's drug control efforts.

In the hustle and bustle of these affairs, Kabir wanted to look around the Hotel. Some of the construction had changed. Out of curiosity and remembrance, he decided to take the rear door, yet again. In a long time, he got a chance to revive his old memories. This is where everything had actually started for him.

As he was returning from the outer exit, he stopped. He saw Michael talking to someone familiar; he got curious, and hid himself behind the door. The man looked familiar. He wasn't sure about him, yet. But that look carried deception now.

He tried to overhear their conversation, but failed. He did not want to lose this opportunity. The conversation stopped and both had disappeared from the scene within a few minutes.

Kabir took the back door, which lead to the lawn. All this while, he scratched his head; held his eyebrows with his fingers and pressed them hard, only to find himself lost. He wasn't able to recollect anything at all.

He could spot the man taking the route to the car. Kabir started running towards him and, on the way, clashed into Michael.

"Who was this man, Mr. Michael?"

"I believe he is a businessman from France."

"What did you discuss with him?"

"Nothing much. He just discussed about the investment plans in the U.S, and was generally asking me about my schedule."

"Oh, okay. So, where is he staying?"

"What happened Kabir?"

"Why are you lying to me, Mr. Michael?"

Kabir remembered, this man was sent to him while he was in Herat. Michael had sent him, and now he did not remember.

"Why would I lie?"

"Either you are lying now, or you lied to me when you were in New York last year?"

Kabir further recollected how he had met him as one of the project coordinators. While Michael was in the U.S, and could not be in Afghanistan, he had sent him to collect a lot of information related to the projects.

"Something is wrong with you, Kabir."

Michael left the sight and mingled with the guests.

"I will deal with you later, Mike."

Kabir began to run towards the gate. He knew he did not want to lose the sight of this secret man. He immediately called on Nur, and asked him if he could recognize anyone leaving from the gate. Nur was parked outside, right near the gate, and was walking around the parking lot.

"Yes, Kabir *saab*, he just left in a rush in the car."

"Where to?"

"That went towards the..." Nur stopped abruptly to think if he could add some weight to his point, and then continued, "I think he was a Russian. He went towards Russian's favourite hotel."

"That man guised himself. I am devastated Nur."

"But what happened, Kabir *saab*?"

"You have no idea, what I am going through right now."

"Really?"

"Yes, but this is not the time to talk. I want you to get the car right now. We need to chase him."

A noise could be heard from far away, like an explosion, these guys were already psyched out and, hence, reacted immediately to it.

"What the hell was that? I believe it is a tyre burst," Nur said.

"Oh, hell, it all looks like hell right now, to me," said Kabir in anguish.

****

Inside the seminar space, Noosh kept looking around for Kabir. It was a very special day, and she thought it was the right moment to let him know that she wanted to marry him as soon as possible. Over last several days, she had been thinking the same, a lot of planning had gone on in her mind. She had spent a few notebook pages calculating everything, right from the budgeting to the venue, menu, guest list, travel plans to India, every small detail.

Where are you Kabir? When I need you the most, you are not around me. Juliet wants to marry you Romeo. Where art thou?, She kept murmuring in frustration.

She decided to step out, and her eyes faded into the car screeching out of the main gate. Oh, was that Nur Uncle with Kabir in the car?

Nikita came around, "Where will they go at this hour? Why would they step out abruptly from this day and event?"

"Oh, this man, I hope everything is fine. I wish I had a walkie talkie so I could speak with him right away."

Noosh strolled around the venue with Nikita, and discussed the matter.

****

The car chase ended in front of the hotel gates. Kabir was out, even before Nur could stop the car. As he began to run, he looked back at Nur and shouted, "Nur, he killed your brother."

"Yes Kabir, get him. Be aware of the security around the room. He might not be alone. May be today he is. May be he is not here. Nonetheless, I am coming and alerting my people here."

Kabir ran up to the fifth floor; there were several men present outside most of the rooms. Those were several Russians who guarded it, with only two rooms on that floor given out to anybody else. These two were occupied by the Afghani businessmen. He made an observation, and hid behind the stairwell door.

Nur had done the smart thing. He managed to short plan some set of activities. He reached the spot, and put the door key of Afghanis occupied room very swiftly in the pocket of Kabir's coat. "Shall I pull out my gun and shoot them all? I mean, his gun; his Barrett that I probably retained with me for this day," said Kabir in anger.

"Kabir *saab*, what has triggered this suddenly?" asked Nur in a hush hush tone.

"Let's save the detailed discussion for later, Nur. We need to do something now. I want to confront this Russian, one last time. But, with the huge security here, we cannot do much, except I want to believe what I saw."

They both started walking nonchalantly, and got inside one of the rooms using the keys that Nur had arranged.

"What is next *saab*?"

"I am thinking."

"I am thinking, too, you need to confirm the person in that room is Yuri, right? I checked with the hotel staff. They mentioned the person is staying under some name that begins with F, and I don't recollect, but it is certainly not Yuri."

"Yes, that I know. The name, the guise, everything, and it must be Francois in the hotel registers, linked with some extreme covert ops. He is at something; we need to figure it all out, and, maybe, we are running out of time," suddenly, Kabir became a little hyper, gathered his courage, and walked towards the security bound room. He asked the security personnel to allow him to meet the hotel guest inside the room. What clicked with the security was that Kabir spoke to them in Russian.

Kabir began to talk in Russian with the security agents.

"Let me get inside, I know him," said Kabir.

"If you do not have an appointment, you cannot meet him," one of the armed security official replied.

"Since when has Yuri started meeting his people on appointment?"

Security remained quiet.

Kabir insisted.

On hearing the commotion outside, and guessing the reason, the guest stepped out of the hotel room.

"In side, my man, come inside, and why do you look so rattled?"

Kabir was stunned. It was a spectacle for the security around before they went inside. He lost his speech. He lost all his energy after what he saw.

"Where is my hug, my son?"

"Professor, it is you."

"You are stretching your imagination, come take a seat."

He could not believe his eyes. He wished that all this were a bad and bitter dream. But it was not.

Professor Sizov was never short of tricks, and he carried many up his sleeves. He had disguised himself. It was all out in the open now. Kabir felt betrayed. He was living the worst horror of his lifetime.

"I made you a man, Kabir. Who knew you? Who would have known you? I established you. I saved your life many times; you would not know about that. I am cold for many, but I protected you like a warm human being."

"You betrayed my trust. In the name of prosperity, I think you mean under the facade of aiding Afghanistan; you kept filling your coffers. In the name of money, you killed innocents."

"What do you mean? I have never killed a soul. We only kill the purpose that goes against us. You have any idea how many billions of Roubles we have funded over the years to this country?"

"I don't need a lecture again."

"There is no facade."

"Then why this mask?"

Professor knew it was not defensible anymore. But he remained unmoved. Unfazed.

"What were you doing with Michael?"

"Don't you know he is my friend?"

"Why did you meet him in this manner, masked?"

"There is a threat to me, so I had to."

Kabir asked him to be truthful to him this last time.

"Why did you disguise and meet me in Herat? What did you do with those project related documents that I shared with you trusting you were concerned with the development, and thought that is why Michael sent you? Tell me everything professor. You and Michael have together ruined many lives, many dreams. Tell me Professor," Kabir continued in anguish.

The Plot and conspiracy, on the face of it, seemed damning. He asked him about the role of Singh. The picture became clearer to Kabir, and he wanted to hear this from the obstinate professor. He repeated his questions, and asked him again "What did you talk with Michael today? Why did you have to be disguised? Truth only. Please."

"Look, you might not know that after the U.S Ambassador's death, the relationship between Americans and Afghans had gone sour. I just wanted to get some information out of you. American agencies wanted to supply guns to the country. To combat us. There was a lot of money involved."

"What information?"

"The demographics. The money going into the current projects. List of people. People who supported Americans. People who supported Russians. You had all the information," Professor continued, "Look, Jafer's murder was a mistake. We found out later that he knew some truth. The plan was to abduct him, pay him money, and send him elsewhere. But he got killed."

Kabir kept looking at him, asking for more.

"Michael had a commission in the arms supply; also, he was given this responsibility to curb Russians, as much as possible. You shared information. I also gathered information. We both had a common objective. We wanted to make money too and keep the secret services alive."

"So, you both are true doubles; no loyalty, whatsoever."

"It was all covert, Kabir. You won't understand. To simplify, we get paid for this, and if we don't, we try different ways to get paid. That's all. It is quite deep rooted."

"Do not weave a maze of words around me, Professor. Tell me what you were doing today?"

"Nothing much. But, yes, the days to come might create history, and then history might safely be locked up. And, yes, the present and future would spell imminent danger."

"What do you mean?"

"Look, Kabir, Afghanistan has been seeking our help for a long time. They have been asking the interference of our intelligentsia. I told my bosses. We are serfs and beggars ourselves, and we cannot change the fate of another nation. The ministers here and the leadership wanted military intervention. Therefore, I turned up today. I wanted to gauge the situation on the ground."

"So, you aren't here to help the country, are you?"

"I do not know the exact details further, however, I believe the nation finally stands a chance to get the military support they've been asking for all along."

"You contradict yourself, Professor."

"You said I am a double, didn't you?"

"Oh, so you benefit from both ends in reality, even now."

"My answer to that is, yes. But it is not me alone. There are many like Michael and me. All over the world."

"And, what about Singh and Yuri?"

"Singh was our operative in Herat. He was code named 'Dar'. We wanted to give the position to Nur as Jack. But he became close to you, so his name was dropped."

"What about Yuri? You have not answered that?"

"Who is Yuri? Who is Leonid? Who is Sizov? You must ask all this."

"Sorry, I do not understand what you mean."

"These are just the names, you know. And I thought by now you would know the answer."

Kabir was stunned. He was in a state of disbelief. He was shocked to the point of being hysterical. He thought back to all the events that had taken place one after the other. The flashes of all his meetings, interactions, and why he never met Professor and Yuri together, kept hitting his memory. "Oh, hell, that is why the person you introduced me the first time, as Leonid was not too visible, and kept some distance. And when I came to meet you at KGB, you told me Yuri was in Czechoslovakia and you created the atmosphere where everybody believed in what you had thought of. So, all the stories were cooked and served well; you really fooled me, old man," Kabir was panting heavily. "You are Yuri, and you are Sizov too. You are one."

"See, which is what my job as a spy is, and I wish you had not turned down my offer. Nobody would have known it. You would not have known either, had I not told you. But, I thought to tell you and do you this last favour before I leave from here. And, who knows, you might have met Singh, at some point, too." Professor had no qualms about the same.

Kabir was only getting sunk in the entire discussion. He kept getting all his answers, though.

"And, what kind of military intervention you referred to earlier? Are you going to guard the country now? Does UN allow you to do so? Can you really do that?"

"If Afghanistan seeks our support, then we do not require any permission from anyone. It is mutual between two nations and two friends."

"You have not done the right thing, Professor."

"I have to fly out in a while. Hope to see you soon. And, yes, pay my regards to Noosh. You make a lovely couple. If possible, you must return and settle down in India sooner. I have always been your well-wisher. Take care, son. I have to leave now. And, yes, before I leave, remember I had a choice not to meet you today. I did not exercise the option. And, yes, in some days, you might hear that Yuri is killed. You would be the only person who would know the truth behind this. I hope you keep it a secret. Now, I have to go. It is getting late."

He left the room with the security and disappeared in seconds.

Kabir was joined by Nur, now, as he stood just outside the Professor's room.

"What did he say about Jafar's killing? What did you find out Kabir?"

"He was Sizov and he guised himself as Yuri. You have been ferrying him around for years, and even you did not know," Kabir was completely baffled, "He stated about some militia, some sort of military intervention, which now shall be met as per this country's demand. He was talking very big."

I told Noosh that I am here for an Epic, and this old man seemed to have overheard me, and he took it so seriously. He spoke of creating history, Kabir thought in his head.

"Really, I cannot believe this man has so many faces. But, why did he tell you all this?" asked Nur.

"He is my well-wisher," said Kabir sarcastically.

Something was drastically wrong here, and they had to figure out their next course of action. He could not even approach Michael now.

Nur tried to think of something, too, and shared whatever he knew of the events and about this man with Kabir.

Kabir was a bit nervous now and, soon, he felt the absence of Noosh, "We need to leave for the hotel. Do you feel the drizzle?

Am I forgetting anything? Nur, we need to go to the ceremony again; I need to meet Noosh. I ran out abruptly from the event; she is uninformed; must be worried."

The time spent in the car, gave Kabir headway into his old memory set. He had been constantly thinking of the past events, "My memory cannot let me down this time, too," as he began to think, his mind was constantly shifting through the moments, which were gone but now certainly seemed relevant.

"Nur", he screamed.

"Kabir *saab*, you must control this habit of yours to shout and scream when you discover something," Nur responded irritably, as he was nervous, himself, after witnessing such shocking revelations during the course of the evening, which otherwise was supposed to be an awards night.

"I apologise, Nur. But the God damn thing just struck my mind,

You know what happened last year. This man asked me a variety of details on the American held projects. He asked me the rail road, hospitals, schools, tunnels, infrastructure, almost anything and everything that a Russian would be interested in knowing from the insider. You know what I mean?"

"Yes, so far."

"Soviets are not here to safeguard; they are here to attack. I can tell you. I know the way he thinks. He mentioned it to me the present is in danger, and you know what – I am such a fool. He even called me Yogi, as I remember, when he met me last year. I just did not pay attention, I am thinking how could he say that, and why I missed to notice that?"

Nur immediately stopped the car.

Kabir stepped out for fresh air, as he began to palpitate. Nur got him some water, and patted his back to calm him down.

"Nur, Nur, can you hear me?"

"I am standing right next to you Kabir *miyan*; say something before you ensure I die of a heart attack."

"That was my last day in Herat last year. I was very excited. I had submitted the report to the bosses in the U.S; and I was told by Michael that some folks might come and meet me further, to get best practices and all the details apply in other areas."

"Aha, and this old man, this Professor, turned up. I don't even know now what his real name is. I always believed he was a doting Professor,

Then, there are rebels, their so called *Dushmans*.

Yeah, I think I was right when I told Noosh that I am here for an Epic. In no meaner sense, is this turning out to be a story for your revised annual edition, or a series of newspaper articles that Times would vie for? This is strategy, this is a war. Nur *ji*, I am telling you, this is a war; mark my words."

"Come on Kabir *saab*. You know it; this country has had a series of troubles, even ever since you have been here; see what happened in Herat; what happened to Amin. Look at the rise and fall of Taraki, Daud, and now Amin is there. Under the rule of Amin, the worst losses have occurred. He has been responsible for killing many people. Russians feel he works for CIA, and that American Ambassador's killing, and the growing dissent in many parts, the whole political fabric, huge loss of trust, execution all over the country, is this any less than a war? There is an internal war already. I don't think anything worse can happen."

"I still feel, the worse is yet to come. I could see it in his eyes. There was anger and hatred; this appears bigger than we could imagine and, you know. The time I spent here, I got to travel across; met with many people, and saw, somewhere, that people are very angry. Russians supplied billions of their currency; internal political rivalry killed many; people are losing trust; the poor have only been at the receiving end; people only lose everything, and it is always like this,

Okay, let us get inside the car. Please drive me, Nur *bhai*."

Nur was also extremely tensed now.

The car reached the spot as Noosh was spotted around the main gate.

"Where have you guys been? What happened?"

Kabir remained silent.

"Can anyone tell me what is going on? Why do you look so troubled Kabir, and, Nur uncle, at least you say something. You have no idea what I was going through, when you guys rushed out."

"Noosh, beta, something worse is yet to happen, much worse than what we have seen here."

"What makes you say that?"

"We just met one of the perpetrators, he deceived us."

"You mean, the guy who gave you the gun? That soviet spy?"

"Yes, Noosh, yes, and I do not know what is going to happen. It could even be a war. That guy is Professor himself. He created multiple identities and fooled us all."

"Can we talk about it with Michael?" asked Noosh.

"Michael is part of the plan and, I believe, by now, Professor would have conveyed everything to him through his people," said Kabir.

Kabir still wanted to take the chance, and decided to shoot in the dark. He did not want to share with Michael that Professor told him everything.

"I am sorry for having doubted you. That was a French businessman. You were right, Mr. Michael."

Michael quietly walked away, showing that he was upset with him. Kabir did not make an attempt to stop him either.

Overall, the situation here had worsened nonetheless. What the leaders from Khalq did to the people was not favourable to the locals, and they found it against their sentiments. That included radical land reforms and women education, however, this aroused deep resentment in the villages. The retaliation began with the resurgence of the Parchams, the party in the opposition, and the revived leadership, which wanted Soviets to provide full military support to counter the growing militancy of the rebels.

A few hours went in discussing the activities; it was now revealed that the opposition leader had reached out to the Soviets in the summer, seeking their support. The Parchams believed this would help in easing out the tensions, and they thought the Russians would save the nation, and no more lives would be lost in cross politically influenced fights.

The Khalqs and the Parchams were the divided parties that were formed after the main party called PDPA was broken.

"It is also a possibility, something better comes out as a result of this Russian support or so called military intervention," said Kabir.

"Every time they think of something better, look what happens," Nur seemed hopeless.

"Yes, and this time again, when he mentioned the military support to Afghanistan, I believe it would come at some cost; at the cost of the lives of people here," Kabir only kept thinking too hard about his conversation with the Professor.

"People are responsible for the actions, Kabir *saab*."

"But, the government is responsible for the people; outside influences can only cause disharmony, deceit, conceit and a huge loss."

"On this Christmas Eve, what we can do is wait for the next day and celebrate Christmas, assuming all shall be fine."

"No concrete designs or plans can be in place at this hour... whatever we need to do, let us talk about it tomorrow." replied Kabir.

They all left for their respective hotels. Michael took the flight to Jordan where he had planned a family vacation, whereas all the media folks were staying in the Intercontinental itself. He was not aware of the conversation that took place between Kabir and Sizov, and he trusted what Kabir had told him when he met him before he left. Professor had to take his flight urgently, owing to the situation so he did not waste any time to take any trouble to inform Michael. It seemed the Russian had achieved what he wanted.

****

Chapter 17

"Bada hua toh kya hua, jaise ped khajoor
Panthi ko chhaya nahi, phal lage ati door."
"In vain is the eminence, just like a date tree
No shade to travellers, and the fruit is hard to reach."

THE NEXT MORNING, after a sleepless night, as usual, Kabir turned off the television, as also it had no images. He was still wearing his clothes from the previous night, and he barely had time to change. He was all absorbed in his own set of activities, for he feared something drastic was going to grip the country.

The television did not show anything, and he tried to make a complaint at the reception; to his surprise, the intercom wasn't working either.

What rubbish, how it could become so fatally incapable; so wrong, nothing is working today. I must wait for the newspaper boy, and he sat down on the couch thinking to himself, Let me go for breakfast and figure this out.

As he reached the reception, he realized he was grossly mistaken to be one of the first ones to be awake, almost the entire hotel was up and about, some were checking out in a worried rush. Some were still contemplating and the rest were either journalists or citizens from other cities of the country.

"What happened here Mr. Akram? Why this madness? At 6 am it appears to be a Pushkar mela here, sans camels and Hippies," Kabir asked the sincere hotel manager.

"Kabir sir, the city has come to a standstill. We see many tanks coming around; I don't know much; all I know is that it looks like a royal siege," said the baffled manager.

"What the heck? Are you serious?"

Kabir seemed to be confirming the truth in his head, what were the Americans and Iranians and Arabs doing all this while, he kept thinking.

"And Kabir Sir, all flights are booked now. May I arrange for a vehicle for you? I can arrange a safe passage for you, and you can always flaunt your press card; they will let you go."

"Hey, Akram, Thanks a lot for your offer; now let me do my business. You worry about yourself. Why don't you return to Udaipur? Like, leave right now, and I mean it."

"Yes, sir, I have been thinking too. No phones are working today, and I cannot make a call either. My boss said, I have to be the last person to leave the hotel, such is the cost of duty."

"So be it; you ensure safe exit for your esteemed guests. Let me figure this out further."

Kabir turned around, gasping; the air seemed to be enveloped with thick black dust.

I never witnessed what happened in Herat, earlier this year. I am sure it must have been a similar scene; this is no less than a war, but who are they fighting against here, hmmm, here to safeguard, something that Sizov said, Kabir thought to himself.

The scene starting turning into chaos within minutes, and people were running amok.

The Soviet army asked everyone to stay indoors. There were clear instructions; so far, it appeared all of this was happening at the behest of Amin; it seemed his plea of getting the army here was being adhered to and, more than that, it was very clear, whatever Professor spoke, a day before, was turning out to be a brutal reality. What was spoken, and what was seen now made a huge difference; the sight looked very dangerous; nowhere did it appear there was an army to protect the people; it was more of a grudge against the rulers and the rule.

The mighty and the powerful who stayed in the hotel and the Tajbeg palace must be clueless, except for very few people who may have been aware of this in advance. This was a part of the most secretive operations; the details were yet to unfold. For now, the speculations would make way; even the newspaper would be biased towards what they felt was right. After Tarik's murder, the Parcham leader who was killed by Amin's people; things had only started getting worse.

Further, stemming from these significant developments, the Russians wanted to control more, and this was the beginning of their plan towards the objective of taking complete control of the Afghans.

"Yes, Kabir, you got it absolutely right. We have been captured, and literally held hostages for now; we cannot even move out."

"Are you sure, Noosh?"

"Yes, I am," said Noosh, as they had begun to discuss these turn of events.

"I want to be proven wrong, Noosh, and if this is right, then war is in the offing, and this is going to be a proxy war; the Americans will fight them out; the Russians will not budge, and we will all die."

"If that is the case, I see many reasons why we need to fight the Russians."

"So do I."

"Come, I know of a way to leave."

"Oh, yes, I do too."

"Which one?"

"The one that I used once to meet Yuri a couple of years ago."

"Yeah, the one from the back that goes under the basement and reaches the mountainous road to the palace." Noosh was also aware of the same; probably, at some point earlier Kabir must have told him about it.

"Exactly."

"Okay, let us rush out now."

The two leave the passage that was only meant for secret ops that took place; the soviets had built this passage many years ago; only a couple of hotel staff knew of it, they were endangered, hence kept quiet.

The duo wanted to reach the palace, as they thought it would be a safer place and they could discuss the actions with the ministers and the ruler himself. They managed to reach the palace. However they were not allowed any access inside. The people out there knew Noosh, though, so there was some chance that they might be allowed upon insisting.

Amin seemed very nervous already; he was getting his ministers to hide inside the palace.

There were some locals gathered around the area and kept talking amongst themselves.

"We are aware of the insurgents having their base in neighbouring countries including Pakistan, Iran and Egypt," said one of the locals.

"We understand that, and then you witness the spread of T62s and the failure of communication system, all of a sudden. All you feel is the threat perception; you don't feel it is there to protect you; you feel it is there to kill you," Kabir responded to him.

"You do not worry; this is part of the larger plans. Come take some rest in the courtyard here; you know what happened under the regime of Amin, and now there are many against those so called reforms."

"Yes, I know and I have been travelling for last two years. I discovered many things myself and, yes, a large part of the region, especially around Herat."

Kabir and Noosh returned to the Hotel and stayed there. They found the conditions at the palace were worse, owing to the presence of army men.

The much hated agrarian reforms that were not acceptable to the villagers, as it seemed to favour the rich, and the effect of suppressed human conditions were coming to an end. People like Sizov and Michael ensured there was enough ammunition to ruin and prove supremacy.

"Noosh, I need to share something with you," Kabir said.

"Tell me first, when do you plan to flee? The Russians are very soon going to close out all the borders with China and Pakistan, and then we shall be left with no place to run away; the situation is only getting worse. There comes a point where the ID's don't work in a war; you see the situation now." Noosh said worriedly.

"I quite agree with you Noosh, and those are the attacks. Precisely, I have come to talk to you about. I still am not able to believe, and hence I wanted your opinion.

You know, over last couple of years, all the documentation that was worked upon by me, all those plans, road maps, series of details, everything seems to have been copied by the Soviets to help them in waging this war; this is exactly how they are going about it. Right from cutting off the communication lines to planning the attacks in a fashion that they can last longer, everything is planned."

"No, Kabir, you are under some misunderstanding; there is enough access, anyway, that the Soviets have, so why would they need it from you?"

"Access and details are two different things, they very smartly placed me here. I mean, even though I never worked for them, but look at it, I ended up playing into their hands, don't you see that, Noosh?

That Yogi code word; meeting with the Professor, revelation of Professor's and Michael's covert designs; journalism course, placement through the professor, so you think, it is all by chance?"

"Hmmmmm," Noosh put her head down, frightened as she was, and now went numb, she trembled, "Kabir, I have never felt so scared in my life; I never feared so much, and it is not just about me, I think we are falling apart; everything is falling apart."

"Look, Noosh," Kabir stopped her in between.

"No, Kabir, I don't want to stop."

"Noosh, here," he gave her water.

And Kabir picked up the conversation from here on.

"Noosh, I am very sorry," as he held her hands.

"No Kabir, why are you sorry?"

"I was betrayed. I was naïve."

"Come on, don't be foolish, you did nothing. Now you can do a lot."

"I prepared a mighty piece of reference material that is aiding them today. I brought your country down."

"What are you saying Kabir? Are you insane?"

Kabir went to a corner of the room, and sat absolutely still in a chair. He kept biting his nails and murmuring to himself. He was clearly reeling under the shock the day's events had given him. His eyes turned blood red, and he shifted to a state of anger.

"How could I trust him, how could I? Professor, you created hell for us here, Sizov, Yuri, Leonid Michael, Singh. Oh, god, I wish you get hell. I wish you get the worst treatment meted to you when you go to hell.."

"Kabir, they will get hell here. You think, invading my country will bring them peace? No, they will not be at peace, for the rest of their lives."

"Noosh, I need to do something," Kabir started talking very fast. He tried hard to be coherent, however, it was not a normal day, and Kabir was never seen in such a bad shape before. He fretted and fumed, banged his head twice on the wall, kept screaming, "I don't know now, and I had not known then what I could have done; I feel I am a very small, a trivial person."

Kabir was feeling very heavy in his heart and, at the same time, he knew he was pitched against the mighty and powerful and, despite knowing so much, he felt, he could not really do anything. He wished he could have done more than merely confront Sizov.

"Kabir, what could you have done? These are international matters, we are mere workers here, and, yes, you have been used, and hence all this guilt." Noosh tried to console him.

"And I won't leave from here, now."

"No, that is not right thinking, Kabir. We need to consider our future too. I wanted to ask you about our marriage plans, and look where we landed ourselves."

"Whoops, you are the most important person to me, Noosh; I shall listen to you."

"Then, listen to me and plan an exit from here, we need to leave like everybody else".

"And, then? Flee like a loser. I will do all that my strength permits. I am not leaving, till this is fixed. Not until I die."

"No, it is for the governments to fight this war, not for us."

"I am guilty; yes, I am. I want to get this load off my chest, and the only way I see this is possible is to fight this war. I want to participate in rehabilitation process. Wherever I can help with my intelligence, I shall ensure there is enough from my end. I will fight this war."

"And, who are you going to support? The ministers are nobody's, the Russians are supposed to be minister's partners and they have invaded us, so the fight is actually a fight within the system; it is us against us, so who are you going to support, Kabir?"

"I need to think that through, but, for now, my enemy truly appears to be across the lines, anybody who attacks and captivates us here is the enemy, for them, the *mujahideens* are and it is part of the larger conspiracy that I don't know, that must be known to Mr. Carter. What we can do in our capacity, we will. Are you with me in this, Noosh?"

Noosh fell silent.

"Kabir, when you are so much quick, and so intelligent, then the other person needs some time to process, understand, and respond; give me some time," Noosh responded slowly.

"I don't need you to respond to the technical part. I am asking you if you are with me."

"Is that even a question to ask me, Kabir?"

"When the brain works in multi directions, then you don't know whether to assume or to ask…I prefer to ask."

"Now, and till the end of times, keep it assumed that no matter what you do, where you go, and what you want me to do, I shall always be with you, I am not leaving you, Kabir."

"Noosh, say that again."

"I am always with you, Kabir."

"Say that a few more times, Noosh, I believe I am addicted to you."

"I am always with you Kabir, and you, would always be my muse, and you?"

"Apply the same assumption Noosh."

"Yes that I know of you, so Kabir, will you marry me?"

"What a day! Really, a woman, a Persian woman, asking a man's hand in marriage."

"Yes, Kabir, I am well educated, intelligent, born in a liberal society, and I am asking a man if he would like to marry this set of combination."

"Who on earth would be such a fool as to refuse? I don't want to regret…umm…possibly regret."

"Regret what?"

"Not saying yes to you. But, dear, you had told me you will marry me when the right time comes and, similarly, you had told your father also that you will marry me when the time is ripe and right, and now when there is a war hanging on our heads, you want to marry me? Is this the right time Noosh?"

"Yes, Kabir, this is the right time; the perfect time to be together because I know you cannot fight the war alone. We need to fight it under the same roof now."

"That sounds like a pretty strategic move, huh…right Noosh?"

"Yeah, learning from you."

During the course of the conversation, Kabir realised the situation outside was better and this was the perfect day for him to give Noosh a surprise. He asked her to accompany her to some place that he wanted to show to her.

Upon reaching the place, Noosh was pretty surprised.

She asked him about the details of this house. Kabir told her it was the house that he had bought some time back, and wanted to surprise her with before their wedding.

"Kabir, you never mentioned about this house to me, how come? Then why do you stay in the hotel?"

"Well, Noosh while I never deliberately participated in any covert ops, yet I discovered a few things, and one of them was to keep changing your location and always have a plan B in place. This was part of my learning."

"That is so nice, so you bought this?"

"I wanted to give you a surprise. I bought this for us, actually, as a vacation home whenever we would come from India, so I bought this a few months ago, before leaving for India. The prices had fallen down, and it was the right time. I began to save more after the promotion, so I could afford it."

"And, now, you got me into this house, and I am not even married to you. It is ethically not right."

"Discussing and strategizing and making a conducive plan, globally, is ethically and morally correct, so do not delve into it, and now after being here for a couple of hours, you ask me this."

"You convince me each time."

"You get convinced each time."

"Yes, because you are able to."

"Noosh, you just look for those positive words from me; the day I agree with you, I bet, you shall turn back yourself and say, Kabir, you have changed, this and that."

"Interesting, sir."

"At some point, we need to take a trip down to Herat. We need to figure out. I hope everyone is safe out there,

So far as I know Russians, will take some time to reach there."

"They can reach there anytime…they are not just a land army…I believe they have airplanes in place too…."

"And, what about our old gang of girls and those boys?"

"They must be taking the plane to Jordan or to India; there is a safe exit for all the foreigners and tourists."

"Do we not meet them? Where do we find them?"

"Well, I think they exited the hotel. Things look bad outside; someone needs to go back there and find out. I am certain they must be under surveillance, all foreigners must be, and they know there might be secret agents and the journalists, so need to be cautious. I will go, you stay back."

"And, if you don't return?"

You asked me to assume, right Noosh, so I assume you are not leaving me, and so you assume too and do not worry."

Kitna Khouff hota hai sham ke andheron main
Pooch un parindo se jinke ghar nahi hotey
"How horrifying are those darkness of the evenings
Ask the birds who have no shelter."

What struck today seemed to have been in the works for a while now. This could not have been materialized in a just a few weeks. Upon investigation by the media folks, the linkages were established to Babrak's visit to Moscow. Some of the eye witnesses even mentioned that on the eve of Dec 24th, Babrak had come with some of the Soviets from Moscow. Kabir missed to see the same. It was later that Babrak also came to see the Professor off at the airport. This Hotel where the Professor had stayed was actually a favourite spot for the Soviets. Many a time, the ops were so secretive that within the same directorate of the KGB, there could be multiple sets of information.

It was still hard to believe why they would choose Afghanistan, a vast nation with a population of about 15 -16 million people. Afghanistan had leaders and rulers who were given many millions or billions of gold rubles, and they appear sold. Even in the past, people like Amin had shared their vision of Greater Afghanistan. They wanted to expand as the history offered, and their neighbors, like Pakistan, took advantage of it.

Kabir once tried to approach the subject in 1978 with his bosses in the west and he was told that anything that Soviets try to do is always known to the Americans. They were busy in Iran, however, they were completely aware of the activities in Afghanistan, reason why they developed their aid centers in the country, reasons why lot of folks from media were present in Afghanistan when all this happened, but then what happened at Carter's level, or his discussions with E Kennedy or with Germany was not known at that point. Kabir, in all his right minded thinking, kept sharing important information with Michael which eventually backfired.

Kabir did not draw much inspiration from these activities. So, now, he was like any common citizen who was in love with a woman. He was set to save lives of many in many ways and see how this invasion could be thwarted.

The rumor and speculations in the corners of the country were doing the rounds as people were talking of the attack by the Prachamists on the Khalqs. The Parchamists were considered the Intelligentsia, and The Khalqs were considered the military party. With the situation at hand, it was felt that Babrak, who was part of the Parchamists, might attack Amin and all those in the Khalqs who were sensible and believed in goodwill of people will join

Babrak, and also the PDPA might be united again. Amin was considered a dictator.

Some of the happenings in the country were also ignored due to the fact that some of the Soviet people in Polit Bureau were considered close to Amin, so they never gave the actual account to the leadership. Later, they found out about the independent agenda Amin was running that would have turned against the entire objective of communism and, also, they felt this would spoil USSR image on the international front when USA and the allies would look for any opportunity to take USSR as the hostile nation on international front.

Overall, when the activities started taking place on Dec 23rd, 24th and 25th, people did not have much clarity. Some thought this is in support of Amin while the others believed this is was a coup d'état, to topple the government of Amin.

In the air, Afghani pilots could be seen flying at the height of 60-70 meters for the first time in their MI 25 Helicopters.

During this time, Amin did reveal to his closer aides that his proximity to the westerns did not help. He said he did not care anymore, as to what the west wants; all he could see was his empire toppling, and only the soviets seemed dominant as he had a broader sense that he might be killed.

The evening of 25th and 26th saw lot of activities as the troops began to close in and the tanks nearly capture Kabul.

The operation Agat, as was known, was to take complete shape on December 27th.. There were many members of KGB who had come to Kabul to ensure the success of this operation which aimed at eliminating Amin and all his men. The arrests would happen, and the blood bath was in the offing. The soviet troop, that included Spetsnaz, were dressed in Afghan army uniforms, and there was an explosion at the residence of Amin. Many members were arrested and killed, a few people from KGB also lost their lives. This caught international attention, and some of the commanders in KGB did not appreciate it. Babrak wanted severe punishment for Amin's men, and wanted to assure the Soviets of relentless support. Communication between Moscow and Babrak and his men became stronger. Dec 28th saw the end of the operation Agat. This operation had support of the people from the masses and all those who opposed Amin's rule including the Soviets.

Any resistance from Amin's army was crushed before it could grow; the army started taking orders from the Soviets knowing the situation was only tensed and against them. On the other hand, the rebels started growing in other parts of the country to counter this insurgence.

All those who were close to Amin, now showed their proximity towards Babrak. Some went to the extent of stating they wanted their lives to be saved, and hence supported Amin's sentiments. A lot of people in the Afghan office contemplated this to be the hand of Americans, and some thought this could be Parchamist. The people were left divided and opinionated; some even believed now Babrak will take over and, hence, the situation will improve. One thing they commonly believed was that this war will not stop any sooners and this will continue.

There were Maoists, rebels, Parchamists, conspirators, Akhvanists, Khomeinists who were held prisoners under Amin's rule. Things started coming out now; it was a tyrannical rule; many were convicted and many were killed. The prisons were now filling up with Amin's loyalists and all those who were behind the killings of the innocents.

The Kabul times carried the news that the will of the people will be the deciding factor. While the people were not aware of what was happening, and it said 'down with the interventionists'. This seemed to be one of the last ditch attempts of Amin to solicit the support of the westerners; since the print was in English, not many Afghanis could understand, so the intent was to garner the support of the westerner and to let them know Amin was against the Soviets.

On the other hand, communication lines at Amin's residence had already been studied. Come December 27 and the residence of Dar ul Aman was attacked. Amin was planning a counter revolutionary coup, later, for the month of December, however, he was executed on the 27th itself.

There were airborne divisions and paratrooper regiments that guarded the capital…this would dissuade any attempt by the Afghan army to do much. It was all well planned.

Kabul radio was in the hands of the soviets, and it was difficult to decipher whether the announcement were made or written in USSR or it was actually being broadcasted from Kabul. Soviets had completely taken over the control in Kabul. The actual announcements on the radio were being made from Tashkent, and people were made to believe it is being done from Kabul.

Babrak wanted normalcy to return to the country, and he shared the same with Dedov. There was gendarmerie force that was created under Doud, called Sarandoy, carried by Khalqs, and now was to be reorganized under Babrak. There was a treaty signed with Soviets in 1978, and Babrak was following things in accordance with the same.

Kabir had met up with Babrak, on a couple of occasions during this time, and he was comforted that sooner things will be back to normalcy as the Russian and Afghan troop would flush out all the rebels. Kabir kept providing all the ground details to the western media, and ensured they were kept informed on how the government machinery was operating in this crisis situation.

Overall, this was being viewed as an anti-feudal, anti-imperialism revolution that protected the rights of the people and sovereignty of Afghanistan. Soviets started talking to the Socialist countries, justifying the acts of USSR in Afghanistan and that included Romania.

At some point, it was believed that Americans wanted to seek Soviet's understanding of American Iranian conflict, however, Soviets rejected it, and the issue had become very international now.

Some of the factions in the Soviet Union did not approve of the actions taken by the Russians. They believed this was an interference. Also, they went on to state that first the soviets invade, and then try and seek western approval for their actions. They were really not able to digest the fact that Soviets had chosen Afghanistan, and felt that their own economy needed to be improved, and they were turning their neighboring country into a poor and distressed place.

Kabir spoke with Andropov, around this time, and he confirmed that there were many in Russia who opposed this move. He went on to mention that the Soviet propaganda was misleading the international community with false information and their justification of the act. The Soviets kept maintaining that the Afghans wanted the support of Russian troops and they have been rejecting those offers that included Babrak and Amin.

It was a fact that USA and Iran relied on Amin and, later, he got no support. The Americans had developed sore relations with Afghanistan when their Ambassador was killed in a planned attack earlier in the year.

Next many days would see Soviets carrying out sorties in the air with troops all over and tanks blazing across the streets, the army taking command of the country. The city was undersiege, and now it seemed to be spreading across the country.

Most of the countryside was in the hand of rebels, and that is what Soviets wanted to break. The war would actually begin and might never end.

Kabir kept working hard from his end to ensure he found the right information and in the interim, he gave Nikita all the information that would come in handy. This included supposed war plans that Soviets were designing and also all the material he gathered from his informers. The western media friends were still in the hotel.

****

On the other hand, that day Noosh waited for almost a few hours alone in the house, and she was running her biggest fears. Being very positive in life, such sharp life changes helped her in no way to retain the same though she kept trying to be composed and sane.

She had never faced a war like situation. The option of fleeing the country was ruled out, though she was not giving up all hopes. She kept thinking there would be that perfect moment in life, when Kabir would come to her and ask her to leave with him for Bombay.

Such thoughts helped her to a large extent to look forward in life. She got a chance to look around the house, and kept her fears in check.

Wow, this is a beautiful house. I cannot believe Kabir is so fond of collectibles, she said to herself.

There was a beautiful chandelier, inspired from the Hotel Intercontinental; then, wooden furniture, beautiful Persian framed pictures on the wall, some from his family and the others of his friends and, in one corner, a beautiful group photograph with Noosh in it, taken in Herat.

There was a huge wooden cabinet, a buffet which had many photographs in plastic albums. This was way different from all the official pictures that were collected.

Noosh started picking out photographs from those albums, and began to put them in the album that she had beautifully crafted. This was covered by the Persian Scarf that Kabir had gifted to Noosh.

Noosh had a particular thought and design in her head, and wanted to weave it with the gift that she cherished the most, so far, and that was the scarf.

In about an hour, she was all done; the album was half filled with the lovely pictures, and she ensured this would continue for long time.

It was around six in the evening, and there was a knock on the door. Noosh could view the visitors from the gap between the doors, and opened it with nervous excitement for familiar faces.

"Did you bring me food?"

"Noosh, we thought you'd be happy and excited to see us alive."

"Are they murdering people now?"

Nikita held herself back with some sadness as Jemima came forward and put her stuff inside the living room.

"Guys, you can keep your stuff inside the guest room. And, do not freak out if you see many wires lying around, that is my bypass communication system that I have set. We can still send our telegrams from here, and I have wired it with Tashkent. I contacted my friend and sent a message to get this set up for us," said Kabir

"My food," shouted Noosh again.

"Wait, we got food that will last us three days, and, Noosh, I forgot to tell you there was food in the refrigerator. My bad, I did not know you will not look around for food."

While Kabir was talking to her, his eyes went towards the new guest in the house, the photo album.

"Oh, my, look at this. Isn't this beautiful? Now we know why you did not eat anything. Noosh, you made this? Cannot believe my eyes and your choice of pictures too. But how did you get this idea of neatly covering it with this Persian cloth?"

"Well, Kabir, these are memories. I might have misplaced it here, now or later, thought to wrap up our moments in it for now, and shall continue to do so."

"Hey lovers, can we eat now?" Nikita asked.

"Come on, of course."

"So, guys, what is the plan to return home now?"

"Not any sooner, Kabir. It is risky and most of the journos are here. The airbase looks like a military camp, as someone said; let the situation ease out, another couple of days, maybe."

"But they are not going to hurt any of us; we are safe here."

"Yes, correct, and there are no flights, as of now."

"Oh okay, we received a message from our boss that there is nothing to worry and we shall be safely evacuated."

"Tell me, Kabir, why did they come to haunt us all?"

"It in an unwinnable war, and they will regret coming here, one day."

"I have never seen so many tanks in my life, this might be a WWIII, who knows?"

"Come on Kabir, talk sense, we don't want to die"

"Who on the face of the earth would have imagined a young man from India accompanied by a Brit and a few American colleagues would come to Afghanistan and face these tanks and jet planes?"

"Yeah, and fight a war."

"A full scale war."

"With the Russians."

"How bizarre!"

"Kabir, you wanted an epic, didn't you? God is creating history for you," said Noosh reminding him of Epic that even he won't ever forget.

"Guys, take it easy. We need to plan our next steps."

"And, Kabir, before you take next steps, do not forget to marry me."

Kabir went to his personal vault, and pulled out the balance of the secret documents, mostly classified and handed them over to Jemima and Nikita.

"There are many papers in this; these were not part of my initial lot that landed with Professor and Michael. This has more details on further areas. I don't think Soviets know this terrain as well as we do. They will only try and seal their borders, but there is a lot of activity that will happen inside. I am aware on the some basis of my conversations with Sizov. They can always disguise in Afghan clothes, and they will try and make use of Sarandoy, local Afghan network of army. Their forces are not enough so they will rely on the forces now commanded by Babrak... Lot of other details are inside. Give to the boss and see how best we can show the truth to the rest of the world. We know what the radio broadcasted was just a sham; it was actually from Tashkent. Let the world know, too."

"Oh, I thought you would ask us to stay back and cover the war."

"No, there are enough people here to cover the war. I shall keep providing you guys with on ground intelligence inputs."

Noosh suddenly looked around, "Guys, where are the rest of the folks? Salem, Meer, Babu?"

"We tried our best to look for them, no one had any clue and we did not want to waste much time."

"Kabir what do you mean? Let me go and find them," Noosh said compassionately.

"Oh, come on, you really think I would leave them? They are working on the logistics for our travel to Herat and also for you guys," as Kabir looked at Nikita and Jemima, "for your return arrangements."

Nikita jumped at Kabir, "Oh, Kabir, you are the sweetest man I have ever met."

Noosh, was completely red with envy. "Nikita, I thought you had already found your sweetest man back in the States."

"Oh, come on Noosh, my darling, he cannot match your Kabir, and don't worry, I am not taking him away from you."

"Hahahaha," laughed Noosh, as she wanted the topic to be over soon.

"Thank Goodness, we seem to be the only people laughing, eating, and joking in this situation."

"You really cannot say that, Nikita; people try and find a reason in tough times to laugh. They try; it is when they don't get a reason, that they remain depressed."

"And, yes, there are some like us, who don't try; we just get some reason or the other."

While the talks were on, it was already about 8 pm in the evening. Kabir pulled out the bottle of wine. "My traitor professor gifted me when he returned from Paris; he said, when you don't feel fine have some wine, so here we go."

There was some noise in the other room; it appeared to be a telegraph, and the machine read out a note; it had come from his friend Andropov.

"Long live, Andro. I believe there is a reason why dad forced engineering upon me. I understand setting up communication, and also I am good at reading maps, however, when I come to think of it now, I should have pursued an additional course in Psychology, then I would have been a lethal value add for all of us."

"I agree, Kabir," said Noosh with a firm gesture.

This tone, trust, faith shown by Noosh set the beginning of a beautiful love and understanding between the two.

"I am free now; I am completely free; I fear no death; I fear no obstacles, when you hold a faith in me," said Kabir.

Noosh felt blessed and Kabir elated. And many tissue papers from Nikita's bag were feeling used worthily.

The next morning, the crew was seen off and Salem, Meer and Babu turned up in the jeep to drive down to Herat. The setting was all military like. The skies that had beautiful stars when they would compare now had fighter jets and helicopters showing their strength.

Kabir was busy taking pictures, whenever he would get an opportunity, and videos too. Noosh kept engaged, reading the accomplishments she and the team had achieved over the past couple of years.

After covering about 250 odd kilometres, suddenly, Noosh began to speak.

"Gosh!! I cannot believe all of this might just go in vain; there are some great projects that would have now started taking shape, and now the infrastructure, economy and the social agenda might just cripple."

Kabir immediately put his camera aside, and asked Babu to stop the jeep.

"Wait here for a few minutes. Come, Noosh, I want to show you something."

"Look that far; tell me what do you see?"

"I see Buzkashi. Yeah, this is a very famous sports here."

"Yes, this is called positivity."

"May be they know nothing."

"Yeah, do not look at it from their point of view, watch from yours."

"Yes, there is merit in what you say."

"Yes, at times, we need to see things the way we want to; it gives me a lot of strength. You know when I spoke with that paratrooper, I asked him how his parents feel about all this,

You know what he said."

"Tell me."

"Well, he said, he does not know that exactly, as he did not get much time to spend with them when the announcement of his appointment came."

"So, what did he say?"

"So he said he told his parents, that he has got a promotion and a pay hike, rather than saying that he might not even return alive."

"Hmmm."

Salem said immediately, "Saab, hope we can send the same message to our parents too. By the way, ever since we joined you, our parents are very happy. You know my sister is getting married next month; they wanted me to come. I am not sure now, if I would be able to."

"Of course, Salem, I shall ensure you visit her next month, do not worry we will find a way."

"Right now, the mines are being laid on the borders, especially the northern border adjoining Soviet Union. We can find a way for you to go through Peshawar, but, yes, then we can plan a safety exit for you thorough Jalalabad. I have some good contacts there, keep the faith."

Babu also wanted to find some opportunity, and Meer kept thinking hard to make the best of Kabir's mood.

Meer spoke to Salem in a very soft tone, "Did you notice something about Kabir saab, Meer?"

"Yeah, he is very smart."

"No, not that; ever since Noosh madam has entered his life, he has become very positive and his outlook has broadened further; he is more confident than ever before."

"Oh, yes, you are so correct."

"Guys you haven't still changed, you still talk in whispers." Kabir said in a husky tone.

"Hehe, *nahi saab*, we were generally chit chatting and did not want to bother you."

Upon reaching Herat, they witnessed a different world. Things were a whole lot different than they had left. The local people carrying launchers and guns could be seen around, waiting for their turn to fire at the enemy; their enemies were within the establishment and the Russians. Some of them were rebels, and some who were earlier part of Sarandoy, and now would fight the regime."

Noosh's father was outside the house, on the lane, to take them inside. He looked completely baffled at the state of affairs.

"So, they got the man they wanted, but why would they need such a big force to get one man. It is a war, isn't it? Tell me now," Shir was referring to the execution of Amin.

"Dad, relax, will you?"

"Yes, I am fine, a little worried for my children. All these young boys, you see, here have grown up in front of my eyes; their life should have improved; look at them now. What does anyone gain?,

Watch your steps, my son, come in,

Nur is also here; aha, good to see you."

Noosh, somehow appeared blushed, as she had come with Kabir. Her father was well educated, of liberal views and, at this juncture, the society was not very conservative.

"Kabir, our ancestors settled here from Iran, many years ago. We follow all our traditions, however, I am not very rigid, especially considering the circumstances.

Nur bhai spoke very highly of you last time and, ever since, I have been thinking to discuss yours and Noosh's marriage with you.

No matter how much Noosh refuses to get married, and wants to wait for the right time. I believe there could not be a better time than this. Also, I am turning old now, I want you two to get married and Noosh should settle well in Bombay with you. I will also get a new city to come to. I have been to Udaipur a couple of times, though. We have old connections and associations with India. Few of my dearest friends live there. Been couple of years now, we have been occupied and hence lost touch."

Nur joined Noosh's father, "So Kabir *saab*, we assume your first and second *Khastgiri* process, our tradition of meeting and approving, is over. We are liberal, and yet follow some of the traditions, however, not too rigid. You and Noosh have known each other for quite a long while, yet I would like to ask you and Noosh together if you are both fine with this wedding."

Kabir knew of Persian culture through Noosh. He felt a little sad as his parents were not here at this point, and also he found it a little surprising that her father immediately started talking about their marriage, in all this situation. Noosh wouldn't be around. However, upon her father calling to seek her consent, she came running, said yes, and went back soon. Kabir did not have any company, and suddenly there was a knock.

"Salaam," came Meer's voice.

"Oho I am so sorry. Why did I not ask you guys to come inside?"Kabir said.

"Why would you ask us saab? You only kept looking at your 'would be' bride," Salem said with a smile.

"God heard my prayers," Kabir said.

"Really, I thought so saab," Salem said.

"Okay, so Salem, tell me in what context did I say God heard my prayers."

Salem, with a hidden smile, "leave it, saab, you will be embarrassed."

"No, no, you tell me now; I want to know." Kabir insisted.

"Okay, okay, saab, I thought since we are from India, so you might be shy talking about your own marriage and therefore…"

"You are close enough. I was feeling absolutely alone, and Noosh could not be here. *Ladki nahi baat karti na apne rishte kee.* So, naturally, I am the only one; plus, dad and mom must be enjoying cricket match on Doordarshan, or may be dad is listening to All India radio news about Afghanistan, I am not sure, but then they are not here. By the way, I was able to send them the telegram, remind me tomorrow to follow up."

"Kabir *saab*, you know what, you have cold feet already. I have never seen you going so mad, even when Soviets came or when you came to the hotel to look for us; you seemed pretty okay, but look at you now; it appears you came to this country just for your wedding, and you will get the 21-gun salute from the army. I mean, look at the situation, the war, and then your love story, and then this. I mean you have all the reasons to go crazy."

"So, Unclej*i*, we are from boy's side," Salem said immediately, joined by Meer, and Babu also came forward, "all of us, he means, all of us are representing Kabir *saab*."

"Kabir, I wish I could really follow all the traditions of the marriage. I just have one daughter, and all our relatives would like to be part of it. I am still thinking if we could pull off some traditions, yet keep a low profile. Kabir, you follow your rituals too, I assume, you would like to go to India and do the same in your ways too."

"Yes, sir... uncle... dad... abba... I mean, yeah," Kabir started stammering. He was extremely nervous; for him to see his love come alive was no less than a wonder. It was all happening very fast and rapidly, that he could not believe it too.

"I already have a ring with me."

"No, no, son give me a couple of days. We need to let all our relatives know and you can let yours know too."

"I already told my parents, and they are very happy and excited, and looking forward to seeing you and Noosh this time in Bombay, hopefully in a few weeks. By the time, this Soviet troop withdrawal should also have happened.

"Okay great, soon, we will decide on the wedding date. I shall be completely free then, you can take care of her, that would be a big reprieve," he got emotional as he had already begun to feel that Noosh would be gone very far from him.

"Tell me, Kabir, how far is Bombay from Kabul? After the *Agdh,* we can also plan to come over. Hopefully, this saga of terror will settle down too."

"Afrina or Air India, I think both have direct flights, it should be around three hours or slightly less from Kabul, as Kabir remembered from his visit to parents some time back.

There were many discussions that took place about culture, tradition, future of the two and much more. From all the interesting discussions and new forming relationships, it was very difficult to believe these guys had just returned from the horror of war, and they wanted to stay here until Kabir finished his purpose of getting enough world attention and saving lives.

Her father made nice arrangements for Kabir to stay in the same hotel. The best rooms were chosen, however, it was not as exciting as it used to be last year. As for Salem, Meer and Babu, they enjoyed their compound more than this hotel stay, and requested if they could stay there rather than staying in the hotel where it would be hard for them to adjust. At first, her father could not understand, but, then, he gave into their request.

Kabir went down to the reception area.

"Asad, hello, how are you? Look, you might receive a phone call here or a telegraph. Keep me informed at all times. It can come from Tashkent, Moscow, Bombay or New York."

"Yes, sir, always at your service. But, sir, I heard the news and I read in Kabul times also, and look at these pictures," Asad, the new manager, pointed towards the newspaper, "What is this going in Kabul? I tried reaching out to my friends, but there is severe communication failure."

"Yes, right, things are bad. It seems to be a war like situation that will only worsen over a period of time, and do remember my telegraph. Don't forget, it is very crucial."

"You just don't worry, *saab*; only people like you can save us. We have couple more journalists from France and Germany who are putting up in our hotel; they also seem to be waiting to get in touch with their bosses in Europe and the West, some coverage I suppose."

"Oh okay, that is definitely a good information. I appreciate it. What is your code name?"

"Sorry, Sir?"

"Just kidding," Kabir said with sarcasm.

Kabir zipped up to his room, and tried to get in shape. It was a long journey, not tiring as it was duly compensated with the marriage proposal and near exchange of vows. He missed his parents a lot. On such occasions, he felt their need the most.

Well, I hope, all goes well and we can be with them soon, he thought.

He tried to gather as much information from the available newspapers, and sent as much info as he could to the western media. He already mustered his resources and started making all possible efforts.

He dressed casually for his evening meeting with Noosh. In many weeks, this was the first time that Noosh and Kabir will be able to spend some quality time together. Asad had already decided on the table and, this time, it was the preferred table of Noosh's choice that she had always loved.

Around six in the evening, Nur dropped Noosh at the hotel. She also had some visitors from her previous NGO.

"Kabir, hello, you know what, I lied to my father that I am meeting them exclusively."

"Lied, hmm, the first time?"

"Yes, I mean, to my father, yes."

"Oh, it will take a few days, then to let this pass. Afterwards, you won't need to, anyway."

"I am looking forward, and did dad tell you about his wishes to come to Bombay."

"He did; my family would be delighted. Just before you came, received this telegraph from my parents. Read, these lines are for you, and they also sent some silver coins and gifts for our wedding."

"They seem upset they cannot be here. But they wish us good luck, and I want to meet them soon. I wish I had joined you to Bombay the last time."

"You and your work, phew. That would have been the best introduction."

"It is okay, even now we will go, more openly, as wedded husband and wife. I really want to be called Mrs. Kabir real soon."

"Ask me. I want to call you Mrs. Kabir soon."

"And what do you want me call you? Boss?"

"Hahahahahahaha, my dad calls my mom wifey. And, you know what, when mom gets upset then he calls her Boss."

"That is funny; my dad used to call my mom Rani. I don't know which Bollywood movie he picked it from, but for many years, there was a time when he could not sleep without listening to Hindi songs or watching a movie."

"My dad is a big Ghalib fan."

"Oh, so that is where the genes played a vital role."

"Arey waah, isi baat par arz kiya hai." (So on this note, let me share a poetry)

"Irshaad."(Go ahead)

"Hum toh fanaa ho gaye uski aankh dekh kar Ghalib

Na jaaney wo aaina kaise dekhte hongey."

"I have gone insane, seeing her eyes, Ghalib

Only heaven knows how she looks in the mirror."

"Lovely, I like your shayari. Is this rose in the glass here your idea, Kabir?"

"You like it?"

"Yes, it is nice."

"Of course, *Jahapanaah*; this is my idea."

"Then, do what Shammi Kapoor used to do with a rose. The way he would pull it out and dance for his opposite stars."

"Really, Noosh you are so funny."

"You cannot even dance like Shammi for me?

"How about Dev Anand? I can do his steps for you, but then, you be my Wahida Rehman."

"I knew this was coming."

"Hey, I want to say something to you."

"Go on, Kabir, you never have to seek my permission."

"You and I do not have a picture exclusively together in my camera."

Noosh moved left to the sofa chair and created space for Kabir. Meanwhile Kabir called the bellboy, Rehman. It was tough; the staff could not handle the camera.

"Sir, this is far too complex, is this a new model?"

"Yes, it is not very old. I am not asking you to do anything. I shall set it for you, all you need to do is look here and click the button."

"Is that all?" said Rehman in relief.

"Yes, that is all my dear friend."

"Okay sir, please shift further, put your arms around ma'am."

"Listen Rehman, are you a photographer? Whatever we need to do, we will, do not give your guidance."

"Oh, sorry sir, I just meant to have a pose."

"Leave it, now click the button."

"Here you go, Sir. You both look very good together, you know; ma'am has been our client for many years, and we always used to wonder who she will marry.'

"And then, hope none of you."

"No, sir, what are you talking? She is highly respected here."

"I am glad to hear that."

Asad called on Rehman, "Come here Rehman, Kabir sir, let him go; he talks too much."

In middle of the conversation, Asad comes around and whispers something into Kabir's ears. Kabir immediately left, telling Noosh, he shall be right back, and asked her to leave for her house with Nur.

"Don't worry, I need to attend this phone call, and might be delayed, cannot tell you much here, hope you understand."

"Yes, dear," Noosh smiled. Inside her heart, she was worried, extremely worried, as she could see some tensed expressions on Kabir's face.

Outside the hotel, Nur was waiting for her.

"Hope you had a good meeting with your team."

"Yes, Nur uncle, I did," Noosh lied.

"I believe we gave those Russians a good beating, earlier last year; they would not want to come back here again. They would be concentrated in the capital only."

"You cannot say much about their plans. Uncle, you never know what they are up to; plus, the newspapers write anything; radios broadcast anything; it is all ambiguous, so we don't know." Noosh parroted whatever she heard from Kabir.

"Did Kabir *saab* say anything? He has connections in Soviet, as well as the ministry here, and even with the Americans; he must be aware of much more."

"Yes, that we shall discuss, uncle; hope dad is doing fine and not too worried."

"He is okay; we discussed about your marriage. He wants you both should get married sooner, in fact, in next few days itself. We shall inform the relatives in coming days."

Noosh remained silent for a brief period. Then she asked Nur to go around and handed him a slip; this carried some notes and details from Kabir.

Nur looked at it, "Okay, I shall ensure I get as much details from the nearby villages; will inform the people, anything else Kabir asked?

"Sorry uncle, I lied to you; I met him at the hotel for tea."

"I knew that kid."

"I am glad I told you the truth. He received a call, and then he lost his expressions. I am certain there is a lot more that will come your way, be on the alert."

"Yes, true, that we are."

Noosh's father saw her coming and, upon seeing them, "See I knew it; these leaders, ministers, are all puppets; they won't think of us."

"What happened, father?"

"Who likes all this? I see young men and boys carrying guns, it is not good. When we were young, we would carry books in our hands. I just received the news, Soviets are planning nationwide attacks."

"Oh, is it confirmed dad?"

'Yes, almost, I want you and Kabir to get married."

Kabir showed up with some papers in his hands "Nur *ji*, we need to make arrangements to send this to Washington and New York soon. The telegraph system that hotel arranged is not working, apparently."

Nur rushed out to get the same done.

"What happened, Kabir?"

"Things are going to worsen, they are getting more troops. They lost people in some areas, they might want to re-strategize."

"There are Guerrilla fighters here; the terrains are only known to them or some of us, but, then Soviets have more air power."

"Dad, I can tell you, in coming weeks or months, more global powers are going to join hands, and this will be a full blown war."

"So, then, where do we find safe havens?"

"We shall overcome these hardships soon, do not worry."

"So there is specific set of news and, hence, our actions need to be very specific. I might go to Moscow, in coming days; I have made plans, too, and arrangements are intact."

"You might as well then go to India, Kabir?"

"You know, Noosh, my passport has some issues, and it just slipped my God damn head to get it fixed. In all this, I just forgot, and now it will be tougher and time consuming. I am not going to Moscow officially; it is all undercover."

'Here," Noosh's father handed him over some information that he had gathered.

"This will definitely be of great help, Dad"

"So when do you return, Kabir?"

"As soon as the calendar decides to change the month, you shall find me here."

"Wonderful, then."

Kabir and Noosh were alone now in the house as Nur and her father stepped out while talking; they actually stepped out after hearing a jet in the sky.

"Noosh."

"Yes, Kabir."

"I want to kiss you."

"And Kabir, I want you to kiss me."

"Kabir, kiss me so deep that it lasts forever."

He held Noosh and kissed her.

"This is the beginning of a wonderful relationship, Noosh."

"I will miss you, my man, and I will beg and pursue the calendar to change the month sooner; only wish, this moment could go on forever."

He stepped out, while she sulked.

He looked up in the air, pulled out his middle finger, and waved it at the fighter plane, "Look, one day, you will be pulled down, and your carcass shall be fed to the vultures."

"It is okay, Kabir; they are all duty-bound, and perpetrators are watching the show in Moscow and anywhere else in the world."

"They will pay for this, one day."

Kabir left, as his Toyota minivan was waiting for him, Noosh came out, running.

"You forgot your camera?"

"I left it deliberately here; it goes when we are together, otherwise it remains with you."

"Oh, okay, baby," Noosh smiled.

"Kabir waved like a child at everyone.

"I see that thing in this man. Look at the way he cares and see the strength that resides beneath his skin," Nur observed.

"You are lucky, Noosh. I am happy for you, and look at his commitment; he received a supposed phone call, and he set off immediately," Shir added.

Over next few days, the entire clan was involved in the wedding plans. They wanted to make the best use of this time.

This family was one of those who would take everything in their stride. It also went on to show that, while the enemy was busy fighting, there were many people who would want to resume their normal lives. As long as they could, as long as their fate decided, till their spirit was alive, and for some spirit never died.

Chapter 18

"Pahuchenge tab kahenge, umdenge us thai
Ajhoo bera samand me, boli bigooche kaai."
"When I reach the shore, I will talk about it
I am sailing right now in the middle of the ocean."

KABIR REACHED MOSCOW AFTER FEW DAYS OF GROUND TRAVEL. The city was almost same as he had seen last time. Except, there were more tanks on the streets. It was no surprise they were warming up to run across the border.

He met up with Andropov and some more of his friends. He was likely to spend a week here.

The first information he gathered was that Yuri might have been killed. Another substantial information was that Professor had defected to London and remained unavailable for anything. Dedov was given more responsibilities now, in the event of war by the Government.

Kabir told Andropov that the information of Yuri's death was fake, and that he was aware how Professor planned it all. He told him about Sizov and Yuri being the same person and the entire plot.

Andropov was shocked on hearing the plot. He further added that the newspaper carried negative news of the country and the nationals do not subscribe to the idea of the invasion.

"I am at a cusp," Kabir said with deep anguish.

"That you are, but then who is listening to you here, Kabir?" Andropov responded.

"Despite belonging to both the nations and, since I feel a lot of pain, what is it that the Soviets are not able to feel, what is to do with Marxism, so much that you stop caring, and, then, these are your friends how can they stab."

"This is deeper indeed," Yakonov added.

"Your phone call stated the same Yakonov; this is deeper," Kabir said.

"So yes, the point is all this is a deeper conspiracy; it is out of bounds for us."

They discussed everything in detail. At the same time, these guys had prepared a set of fabricated dossier that needed to be delivered to Michael. They discussed a secret plan. Michael did not doubt Kabir yet. He was not aware that Kabir knew the truth. Once Kabir ensured the documents reach Michael, it will help a big deal. The documents will appear to be classified and stolen. All these include information that Russia is planning to build a nuclear base in Afghanistan and also readiness to combat America. This would shock Michael, and he would want to share the info with American defence to gain a promotion and a bigger role. In any condition, Afghanistan will stand to gain, as this will help someone in the world to pay attention and deploy strength accordingly. There was nothing to lose. It was a shot worth taking.

Also, they shared with Kabir on how he could help build bunkers in the western Afghan region. None of these tasks was ordinary. The work had to be executed.

The entire week flew by. Much ground was covered in this time.

"It seems it was yesterday, we had such a great time."

"Kabir, over next few days, we hope to sort out quite a few things that should help us provide clarity."

The strategic discussion continued in their own limited spaces and world. It was very interesting to see a group of youngsters who were well connected trying with all in their might for common interest, to save humanity, and much was also driven by Kabir's desires. These were all good friends of Kabir. In fact, one of Kabir's cousin was planning to get married to Andropov and this was discovered only during this visit. Kabir left the country, and vowed to never return for work. Only factor would be his family in Russia now.

****

A few days later, in Herat, groups of people could be seen gathered on the streets. There was very little that anybody could do anything about it as it appeared to be preparations for a war.

Some of the kids could be seen flying kites in the sky, and the others were shouting. One of them said, "Can you cut that plane in the sky with your kite?"

"See, this is how it is; when kids of this age talk about violence and revenge and you see their blood seethe, you know something has fallen apart drastically, and when this happens countrywide, it takes less time to fall and then it gets irreparable," Shir said.

His elder cousin made a note, "You are right, *bhaijaan*; I wish we had a democratic set up like these Americans and Indians. I mean, you have issues, you raise your voice, but you do not go for a war; such a plight. We don't want rulers, anymore; we want servants who can serve the people."

"I hope God is listening."

They both look up together.

"Listen *bhaijaan*, keep your worries aside. Being worried manifests negativity. Your daughter is going to get married; your son in law, rather your son will be here any moment; look forward in life now."

"Yes, harder I think, more depressed I get."

"Plus, you have not taken charge of everyone. We are here to do what God has designated us to, so we shall try; why waste time and energy."

"Yes, you are right."

"Yes, and your Bhabhi is arranging for all nice clothes for our Noosh."

"That is nice. Had you not been here at this point, how I would have managed all this alone?"

"Bhaijaan, if you did not do so much for us, we would be nowhere; you helped me and so many others settle."

Shir had leveraged his influence when he was in the ministry, through all legal means, to help establish his brothers and cousins. It just helped them get a good start, and now they were well settled. They were mostly into manufacturing and selling of Persian rugs and jewellery items.

A few hours later, Kabir arrived and there was an atmosphere of celebration in the air. He was welcomed by the clan. There were rose petals and saffron water being showered on him.

"This is the best welcome I have ever seen. The last I know was when I was born. I did not witness it or, rather, I don't remember it, but, yes, I saw how my cousins were welcomed in the world, especially my cousin sister. When she was born, there were similar celebrations.

Dad, it feels I am born again, rather I am born today."

"You have given us life, son. We were hopeless otherwise; you showed us light. You showed us life in trouble. You gave us wings, else we would be crawling."

Kabir hugged his would be father in law. There was a lot of warmth in this. He kissed his forehead and blessed him with happiness and togetherness.

"Son, I am giving you my most precious Persian jewel. Shine her, for she would sparkle, love her for she would prosper, and together you both make a beautiful couple."

"You need not say that. I am thankful to you for giving me the jewel of your heart."

"All our plans are in place for your wedding, day after; any message from your parents?"

"In fact, I was in constant touch with them from Moscow. They really miss us, but they do not show so that my resolve does not weaken. They are strong parents. They just want us to be married and be happy. Mom has kept jewellery for Noosh, for the marriage back in India. She has been waiting for this day."

After a few days, Noosh and Kabir got married in a low key affaire.

Most of the rituals were followed, and the women kept asking Kabir if there was any ritual he would want them to follow.

One of them even asked him, "What is your religion?" and he very quietly said, "I don't remember."

There was a silence followed by some light jokes.

Kabir had to spend some more days to execute his plans. He gathered the local force and guided them to do the much required construction.

He helped build bunkers, escape passages, and even handed out maps to the locals. The activity to build bunkers had started, for it would solve two purposes: to save lives from the explosions itself, and to take shelter and escape any ear injuries from nearby explosions. It was a different thing that later Guerillas would use these bunkers to fight the war.

Some of the installations were inspired from Maginot Line, from World War I. Kabir knew how Soviets maintained huge bunkers, and even the deeply dug metro system in Moscow was for secondary use as Nuclear Shelter.

Primarily, trench bunkers were built as their construction did not take much time.

Considering the tight budgets, trap door design was used. Door was of steel to keep weight less, with a fitted lintel and frame. Ventilation was considered, as it was missed out earlier on. Kabir realized this might help in case the stay stretched here. Most of the grenade attacks could be escaped from here, except for heavy and bunker buster attacks.

Further, Kabir shared as much information with Noosh's father on the escape routes, prohibited areas with detailed markings. The regions where the mines were most suspected to be laid were explicitly drawn out.

Crossing across Soviet border was a big no as the neighbour would never want Afghans to form refugee camps in their country, therefore the mines were laid on the Soviet border to begin with. Kabir only wished he could make mine detecting device too.

The development funds towards the rail track was diverted towards security, and the secret supply of arms was in progress.

It was yet to be seen, what was the response from the west to counter T62s and fighter jets. For now, it appeared to be a war between a nation and the Guerillas. For the terrains it was a great way to combat a war in long term.

Like they say, wars are fought on the basis of intelligence, and not necessarily the number of troops. Afghans, Mujahideens and various other groups were trying to put their rebel army together to fight this war.

At a personal level, Kabir had a huge army of followers now. This pepped the brave man further. Noosh felt extremely proud of him.

At the end of it all, the newly wedded couple finally began the preparation to leave for Kabul.

Many of the relatives tried convincing them to stay locally, but they both maintained they could do a lot more in the capital city than here, so they had to leave.

"No, auntie, don't worry, Kabir has bought a place in Kabul, and it is quiet safe out there," she wanted to pacify the ladies, so that later her father does not have explain as to why he let them go.

Both of them were seen off with many presents and gifts.

"Noosh, I did not know your folks are so rich," Kabir noted with a smile.

As the minivan began to leave, it had Babu, Salem and Meer in the front of the wheels, and the couple sat in the rear.

"Oh, yes, they are rich."

"I believe your father has done an extremely good job in helping them settle, but they all are very insecure about their work. In fact, one of your uncles even approached me asking if they could establish something in India."

"Really, you know how relatives can be at times."

"Ask me, universally it is a fact, but there is nothing wrong. They are all our people."

"First let us see what is it that we need to do."

"Have you decided on our honeymoon, Kabir?"

"There are sorties in the air, fire right off the canon, gun salute all over, have you ever seen such a welcome?"

"It also appears Kabir, perhaps, we are the only couple who has got married at this juncture."

"You never know, maybe there is love thriving somewhere, where there is war, where there are guns, I would still believe, love never makes itself a slave of such circumstances."

"Hmmmm, yes, possibly yes."

After a short distance being covered, Kabir stopped the van.

"Noosh, hope you don't mind if I remove these pamphlets."

"Hahaha, I forgot, I wanted to tell you the same."

As Kabir begins to remove the wedding pamphlets that were stuck to the rear glass of the van, there was a big explosion nearby and the van shook in thunder of the noise.

Surprisingly, nobody was shocked or scared.

"Did you notice, Noosh?"

"Kabir, it was loud enough. I think it is about a few miles from here."

"But none of us is worried and this is a step number one of our victory."

"True, and also we did not lose any lives here, come inside, quick."

"*Saab*, please tell your friends not to harm us. Let them give us a safe and free passage," Salem said, referring to Soviet army.

"And, we would stop over in the *chaikanas*, a few overnight stays, cross through Kandahar again," Babu crossed his heart, "Let us have faith in God."

"Have faith in yourself too; let us be very watchful. Fortunately I have got much intelligence, Babu. We need to change our route midway and, yes, the mines are not laid here yet, so don't worry. This bomb must have gone off in Panj e sharif."

"They are targeting areas which have rebels. Later this year, they might want to spread across, for now it is Kabul and nearby areas."

"Okay, *saab*, thanks for sharing the information."

Salem asked Kabir, "*Saab*, have you done anything about me?"

"I remember what you had asked me. Next week or so, hopefully I shall have an exit plan for you."

"Saab, one more thing, please add one plus two; I want to take my best friends Meer and Babu along with me."

"I had already thought of it, but, I want something in return."

"Anything for you, *saab*."

"Well, you need to arrange for the movie cassette of Amitabh Bachchan's Zanjeer. It was released last year, and I so much wanted to see. It was running houseful in India when I visited, so I could not see it in the movie hall, and I did not want to pay the black-marketer who was selling at double the cost outside, so I missed it."

"It is a deal, *saab*. I shall get it for you."

"Is it a romantic movie, Kabir?" Noosh asked.

It must have some romance in it certainly, but, yes, he is Mr Angry Young man.

"The way you are."

"That is the best said thing to me ever."

"You are, and you have a soft heart inside. You are someone who any woman on earth would like to be wooed by."

There was music from the movie Silsila that played on the recorder inside the van. It sounded a very nice and deliberate attempt from Salem to please the fans inside.

Ye kahan aa gaye hum…

Yu hee sath sath chal chal ke…

"Kabir, I thank you for teaching me a bit of Hindi apart from *Ghalib's shayari*."

"So for you Noosh, do not thank me, for if I start then the list is endless."

After days of travel through the rough terrains and new found roads, they spotted tanks coming their way…

"Whoops, we see trouble coming."

"Don't you worry. I am well prepared, and they don't attack an individual minivan."

The tanks came and crossed them; nobody cared to even look inside as the tanks passed.

"See, I told you, they have no intention to pick on us."

"Maybe, they know you guys are inside."

"Yes, maybe; keep that faith alive guys."

"*Saab* you remember how we enacted those scenes from *Sholay* when we were coming from Jalalabad to Kabul?"

"Yes, now don't tell me you are going to repeat the performance."

"No, but now I remember some other scenes."

"Which one now, Salem?"

"The one which has Manoj Kumar in it; I don't remember the name."

"Yes, that showed struggle against oppression. I feel somewhere people here need similar motivation."

"Yes, *guru,* I agree."

"The *chaikanas* on the way seem to know us all."

"People here are hospitable, Noosh. I have not seen such hospitality anywhere."

"They wanted their pictures to be clicked, and were happy to receive us."

"And we are their own; know that humans understand the difference, skin color, ethnicity, nationality does not matter."

"So true."

"Finally, we are back in Kabul."

"Yipppee, finally we made it in once piece." Noosh screamed in joy.

"Yeah, and do not forget, Noosh is our lucky charm; nothing would go wrong when she is with us."

"That is so nice of you, Kabir, and I accept it humbly."

"Yes, you are the woman of my life and, together, our luck is enhanced."

"Definitely."

"This is like a fortress here; it is a mini war field."

"To protect us."

"Exactly, hahahaha."

"Watch your steps, Salem," Kabir paved the way for them to come inside.

"Settle here, feel at home."

Kabir rushed inside the house, and tried to follow at least one ritual.

"Welcome to our home, our *ren basera*, Noosh."

"So, finally, we are legally together, under one roof."

"As husband and wife."

"As the wedded couple"

"Who can never be left alone."

"For, our luck works when we are together."

'Forever."

"Kiss me, Kabir, like you have never kissed me before."

"Let these men go, Noosh."

"They are gone, Kabir."

"I mean, let them go to the hotel; let us get our time."

"But I want a kiss now; they will take a few minutes. Don't forget, it is still some walking distance to reach here from where the car is parked, and don't waste time."

Kabir gently pulled Noosh towards him, held her firmly with both his hands wrapped around her waist.

"Say something that you have never said before." Noosh whispered.

"God had a lot of free time, Noosh. He must have made you during his break, in his happy mood."

"Hahahaha, thanks Kabir, you are good with words."

"I am good with action too."

"I am waiting."

"Then don't speak a thing."

"Till you make me stop…"

"…a kiss, the most astonishing feeling."

"I love you, Noosh."

"I love you more."

"Till death do us part."

"Sssshhhhhhhh, in heaven or on earth, never ever."

The couple was high on romance as they kissed. The boys arrived with the luggage, and the serious work of settling down began.

Salem, Meer and Babu began to leave, and the house was planned to be set up sooner.

Kabir handed them some cash; Noosh gave some of the stuff to eat and a book of daily prayers, "Keep this with you guys; this will keep you strong."

"Okay, madam, we will pray for you everyday. God bless you and, *Saab*, thanks for the cash."

"God bless us all."

****

Chapter 19

"Akanth kahani prem ki, kuchh kahi na jaye
Goonge keri sarkara, baithe muskaye."
"The story of love defies narration
Similar to a mute enjoying sweets, can just smile."

THE NIGHT CAUGHT UP WITH THEM SOON, both were extremely tired and fatigued.

They were totally, irrevocably in love with each other.

"Kabir, I shall always love you selflessly."

"You make me remember what one of those great philosophers had said once, and it holds true for us and anyone who loves."

'And, that is?"

"Look at the love between Sun and the earth; it is pure, pristine. Sun gives its energy to earth, and never demands anything in return. That is the definition of true love, and look at what such a selfless love does, it lights up the sky."

"I so agree, Kabir. Initially I thought you were not a man to be trusted."

"I wish I had a clue. But, then, everything happens at the right time, and there is a right place too."

"And, Kabir, in my case, yes, all of what you said plus God's right mood also to be factored in."

"Hahaha, that is a good one, Noosh. I shall remember."

The telegraph system was working fine now. Kabir decided to look at the information received.

"Kabir, spare it today, please."

"Oh, I am so sorry; spared, I won't enter that room today."

No, it is okay baby. If you think there is something important, please, I was just getting carried away."

"Are you sure?"

"Of course, I would have told you in case I was not."

"Okay, decided; will do it tomorrow; come, let us not waste time."

The house was set up nice. There was music in the background, one of Kabir's favorite scores and Noosh was holding 'Gone with the wind.'

"Wine?"

"Yeah, I don't mind wine and you together."

"So the mood is also in place, thankfully."

"For you, it is set all the time."

"Here you go, *Madame*."

Both of them were disconnected from the outer world, however, the outside war scene caused some disturbance. In fact, even Babrak, the new ruler was troubled. Soviets had been taking control of the situation, and he needed to intervene a few times.

It seemed to be slipping out of his hands. But, it did not appear like this to the locals and the outside world.

Kabir had thought he would try and work closely on the ground, continue to monitor the situation, keep western media warm with lots of news and information. He did not know how things would shape for worse in the coming days.

"I wish the skies were a bit calmer."

As the lights turned off, the ceiling shone, it had dazzling artificial stars and the moon.

"Aha, at least our skies are calmer and soothing."

"And, so is our world, Noosh, you like it?"

"I love it."

Every breath you take...

Every move you make...

Then, at the sound of music, they both sang to each other.

Within a minute, Kabir held Noosh's cheeks with his palms; kissed her deep in the mouth, and began to then move his hands down her body. They both had not felt like this before. He fondled her, necked her and began to caress her elegantly, slipping his hands between her breasts. They both undressed each other for an exciting foreplay. Kabir was on top of her, as he gently began to move her hands to the side. He kissed her on the breasts, and played with them. After a while, he went down her tummy and licked it with his tongue. Noosh was aroused by now as she began to moan in ecstasy. She spread both her legs, as she played with his hair, while her body shivered. He went down on her and licked her till Noosh reached a few orgasms already. Kabir was hard with erection, and he pulled himself up to penetrate inside her. Noosh kept pressing his body and even scratched his back with her nails a few times. That night, they had sex a few times. Their relationship went up to different level of intimacy.

The next morning, they woke up on each other's side. Noosh and Kabir hadn't moved through the night. Noosh slept naked with her head on Kabir's chest and hands around his abdomen. Her legs were curled up between her man. Kabir's hands were beautifully wrapped around her arms. They woke up like they had slept.

"I don't want to get up, husband."

"Who wants to?"

"Can this happen every day and night? I feel dreamy."

"Yeah, this will happen every day and night."

"Let me make some tea for us, Noosh. I know you prefer less sugar."

"Don't go anywhere, just stay here."

"So much love, already," Kabir said as he kissed Noosh on her cheeks, forehead and lips, reciprocated by Noosh, with an extra on his ears.

"Now, who wants to go anywhere?" Noosh said.

"Who wants to let you go, anyway?" Kabir said happily.

"Can the tea wait?" Noosh asked.

"Hahahaha, you ready to let go off tea for this."

"Anything for this moment, Kabir. Why do I love calling your name time and again?"

"I wish I had the answer, Noosh, Noosh, Noosh."

"Kabir, Kabir, Kabir, Kabir."

"Aha, always a step ahead."

"I told you, I love you more; by the way, Kabir, go and check for messages, it is important I know."

There were a few messages from Andropov, alerting them of the imminent danger the place held. He also sent him the address and details of the hotel where Michael was staying in Jordan for his vacation.

"Well, we have gathered as much, there is a warning for us, and it says that all the foreigners must leave the place."

"That, we are prepared for, aren't we?"

"Yes, but we must get our act together."

"What shall we do?"

"Need to inform the embassy and Nikita, too. From the information I have, the residents of the Soviet embassy in Kabul have ten times more people locally situated now, and all the other western embassy have gone thinly on their staff."

"Yeah, must be."

"Per the info, there are local attacks being planned in the next few days. I must figure out this one, in little more detail."

Noosh entered the room and tried to decode the other message.

"Kabir, you did not even pay attention to parent's message here. They sent us our blessings, and there is one from Nikita too. Wow, this machine is working so fine."

"Wonderful, so nice of them."

Kabir had nothing else going on in his mind, "Look, Noosh, I need to go around; I shall be back by lunch time; you stay at home; hope there is enough to keep yourself busy," he held her hand, "Do not worry."

"Okay, Kabir, tell me where are you going?"

"I just need to go to the hotel. It is a hub of activities, not the one where you and I stayed. It is the one that Russians do not seem to be leaving now."

"Isn't that dangerous?"

"Don't worry, I will come back alive."

"So, you mean, our honeymoon is over," Noosh hugged her man tight. "I wish you good luck, my man. I am with you."

"That gives me the best boost up, more than anything else, besides sex," he laughed.

Noosh retained her fears. Now I know how his parents brought him up. This man's conviction does not allow you to let him think otherwise, she thought.

"Be fearless."

"I am. You got to take care, my barrel chested man, are you taking the van?"

"Yes, it has a soviet sticker on it and I can speak the language, will be of help."

"Okay."

"Noosh, do not leave the house; this is still safe inside, I assure you."

"Okay."

Kabir left with some papers and his gun, then he returned, "I will leave this gun here. This belongs to the man who has supposedly escaped like a coward."

"May the almighty save us," Noosh returned to their room, she was extremely worried and confused.

Oh, God, why do you always keep testing good people? I am sure there are many in this country who are going through this ordeal right now, she thought.

As she went to the kitchen and began to prepare breakfast, she realized it was tough on her to eat alone. In fact, she lost all her appetite.

Suddenly, she decided to jump to prepare lunch, since Kabir mentioned he will return by lunch time.

She prepared her favourite delicacy that she had learned from her favourite *Khansaama* during the days spent in Herat working with the NGO.

In some time, as she began to sift through her papers, she found out a folded one. It was a note written by Jafer, that said during her wedding, he will drive her and her husband around the town.

There goes my appetite, she said to herself. She sat down quietly, and began to ponder over life and its many situations. Look at us, we plan and prepare, and then God's designs are unknown; I cannot believe he is no more. She sat next to the album, with her eyes moist, as she looked at everyone in the pictures, and kept her conversation on with God, while flipping pages.

God, I don't want to lose any more people. I trust you; I pray to you, every day; I have never harmed anyone, and this is the least I expect of you in return.

I wish, God could ever return the discussion, verbally, my heart has your answers God, wish we could talk face to face, wish we could predict. You have made us humans, and we are mortals, she kept talking out loud.

She went back to the kitchen; the recipe was crammed into her mind, by now, and she prepared the choicest of delicacy and *khubhani ka meetha* in dessert. Hope Kabir likes it, she thought.

The man returned by noon. He was soaked in sweat. Noosh was concerned, and she offered him water, "Looks like you have been running around."

"Yeah, the world is making me run, Noosh."

"What happened? You seem disappointed."

"I tried my best but nobody let me go in there; language offered no help."

"Okay, Kabir, may be there is some right time; do not weaken your work."

"No, I won't; I need to send this info across," he was still panting heavily.

The house smelled of good food.

"Kabir, this is my first food serving for you. I did not want to compromise, at all and, you know I kept talking to God today, while preparing this."

"There seems to be a pretty good connect between you and Him, Noosh; see, the food turned out to be so nice."

"But the topic with God was all about life and us, and people we love and the fear of losing,

Kabir, I don't see you praying ever."

"Noosh, I have him in my heart, and I do believe in him but, yes, I don't pray like you do."

"Okay, that is fine, how about our parents in India."

"Well, they do, all the time; they pray on my behalf too; maybe, that is another reason why I don't."

"Come on, let us enjoy this delectable meal."

The day was spent knowing each other, parents, cities in India and much more. With each passing day, Kabir and Noosh developed a very strong bond and understanding.

At a strategic level, Kabir would leverage his intelligence and share it with the folks. He kept on attempting going to the hotel every day, and, one day, he made it in successfully. The hotel had literally been converted into a fortress. Few of the journalists were still staying over there. Kabir was least bothered with anyone over there. He simply focused on his job. That day, Kabir was able to send out the details in the name of Michael. This was the set of information that his friends in Moscow had shared with him earlier.

Also, the communication channel was built with the right set of people. His parents were extremely worried. In fact, at times they had more news to share with Kabir than the latter could. Once in a while, he would call them up and speak over the phone, too. The situation was not too acceptable.

Here, he leveraged the key information sharing, and a lot of what he shared did begin to be highlighted in the international media.

Overall, Kabir had access to a lot more information than the journalists that were even present there.

He was the first one to even reveal that the first radio announcement that was shown to be made from Kabul about the friendly support provided by Russia was actually from Tashkent. Apparently, all the leadership were too busy themselves solving their own issues, that they hardly paid attention to how the world was thinking about them.

Soviets did not seem to be concerned either at this stage. Every passing day, things would turn ugly. The world realized that this was a proxy war between Americans and Russians. It was commendable on part of people like Kabir who gave up their own interests to support people on foreign soil since they believed in humanity. As the media began to show more about this scenario, information exchange began to reduce. The operations began to be a lot more secretive. It was also believed that quite a few exchange of dubious information was shared in the name of classified and confidential. When Kabir got to know from Nikita that Michael had been sacked, he could immediately connect the dots that the information he shared must have resulted in the action. Also, during the war, lot of dirty games must have been in full swing.

The information that Kabir shared so far, did help Afghanistan in the western region. Soviets undermined Afghan rebel presence in that region and, when they began to attack, they were almost wiped out. The Guerilla warfare, proactive supply of arms by Americans, and an experience from Herat Uprising, all combined helped the locals to throw Russians out of there.

All the options that Kabir had were gently exercised. He had to keep a very low profile. He never mingled with normal public in the region, and kept his actions under the wraps.

Noosh was waiting for Kabir to tell her when they could plan to leave. She had been waiting for a long time now. Her patience was running thin. In the past few days, the borders had been sealed, air travel banned, and everyone was under the scanner. There was a lot of wait, already, and patience was their second nature now.

This family of two, and the three boy trio were waiting for the right time and the right moment to arrive to leave the country.

Chapter 20

"Jaisi much tai neeksai, taise chalai chaal
Paarbrahm neda rahai, pal me karai nihaal."
"You should what you say
If you do so, God shall take care."

BUT THIS WAS WAR AND, in a war, there are more bad news than good.

In the recent attacks in Herat, during crossfire, something tragic took place. Noosh's father and some more of their family members were killed.

Everything came to a bitter halt. The news reached Noosh and Kabir only a week after the incident.

The war had begun to take its toll now. Noosh loved two men the most in her life. One was gone forever.

She was simply not prepared to handle this situation. When the news spread to others in the neighborhood, some women would come to comfort her. It was quite strange to notice that in times like these when somebody went through such a condition, how humans would come together. In the moment of grief, they did not bother about their own lives.

Kabir was the only family around her now. She began to feel very insecure and was more vocal with Kabir about her fears. This was something, she was reserved about for a long time. She always suppressed about how much scared she was. Now she was more vulnerable.

Kabir's thoughts remained on the pain that Noosh was going through. He felt far more responsible towards her.

He only wished and prayed for conditions to improve so they could move out of here and also that will bring some happiness back in their lives.

There was not a day when she wouldn't cry. She functioned almost mechanically and it was disturbing Kabir.

Salem and Meer visited the house on a regular basis. It was more important to have more people around them, so that she felt the change.

"I miss him a lot, Kabir."

"Come here."

For last few days, she had remained quiet. It was a deep emotional outburst as a series of memories revived her mind. She kept holding him, murmured something and cried.

Time only would heal her wound. It was only after sometime, that she began to talk normally. The deep pain remained, but in a few days, Noosh knew she had to divert her mind. She did not try alone. Her man supported her and loved her all this while. He never complained. He just remained by her side, mentally, emotionally and physically.

God seemed to be watching over this couple from somewhere in some corner. The Almighty decided to let this family get some good news, the family who has been seeing a lot tragic lately.

As luck would have it, Noosh found out about her pregnancy. For a moment, she could not decide how to react. She wept. For her, it was her dad's rebirth. In some cultures, it was believed that when a good soul goes away, it takes the shape of a new born in the family and, if the two coincide, then the belief takes almost a factual view. As this feeling sunk in, which took her a few minutes, she looked up thanking God, and ran towards Kabir.

After a long time, Kabir saw Noosh come back to life. She did not speak anything yet. She just kept kissing him and hugging him. Then held his hand and placed it on her tummy. Her expressions, shared the million dollar news.

Kabir's excitement could not be controlled. He jumped with joy and held Noosh in his arms as he lifted her towards the bed. "Now you need to take a lot of care. Congratulations to us." He said, all smiles.

"Kabir, today is the happiest day of my life."

"For me too, Noosh."

The two began to plan everything further. The more they discussed, the more they realized how much they needed to do to get their life in order. The most crucial task, without a doubt, was to now move out as early as possible.

"I have begun to fear now Kabir. I beg of you, let us leave, for our child. You have given more, lot more in this whole process. Hope you do not hold the guilt anymore. You have not waged this war, my man."

Kabir put his hands on Noosh's shoulders, "Okay Noosh, we will, trust me."

"Yes, Kabir, please."

Suddenly, a fierce gun battle could be heard, this was more offensive than ever before, the communication was completely lost now, power went off, and nothing was working, except the fear.

"Noosh, I understand all this is not good," he hugged her, "Don't worry, we are together, and understand grief of losing someone. God, you know, God, up there, he listens; this new born is his rebirth, trust me."

"I think too, Kabir. Three of us are together in our world. Hope you understand my voice, as a woman, this is all I need from you now."

"I am on it, Noosh."

They offered prayers to her father, and spent time together remembering him. A couple of days passed, just talking about him, the child, and life in Bombay.

During this period, the newspapers stopped printing. It was mostly dust and fire that could be viewed far away; any moment things could worsen.

Kabir took Noosh to the room that he built in the basement.

"It is very humid here, Kabir."

"Yeah, but this is safer; there is an inlet and outlet too. Let me open it; this is like our mini bunker; it can absorb some shock."

"My child needs to breathe, baby."

"Don't worry, trust me; this will be fine in a few."

"And, you are not leaving me here alone even for a minute."

"No, I am not going anywhere now, okay? That's my promise."

He was thoroughly disappointed with himself, and dejected too. Such an unprecedented state of affairs left him in dismay. He did not know what to do.

"In a war, we all lose, only the ego of the Governments win; look at the situation now. Who is doing what? How can everyone on this earth be insane? What is your connect with the western world giving you?"

"Noosh, please calm down; you need not get tensed," Kabir held her hand firmly.

"I was so joyful, and wanted to share the news with dad, Kabir; we are going to be parents, aren't we?"

"Yes, why do you doubt?"

"I am losing everyone I love the most."

"Don't be so negative, Noosh."

"I am, I have all the reasons. These Tanks, this gun battle, these bomb explosions, noisy nights, what else is left? Our small world exists amidst all this. I don't want to lose you. Oh, gosh! I am going crazy in my head. I cannot think straight."

"Let me get you some water."

"You are not going up; we are not going alone," Noosh did not leave him and wanted to go with him.

"Baby, the basement is connected, so I am still here."

"No, this is a big distance. I don't want you to get out of my sight ever; now, do you listen to me?"

"Oh, okay, okay, got it," he sat beside her.

She was completely psyched out; not for a single moment would she let him go away from her sight. Also, her body was naturally undergoing physical changes. She needed a lot of care. She was getting no less from Kabir though.

She was red. Anxiety, fear and many elements of her life were not known to herself. She was in a new world of discovery altogether.

"Kabir, this is new to me. I just did not know I can be so well under shock," Noosh said.

"Noosh, for me, you are still the same woman, do not think too much."

Worried and tensed, she caught on a brief nap.

"I don't know when I fell asleep, did you eat anything?"

"No, let me get something for you."

"Okay, listen, there is rice in the bowl next to the refrigerator. Please check it, we need to keep food out, since there is no power."

"Okay."

"You know it right, I need to go with you when you go up."

"Yes, baby, of course."

Kabir had a few things running on his mind, the storage, the power and the communication. Noosh had just one thing on her mind, be together with her man and travel out to Bombay.

"Noosh, come here, sit down, hope you feel better."

"Yes, baby, I do. I don't hear any firepower, any more; that is a relief."

Kabir did not elaborate much. He knew whatever the aim was, they would have wiped it out and were moving on to the next one, but he preferred to stay mum. He had decided to cook some stories now so that she felt better.

Before he could say something, she asked him if there is any way to contact his parents now.

"It is okay; you don't worry. They are not fighting a war, we are."

"Do we have enough supplies? How long are we here?"

"I am checking that."

"I kept some dry fruits, fruits there, out there, in that storage."

"Okay, this one?"

"No, no, the left one."

"Okay, I got it; yeah, this is good."

"So this will last us 3 days, without the refrigerator?"

There were reasons and moments for Noosh and Kabir to now support each other; he felt more responsible than ever before. she discovered her fear of losing sooner in life.

"You knew, Kabir, right, you knew this was coming; you wanted to do wonders, and you have done wonders."

"Are you upset with me?"

"I cannot be in a state of denial; I am taking a position. I cannot be wishy washy."

"So you are upset with me."

"Kabir, understand my point."

"Noosh."

"No, let me speak; let me complete what I want to say; I am not happy at all."

Noosh continued hammering Kabir. Kabir gave her time to heal. It was important for her to release the stress a little, not much, as then it would hurt her physically.

"I understand you completely, we have suffered losses we were trying to curtail. We attempted and that is what made us be here. Who knows, if we had fled that we would have survived. People are losing lives even on the border, while fleeing, while escaping. The country has been captured. It is under siege."

"But we had the option to leave when it all began; we could have left around the same time when Nikita and those ladies left. I know your answer, so I don't want to hear that anymore."

"Okay, okay, relax. We still saved many lives."

"Exactly, how is it then we could not have saved ours?"

"We are still alive, aren't we?"

"Come, Kabir, come here. I am sorry, I am just upset."

"Do not say that. I just want you to keep the faith alive. Losing father is the biggest loss, and we will never be able to retrieve that."

"Yeah, I know, I think we need to survive, we need to bring our child up."

"Yes, exactly."

"I feel better now, Kabir, cannot thank you enough."

She tried hard, however could not stop her tears.

"Tough times, remember we are together, pinch me, see we are, that's what matters the most."

Noosh was quietly weeping, holding Kabir. They had food together. After the food, while Kabir was getting up, there was a knock on the door.

Salem and Meer turned up, "How long shall we be holed up in the hotel *saab*? It is a prison; we have no idea how we came, but today we decided we will come to you. Even if we had died on the way, we won't have cared."

"Really, what happened guys? You know, you have been sent by God. Noosh does not want me to leave her alone, there is no power."

Salem knew what to do next. "*Saab,* you know I am sure I will find out. Local homemade generators that run on diesel can be found in some places. I shall arrange for one."

"Who will spare you any?"

"There are people who have fled their homes, you know, those beautiful looking white coloured houses are vacant, and the city is on the run."

"Before you leave, *saab*, are you really planning a long term here? Now in this situation."

"No, no way," Kabir said with much emphasis. Then he continued, "Only for a few days; I mean, till we plan and strategize. The safest exit would be via Jalalabad. Will they still hurt the journalists?"

"Sir, if you were with Jemima or Nikita madam, maybe, they wouldn't have, but you look like a local citizen, so before you prove to them anything, you never know what they do."

"Yeah, they can just practice a shot or two on me."

"Are they hurting pregnant women too?" Noosh asked.

"We saw women fleeing the town."

"Congrats, *saab* and madam, that is a good news. We did not know. May God bless you and your family," Meer said.

"Thanks, where is babu?" Kabir asked.

"He is working with the ministers, those survivors out there. He is driving them around to earn some money. He wanted to save as much as he could as he is getting extra pay. Not many drivers are available during this time."

"What about you guys? I know I let you down as I could not do much for you. I had my own thing, you know. New marriage, settling down and all."

"No, *saab*, it is okay. All we know is we can all escape from here. All we need to do is find the right day. The situation is out of hands and out of control, everybody is fighting everybody it seems."

"That is the worst part, so whosoever has a gun shoots the one who doesn't have, be it civilians, including women and children. They are the worst affected and therefore we need to be cautious."

"Yes, true."

"So we understand that, *saab*. You know I have found out some stuff, locally. In lieu of good money or jewellery, they let you come in their trucks and take you to Peshawar, mostly, and I have heard some trucks go far even till India."

"Really, what did you find out?"

"Sir, this war has brought many commercial aspects here."

"Like what?"

"Well, few of the local people have engaged with the soviets and even some from the west in opium trade. Illicit money that seems to be flourishing."

"Oh okay."

During this conversation, Kabir ensured Noosh got some rest.

"Carry on guys, tell me all about it."

"Yeah, *saab*, even a few transporters are making money. They are helping people flee the country. They pay money at *naakabandhi*, you know those guarded check posts; there are Afghans, and they let you go for money."

Kabir could not stop now, "I had lot of information on these appointments; they have got a good raise; soldiers have even got double promotions, double salary hikes, mostly Soviets and some Afghans too."

"Yes, where is this government getting money from? Where is the economy?"

"Yeah, you have a point."

"Exactly, the exports have been controlled by the Soviets indirectly, for quite some time now."

"Money allocation happens according to your influence Meer," Kabir said, "Some of the local people are getting good money to keep things mobilized; they give out the information; they do not join the rebels; keep people by their side, and all those things."

"Oh, okay, got it *saab*."

"So what do we do now, Meer and Salem? Look at the situation here, we have resources and supplies that won't last more than a few days. Even if you are able to manage a generator, it won't last more than a week."

"Yes, *saab*, I agree."

"And it is not safe, anyway, from here to the Hotel, to cover that distance. While I salute you both for taking such a big risk, I wish our minivan had a hundred litre tank and all full."

"Still, *saab*, that won't help, to cross the border you need those informers, at least, that one alternative is now available. It all started yesterday."

"Really, that is a great news. Look at these people, how they get networked. I too had a great network at one point, but no more. The communication is all shut, and I can't do anything further."

"*Saab*, knowing you well, you would have managed to still find some way."

"If it were that easy, I would have got you both out."

"But tell me something, why did you not leave with one of those *informers*?"

Meer jumped in the conversation, "*Saab*, we did not want to leave you both here; ever since we saw a few bomb explosions around the city, we decided not to go."

"You mean after seeing explosions, instead of making the other choice, you decided to stay back here."

"*Ji saab.*"

"And, all this while, all these days, all these weeks, I kept thinking I am the only surviving maniac or rather a living helpful soul."

"*Saab*, come on, please don't say that."

"No, I am serious, and I made a very big deal out of it. You know, I tried to show myself as a martyr."

"You are, *saab*, you are selfless."

"I may be a good soul, but why did I have to think the way I did?"

"You did not do anything wrong, you just confided in your family, and it is okay."

"Meanwhile, *saab*, let me make some generator arrangement for you." Salem said.

"Really, isn't it risky?"

"More than the risk, we were actually and honestly worried for you. Unlike other days, for last few days we did not hear anything from you, so we came rushing to see how you both were."

"Oh, so that is the whole story. You are the future in Bollywood guys. I am sure Salem-Jaaved would be given a run for their money, so it will be Salem- Meer now. I will keep Babu out, as I have not seen him do much except sitting next to that fountain in Herat."

"Hahaha, you remember that *saab*." Both the boys left to arrange for electricity.

Within a few hours, the unit was up with the power, and the boys took their leave stating that, in the next few days or so, they shall make the arrangement for the truck, so they should be ready and prepared now to leave anytime.

Noosh slept more than usual; with the power on, she did not seem to wake up...

On the contrary, Kabir was not sleepy at all. This gave him a chance to look at Noosh more closely when both were quiet, one by default and the other by choice.

He held her hand, the left hand, softly, like a man in love, and kept looking at it. Noosh's right hand was beneath her back, it was left in that posture as she would have slept. Kabir now pulled her right hand slowly from beneath her back, and began to look at them both.

Your hands are so beautiful, artistic, very artistic, Noosh, and all this while I kept considering myself as an artist. Look at your eyes, they speak a million words right now. I am able to converse with your eyes closed too, Kabir kept going on expressing all his love and then softly kissed her tummy. This is for our sweet to be born child Noosh. I want a girl like you. Kabir slept to the right side of Noosh.

By the middle of the night, Noosh woke up, said her prayers, and kissed Kabir on his forehead. Within a moment, the skies seemed fiercer with the jets than ever before. She wasn't able to sleep at all any further. "Kabir, can you hear?" He remained too tired to wake up.

After some insistence, she was able to wake him up.

"Do you hear this?"

'Yeah, it is horrible."

"Why do they need to patrol the skies in the middle of the night?"

"They just want to be prove to everyone that they are on the vigil 24x7."

"But isn't this more than ever before?"

"They must have procured more of them and sent some here."

"In the night?"

"Yeah, baby, this must be their strategy. I don't know, I really don't know or, maybe that is part of the war strategy."

"I am learning this new subject with you Kabir; don't sleep, wake up. Share some stories, motivate me. Hope you know that now it is me and our child, hence there is this extra rush of blood in me; so you are not just handling me, you are handling two people at a time, so think like that."

'That is a nice analogy; even if there are twins inside you and you are three, I shall be able to manage and handle you all, come on."

"There goes a bomb."

"Now it does not scare me anymore. I can get up with you now, face them and give them a fight."

"Wow, lady, you got super natural species inside you it seems."

"Aha, I am honest with you; my fears have all gone away."

"Because the power is back; you can breathe fine, and you have some idea that we will be gone from here sooner now."

"That does boost my confidence. I believe it is also to do with those natural mood swings, you see."

"I get that."

"So where is my motivational story?"

"Really, you need one at this hour?"

"I insist, pep me up Kabir, are you bored of me?"

"No, Noosh, never."

"What if you get bored of me?"

"Okay, for half our life I shall sleep to your right, like I do now, then for the rest, I shall take the other side, will that work?"

"You, man, I cannot win with you in words."

"By the way, your hands are artistic."

"Yes, I can play the Sitar."

"What are you talking? Why did you not tell me?"

"I wanted to keep certain aspects as a good surprise."

"You can keep secrets?"

"Yeah, the worthy ones."

"What else?"

"Is one not good enough?"

"I mean, any other secret, not necessarily artistic, anything else?"

"No, this was it, my baby, and look at you."

Kabir rushed out to get his camera.

There was a complete photo session of Noosh, her hands exclusively, then many close up shots.

"Well, great job done, Mr. Nikon, I owe it to Salem. You know these guys are very resourceful. I am impressed from day one when I met them in Jalalabad. How time flies; it seems like yesterday."

"Yes, Kabir, I am certain. Listen, our friends must be worried for us ever since the communication has gone for a toss. We are in a limbo."

"I so much wish to communicate with all."

"It is now two of us. Can we go to the city tomorrow? I want to see it; I want to feel it."

"Feel what?"

"I want to see and feel the show of power and prowess. What is it that gives them such a high?"

"They are all employees, Noosh, like anyone else. They just follow the command."

"Yeah, and some get corrupt too. I was listening to some parts of what Salem and Meer spoke."

"Yeah, that happens. Oh, okay."

"So I want to see that part."

"Come on, don't be mad, it is not safe. Don't be a sadist. Let me play some nice music for you."

"Play it, Kabir, keep playing it."

"Our kid is turning six months now."

"And you are going to be a great father, I know."

"Yes, and we shall be great parents and a beautiful couple."

"I want us to keep the romance alive and keep it contagious."

"Noosh, Noosh…"

There was no response. Suddenly she fainted.

Oh, no, what shall I do now? Where can I find the doctor? Kabir shouted.

He got water and some juice, wiped her face with a wet towel, "Come on, get up, super woman."

She had gone feeble, and was not able to speak much; she had some trouble breathing.

Kabir lifted her in her arms and took her out for some fresh air. It had been many days she did not step out of the house. She rarely complained about her health, and knew, in these tough times, she would not want to add further stress to her man. Somehow, that level of understanding was deterrent to her health. Kabir realized this now.

"Noosh, I did read some about taking care of a pregnant wife, but there is not much I can do. Please tell me how you feel as I gently thump your face."

"Play it Kabir."

'Noosh, do you feel all right?"

She kept repeating.

"I am worried for you."

Then she blabbered, and began to open her eyes, "Why did you stop the music?"

"It is inside the house, and we are here outside."

"Oh, that is why it is so dark out here."

"Yes, baby."

"Make me stand, my man."

"Are you sure? Can you stand? You seem to be feeling weak."

"I want to stand with you in the darkness."

"I want to hold you in my arms when it is dark."

"Don't make me so dependent on you my man."

"I enjoy you in my arms; you are not that heavy yet."

"And, if I get heavy, then?"

"Well, if it is dark, I can hold no matter your weight."

"And if it is not dark?"

"Then I want you to stand beside me; you are my strength, Noosh."

"You are my air, you know. I feel all right when you calm me. You take good care of me. What will I do without you?"

"You will never be without me."

"I mean, when you go for work, I will keep missing you."

"That will be the only separation period."

"It is also critical, need that space, so I miss those moments more."

"Noosh, be as you are, never be anything else."

"So for you, Kabir. Be as you are but, yes, maybe at some point, I might keep experimenting with your appearance."

"Really."

"Moustache, maybe; hair too, leave that to me. What do you want me to do? You like long hair on me?"

By now, she was feeling better; she had her arms around Kabir's neck. The breeze was soothing. In the backdrop, there were skies filled with night patrols and, far away, animals' voices could be heard.

They had a good sleep so far, and the night seemed to be going well while they were awake.

"Noosh, I believe there is some trouble set for us here."

"Why, what happened now?"

"You look at these marks."

'Yeah."

"These are trails of the T62 tanks."

"They are marking the place."

"So you mean, they plan to destroy?"

"Yes, they might, I am assuming, to be on the safer side, that is how they might draw out their plan; maybe, they did not see any activity and this is a standalone house."

"Hence, they might have deprioritized for now."

"Yes, but I believe, an attack is clearly on the way sometime soon; maybe tonight, maybe tomorrow."

"Do we run?"

"The answer is no. I don't want to leave you alone and, then, walking is also not permitted in this condition. Taking the van out is a big risk. I am glad it is parked strategically, not to be spotted easily."

"What is the option at hand, then?"

"Let me think, if I need to leave you here for some time and go figure this out."

"What are you thinking? You may leave me here if you think that can help solve the problem, but what will you do?"

"I will figure out twenty one ways to an instant escape."

"Humour alive at this hour? Applause."

"At least something. I mean let me go to the palace or the hotel. We need a safe and a free passage, that's all. We are not harming anyone, and I can state that I am a journo. Hopefully it works this time."

"They have all left, nobody is left here now; even if they are, I am sure they must be in the hiding and secretly covering the ops."

"Yeah, the way we are."

"Kabir, I want to eat sondesh, Calcutta rasgolla."

"At this hour."

"I just feel the urge, please."

"You are in a real rush to go to India. God is listening to you, keep asking."

"God, I want to eat Indian sweets now."

"Wish granted."

"Hmmmmm….boohooooo."

"Humor at this hour, applause."

"No, it is a need. I swear, you cheater cock."

"Okay, so here is the plan. I leave this place in the morning, around 10; you be there in the basement. We have enough power with us."

"And…"

"Then, I won't take much longer. Also, we need your medicines, so I need to buy those, too, and, then, I need to connect with Salem and Meer, as well. I mean, I will try to use my Soviet card yet again this time; how long do we fear? Let us confront it."

"Yaa I agree; I also feel fearless somehow."

"Exactly, tomorrow is a big day, then. Listen, keep backpacks ready."

"Yes."

"And those documents too."

"Keep them all in one place; there is your jewellery, cash, camera, passport, and documents, all of it."

"Yes, sir, leave it to me."

"Come on, we got lot of work to do."

"Yeah."

"I just don't want to sleep, anymore. I want to be awake till we reach Bombay."

"I feel the same."

"Let us make this night so memorable that we remember it forever. Kiss me, make love to me hubby, if it were...."

"No, don't say if it were the last, you know what happened in *Casablanca.*"

"Oh, come on, kiss me now."

The couple looked most beautiful together. Both were trying to keep their spirits up. They were looking forward to a beautiful morning the next day. By now, their support system would have been activated, too.

Chapter 21

"Ik din aisa hoga, sab soo padai bichhoh
Raaja raana chhatrapati, savdhaan kin hoi."
"Please listen King, Ruler, Emperor, There shall be a day
When you lose it all, so be alert always."

THE COUPLE DECIDED TO HAVE KABIR LEAVE THE PLACE BY 8 A.M instead of 10 a.m, so that things can be finished faster. Kabir held a sandwich, bottle of water, some dry fruits in his pocket, and a few photographs for the way. Noosh was in the basement, gathering stuff and packing further. Last minute checks were in progress.

It was very difficult to think straight and logical in this war situation. There was an environment of fear around. With so much happening, no stranger could be trusted. There were incidents of loot, vandalism, killing, attacks, and illicit trade across the country.

For this couple, their togetherness and love for each other created a certain harmony that led them to still be normal. Kabir played the role of a real man. Noosh got the best of him to come out; his core strength of planning and execution were the immediate focus.

Kabir reached the palace first; he was shocked and surprised to see a few people lying in a pool of blood. It took him a while to regain his senses.

Suddenly, Babu arrived at the scene.

"*Saab*, we will leave tonight. I am glad you are here. Salem and Meer told me about our plan. You know they are killing anyone and everyone. I am not sure if we are safe here, anymore. I even let go off my salary, this month. I was working for these people, and now I want to leave."

"I am sad to see, Babu. What is going on? I have been away from all this. They are weakening and crippling all the support here and, now, what I have understood is they are taking complete control of the internal army too. Even the army related decisions do not reside locally anymore. The Soviets are controlling the economy, anyone who comes in their way is finished including the innocents." Kabir said, having anticipated a part of it in advance.

Suddenly there was a fierce gun battle. Some of the Afghan guards and the Soviets soldiers started attacking each other. A few of the guerrilla fighters started shooting at them. The firing was all over and out of control. The tanks also started appearing at the scene.

Kabir and Babu tried to save themselves and began to run towards his house. But they kept ducking occasionally, and even rolled on the ground several times. They didn't dare run in front of them, as they knew they would be mowed down.

Kabir was a very tough man as he helped Babu save himself. He asked him to do what he was doing, and Babu did just that.

People were all over the place. Some could be seen hiding and some began to run towards the shots; they could not figure out what was right at that point.

Lot of troops landed in the city that day. The soviets were firing down on Afghan rebels from the trenches covered by camouflage and bunkers made of concrete.

Several dead bodies lay scattered all over. The gun shots kept hitting the people who were already dead, making the scene gory as the blood could be seen flowing down the streets and elsewhere.

As the gun firing became fiercer and more powerful, Kabir said with halting breath, "Oh, my goodness, this is hell. Did I make a mistake leaving Noosh alone in the house?"

"*Saab*, it is not safe to leave Madamji alone?"

By now, they had reached a safer spot. They were very familiar with this area, and hence it was relatively easier for them to head in the right direction. The news was that the bazaar was attacked last night and many people were kille Kabir saw from a distance that there was a bomb that was dropped creating a dark dust of smoke and fire, and a very heavy sound of explosion.

"Where do we go? This is crazy. Where are they attacking from? They seem to have taken their positions."

"We need to run elsewhere, now."

The point was in which direction.

"I need to run to our house Babu; come, we need to get Noosh."

For now, they were not feeling the pain but they were hurt bad, as they felt down a few times. They reached closer to the scene of dust and smoke. The spot was not visible for some time; both were enveloped in the cloud of smoke.

"We might die like this, Babu. What about the hotel?"

"That must still be safe."

"Let us get Noosh."

"*Saab*, don't you think, both of you should have stayed in the hotel?"

"Only if I could predict things so well Babu, I would have controlled this war too."

"You are right."

Kabir's worst fears began to haunt him as he started running. He kept leaping, falling down, but did not stop.

"I don't want to lose you, Noosh. I did a mistake. Why is it taking so long?"

"*Saab*, how far is it?"

"It should have."

"Kya *saab*?"

"I mean, by now, we should have reached."

"You must be anxious, *saab*, therefore you feel so; moreover, we are hurt too."

Kabir stopped talking now. He only kept looking around.

Within a moment, he started screaming. He howled and pushed his lungs out and, within seconds he was on the ground.

Babu imagined what would have happened. This must have been Kabir saab's house, he thought. So he only looked at Kabir without any reaction now.

Kabir remained locked in the thoughts of Noosh, while walking around and digging the ground. It was extremely hot, so he could not go nearer.

He saw some imprints of humans and livestock remains battered after this ghastly bomb attack. Noosh was in the basement.

Perhaps she was many feet under. He wasn't sure of what was going on as a crowd had gathered around him, witnessing the super human pain that Kabir was going through.

Babu, by now fell down on his knees, crying in tears, and found it extremely difficult to control Kabir.

After endless sorrow and a gap of almost an hour, Kabir began to crawl towards his piece of land. It was all crushed; rumbles were still echoing in the far clouds; shards of glass flew as far as half a mile. Such was the impact, a deep trench was created. Nothing could survive in that fatal attack, not even the birds which were flying just above the ground. These tanks ran at a speed of about fortieth kmph, and now could not be sighted at all. The enemy was gone, causing irreparable damage. Lives came to a standstill.

This must have been the hundredth attack in the country, but, for Kabir, it was the one and only attack. It took away his spirit; his reason to live.

By the time smoke had completely settled down, Kabir was lost in his own memories. Today, he did not want to live.

His pain only worsened, and the idea of dying did strike his mind several times.

I always knew that life is tough, and there would be sacrifices all along, and that is what I have been doing all my life. I wish I had died rather than lived to see this day, Kabir kept repeating to himself.

He knew it was all over for him. He remembered how he came here few years ago for Noosh, all that happened over this time and all beautiful memories, and all this while he only cried and screamed. He knew no other language or expression.

He walked towards the debris, gathered mud, looked into trenches, Where are you, Noosh? Where do I find you? Who do I go to?

"Saab, what shall we do now?"

"I really don't know. For the first time, I am numb, I really don't know what to do. I don't want to believe this. It is the most horrifying dream as I would call it."

Babu kept listening to him, while thinking what to do next.

"I still want to wait here. Maybe she is around; you know what, I asked her to be inside the basement. I sent her further down. I was a fool. In the attack, everything goes away. That was just to ease her out, and did that help? Kabir held Babu's collar; did that help Noosh, Babu, I mean.

What shall I do now? I had promised her, I won't ever leave her alone. I always do what I think is right. You know, she asked me many times before, never to leave her alone.

I stayed back in this country so I could save lives of many, and I could not save hers."

Kabir kept cursing himself.

Noosh, I was cursed. You got my blessings, now you are gone. I shall get my curse back. I want to be cursed. I could not save your father. I could not save you. I could not stop the war. Kabir kneeled down and kept knocking the ground with his hands and elbows, in tears.

Babu tried to console him; he did his best.

"In a war, you cannot even register a police complaint. The crimes are considered normal. Isn't that weird?"

Now Babu held his hand, and helped him stand up on his feet.

Kabir was not ready to believe what had just happened, and he insisted this was not true. On the ground, from what he saw, he had no reason to believe otherwise.

All he needed now was a lot of support and comfort. With only Babu around, it was hard to imagine how he would come back to normalcy. He did not even see Noosh's body after the death. And that only aggravated the pain for him.

On sensing the presence of people, he realized it was important for him to act faster. So he began to ask them if they saw anything here. The answers were not very positive, though some did indicate that there was a plan for many people to flee today and, maybe, his wife joined them too. Kabir could not chose to ignore it. He knew Salem and Meer were supposed to arrive at his house as well, and thus sediment that thought in his head.

Babu suggested Kabir to still file a police complaint in the pretext of missing person. That did not fall under war crime, and hence, it will get some help.

Kabir wasn't sure of the idea, for it was hard for him to imagine if the police was still active in the region. Nevertheless, there was no harm in trying.

Gradually, the thought of taking some action brought positivity in Kabir. It was crucial to remain hopeful. He began to believe that with this, the search will begin and, that coupled with interrogating or asking the locals, it might lead him eventually lead him to Noosh.

He was constantly being comforted in the most uncomfortable situation.

Time to act was right now, right here. One last time, before leaving the place, Kabir glanced helplessly across the entire site of devastation, before being taken away by the clueless man.

On their way, he kept talking to several men, as much as his energy allowed him to. It was scarcely surprising that the help poured from all the corners. They helped him find the local cop and a place to take a short refuge till the matter was all sorted.

On the streets, the view depicted a war zone. There were locals busy with fliers, some on the walls, and some flying around, scattered- all carrying a message 'Go Soviets Go.'

Kabir was a mere spectator now. A ban was placed on the media. No word will go out without their permission. There were talks of sending all the media folks out of the country.

He met up with the cop, who did make efforts to take the relevant information and mentioned to him the possible ways to find in detail. The communication lines in the hotel were shut, but the cop arranged it for Kabir. That day, he could speak with his parents. Time allowed to speak was only sixty seconds. While Kabir spoke about the disappearance of Noosh, his mother only sounded more worried, and consoled her son.

After the phone call, Kabir continued to battle his fears and the decision. He agonised over what to do next. Babu asked him to do, more or less what, his mother had told him - to surrender to God, and continue making the right efforts. Life will guide him the right away. Easier said than done, Kabir thought.

In the course of their plight, the next day, Babu procured some information from the people. He finally managed to get the information on the transport company owner who ran a significant portion of illicitly sending people across the border via Jalalabad.

It was in Jalalabad, so they needed to move out from Kabul to the new city. That arrangement was also made in exchange for some money that resided in Kabir's wallet.

The travel was planned for a day after. They waited.

"Circumstances, *saab*, do not worry. This will not stay forever. Things will take a turn for the better."

"Thanks, Babu. I am glad you talk like the way I do, when I need it the most."

"*Saab*, I think let us go to the hotel; maybe, we can find out something further there."

The streets leading to the hotel were barren; not a single life could be seen. Ever since the bazaar was attacked last evening, every activity had come to a halt; seldom could somebody be seen walking; nobody looked eye to eye; all were under suspicion.

"Is this the hotel we were talking about?"

"Yes, *saab*, this looks all haunted."

"Let us go inside."

The staff was sparingly available. Those present were busy. Today they were not occupied with any guests, rather wrapping up their stuff. They were considered lucky to have survived so far.

"What happened here?"

"Good afternoon, sir, how are you? Things have only worsened. Two foreigners died yesterday, in one of the attacks, and the hotel was immediately vacated."

"Where have they all gone? Do you have any idea about my wife? And these guys, Salem and Meer?"

"It was a big rush, whatever they could get. Some left in the ambulance from Red Cross, and the others were in embassy vehicles."

"You heard my question, didn't you?"

"*Saab,* I did. I don't know. Maybe, they all left; there were quite a few Volvo and other trucks, too."

"Oh, those transporters?"

"Yeah, it was a very noisy scene; people took what they could in just a few seconds. They even left their baggage inside; a few of us are stranded as we were left with no space, and now we don't know how to leave. It is extremely dangerous."

He was miffed at hearing this. He did not let his hopes wane, though. Dismayed, he left with Babu and carried only one mission and aim on his mind, that he shall leave no stone unturned to find her.

Kabir even met up with one of the ministers and put his request.

"You know, mister, we understand your situation, but please understand. There are people in thousands who are leaving this country; some die, some survive and, then, there are some who are able to cross across the border," Minister said.

"But, sir, that is not the answer I expect from you."

"I am not here to please you with my answers. We are already undergoing severe stress due to international pressure. Please do not share this individual approach with me."

"You mean, you do not care about lives anymore?"

"But who are you? I think I have seen you here before."

"I am Kabir, a journalist from India."

"I remember, you were here about a couple of years ago. I was a secretary then."

"You seemed familiar, Sir."

"Come, have a seat."

"Okay, thanks, and this is Babu."

"I know him, he ran away from his job."

"Sorry, *saab*.'

"No, it is okay.

See guys, I know and I understand your situation. I feel bad. I lost my brother in this war. What do I complain about?"

"You hold the powers, Sir."

"We don't. It is superficial. We realise how grave this thing has become, and now we want this to stop."

"But, why don't you stop?"

"You shouldn't be talking like a naive, Mr Kabir."

"Well, then, what is it?"

"It is a whole lot of confusion. Our army moved to the rebels; Soviets took more control. Using our own economy, they are feeding their soldiers. Americans are fighting them, and we are leaving our own country."

"Isn't that sad?"

"So, now you know what we are going through. It is all the fault of our own people and misdeeds of previous Governments, what else can I say."

"I can understand that, Sir."

"Many people have been killed and displaced. You think I can find them all. Journalists like you come, report anything, and it goes against us; now we were forced to put a gag order."

"I am no more doing my coverage. I am just looking for my wife, and she is pregnant with our child. I am hoping she is not killed in the recent attack."

"Oh, yes, there were a few attacks today and yesterday, worst so far; even we are thinking of moving to Saudi. I have my cousin there; he is helping me."

"If you leave, then what happens to the people?"

"Which people?" Minister's caustic comment further surprised Kabir.

It was evening now.

It appeared darker than ever before. Misery and hollowness hung lose in every particle of the air. Life could change anytime for anyone, and, when it hit hard, one would forget any bright minutes from the past. For that particular moment, one might feel cursed. Kabir was going through the same sorrow and agony. Babu was his sole listener.

****

Chapter 22

"Kabir ka tu chitvai, kya tera chyantya hoi
Anchantya harji karai, jo tohi chyant na hoi."
"What are you worried for, what do you gain by worrying?
God will remove all your worries, he will do more than you'd
imagine."

FAR AWAY FROM THE CITY LIFE, A VARIETY OF
ACTIVITIES were noted around the border area as hordes of
people were crossing over the line. Some through Jalalabad on the
east, and some through Herat to Iran. The border to Russia was
assumingly closed with mines. So, nobody would take that risk
except the cattle and livestock.

One such borders went through a small village around Jalalabad.
This was the paid border that Salem and Meer had mentioned
and, now, Babu had the information on.

Many local trucks could be seen in line. Soviet trucks were crossing
without any disturbance. There was specific time allotted to them
and, till then, they could only stop and wait for their turn.

The scene at the border was very chaotic and, for the cops on duty
and some in civil clothes, this was no less than a project to be
handled on daily basis.

This was all based on the communication network between
various borders at national and district levels. The border crossing
management was done discreetly.

A fleet of such transport was operated, and today there were two trucks lined up, one for men and the other for women. One of these trucks in line was driven by Salem's friend. He was from Peshawar, settled in Kabul. He knew almost all the *chaikanas* on the way, all the check posts along with the tough routes. He came with a hefty fees, a part of which went to his owner and the authorities. There was less risk associated with his operations so far. Some others might operate at the same efficient levels, however those were not known.

The trucks have been driving and halting for last few days now.

After being driven for a few days, they came to a halt. At sharp 8:30 p.m, the rear of the trucks was opened. People could be seen tripping on each other, there was a fee for space occupied inside.

Noosh gave away her golden necklace; she made space for two. One for herself, and the other for Kabir. Unfortunately, she was not able to rent out the entire truck. She was dependent on the other tenants inside. Of the entire lot, Noosh was the only one who had remained completely quiet all these days. It wasn't how it all had started.

The day when their house was bombed down, Salem and Meer had arrived just before the ghastly attack to fetch her and Kabir. They had also spotted a tank that was moving towards her house, so the only option left with them was to leave. Also, as the day had progressed, it was observed, there were many attacks. Salem and Meer had proactively moved out, arranged for the transport, and took it near the house, so that Kabir and Noosh could be taken away. In all this rush, Babu was missed and added to that there was no waiting time. That would only mean death.

Noosh was literally forced to go with them, while the lady had resisted and wanted to wait for Kabir. Seeing the tank running towards them, she also felt it was better to leave the place first, as also Kabir was not with them.

The events turned awry when the road to the hotel was completely blocked and none of the trucks was allowed to wait. That would only mean the truck would be required to face a shot from the tank. So the truck kept moving.

This was the last time when Noosh spoke and made her presence felt to everyone. She wanted to get down from the vehicle, every time it would slow down.

She only believed the truck would go and get some more people, including her husband, but nothing remained consistent or as planned in a war. She began to bear the brunt now.

The circumstances caused it all. And, now, there was a big mystery around this whole thing. She was falsely assured that in the men's truck, Kabir must have taken a ride. Things would only be clear once the trucks stopped for a break.

All that while, the lady only kept thinking. She was also in a terrible physical condition. She had no idea that her house did not exist anymore in Kabul. All she remembered was the rush; it was now or never. She never wanted to leave without Kabir; the tanks spoilt her chances.

She wanted to save herself and the child, and she was confident Kabir would find her.

"Come, madam, come out," said the truck helper.

She was deafened out completely. There was a fire place outside; it was getting colder around this time, as the winters began to approach.

After much persuasion and requests, Noosh was being pulled out by a couple of lady occupants.

"Oh, you seem to be from an affluent family, and you are so beautiful," said one lady, introducing herself as Nimrat Kaur.

"Thank you, Nimratji, I am Noosh."

"Where do you belong?"

"Bombay,"

"Where is your man? We waited for him at the Kabul Jalalabad depot for an hour, but then the Tanks were in sight and hence we had to leave, but he never turned up."

"I don't know."

"Okay, come, have some water, and now do not worry."

"I want to go back to my house. My husband must be waiting."

"So sorry to hear about your husband not being here, But, you know there is no point of return from here; it is all one way exit."

"How can I leave without him? You tell me; I won't. I have to return now; I cannot."

Noosh ran to Salem, "You really think this is fair."

"Noosh madamji, we know what you are feeling right now, but we wanted to save your life. Did you not see those tanks coming? I mean, feel fortunate we could save you. As for Kabir *saab*, he will find a way out to find you. There have been many attacks since yesterday. Let us cross this border."

"Are you asking me to leave without my man?"

"No madamji, I am asking you to be alive for him, that is all."

There was a shout all over, to sit inside, as it was 9 p.m. and the border barely opened for a few minutes.

Within a few seconds, the scene was back to where it all started a few hours ago. Noosh was back in the truck again, and nobody allowed her to think otherwise.

The distance was very hard to cover, and the time was tough to pass. Noosh could not blink her eye even for a second. She was completely lost in all the possible thoughts a woman sufferer can go through. She was a victim and she felt apprehended. Tears had also dried by now, and all she was left with was a choice, to hope.

A few miles before Peshawar, there was another local border. As a rule of laws, all the trucks needed to stop in line and wait till the green signal was given. Another truck which joined from other Afghan town was ahead of Noosh's, and now was being checked. It seemed to be carrying smuggled wood and exotic items; the cops held it there, and let the others go.

Nimrat tried to open conversation with Noosh, "See the difference; same land, one set of people kill you and the others protect you; this is beyond my comprehension."

Noosh preferred to stay quiet. Nimrat did not insist. However, let her know she can tell her anytime she needed anything. Then she went off to sleep. Noosh was in pain, mental and physical both. She had been missing Kabir a lot. All she had been doing was crying.

After a gruesome ten day journey with a few stop overs and some arguments on the way, the truck was able to cross over to India and reached a place called Pathankot.

This was the final destination point for the transporter. Everyone began to thank the driver, helper, and the fellow passengers for immense cooperation.

Noosh stood firmly in one corner with bags in her hand. She had come to India for the first time. The place she wanted to live in and spend her life with her husband, she had reached alone. The thought kept eating her from within and she kept thinking.

Again, she asked the same question, this time from the driver, "What do I have to do to return to Kabul?"

"You need to go to Moscow. Tell them you are a soldier. Join their army after you clear their exams. You will land in Moscow. No sane mind wants to be there. Who wants to be in the war except the soldiers?"

"Come on, Pasha, do not psyche madam out," said the helper.

He took bags from her, "Madamji, we will ensure your travel arrangements. You are traveling to Bombay now, right?

"Yes Pasha*ji*."

It seemed Salem and Meer's truck was left behind; she wanted to wait, but the time for the bus to leave towards her destination was almost there.

"There is a bus from here that goes till *Dilli*; from there we will arrange a seat for you in the train.

Madamji, please take some cash from us; we got Indian Rupees exchanged, already," Pasha said. He was aware that the jewellery given by Noosh was quite expensive, hence the cash to her.

"Please do not worry at all. Your *saab* will come back soon, we assure you," helper said.

"We have also informed the other driver; he goes there, once a month. Next time when he goes, he will find out about him and let him know that you have reached your in laws in Bombay. I will do so in case I find him when I reach."

"Thanks so much, all of you, for being so kind."

The frail and weak lady was on a never ending painful trip. She was not in her senses anymore. She was travelling like a programmed robot.

There was so much history that she carried, it was not at all simple for a human in that condition to be able to cope with it. Noosh was cracking up.

She had completely switched off, and, somehow, managed to reach Bombay. She had no idea how she was going to face the new family of her life. She began to cry. In fact, she was always on the edge of tears. In a whacky depressed state, Noosh reached Bombay and managed to find the house with the cops and neighbors' help in Colaba.

She stood before the door for some time, before gathering courage to ring the doorbell.

"Yes, beta who are you looking for?" Within another minute Kabir's mother hugged her as she recognized Noosh.

Noosh could not control her rush of tears.

"What happened? Where is Kabir?"

She was quiet.

"*Arey*, why are we standing outside? Let us go inside."

Mrs. Prakash immediately rushed inside the room and got her glasses.

"Where is he?" she questioned repeatedly.

"It is a long story, mom."

In the meantime, Mrs. Prakash arranged for all the rituals that she possibly could perform at such a short notice. Most of the excitement was dampened due to the absence of her son.

"So, you never got together with him? He had called me talking about your disappearance. He sounded worried."

"Oh, my God, did he speak with you? Tell me more mom."

Mrs. Prakash kept looking at Noosh, and hugged her a few times. Noosh touched her feet to seek her blessings after a while, as she had forgotten earlier owing to her state of mind. Both the women kept talking about this in detail. Mrs. Prakash asked her to elaborate all that had happened.

"I don't know where to begin, but yes, there was a tank, he had gone out....then…"

Noosh narrated the horrifying tale that gripped her over past almost two weeks. She had gone completely pale, the beauty was still visible though.

Mrs. Prakash went inside and completed the rituals. She gave her blessings, and told her not to worry. Old lady had her experience and instinct guiding her. Either way, she was only trying to comfort her daughter in law.

"You know, Noosh, many years ago, we did not hear from Kabir for about four months, and that is when we engaged the embassy and found out he had gone to some wildlife adventure."

"But this is a real war, mom."

"I assure you, have faith. He is all right."

Upon hearing the story, Mrs Prakash sympathized, "I feel sorry to hear about your father; till such time, there was an active communication, we felt okay."

"Yes, mom, things were messed up for last few days."

"We keep hearing it in the news, all the time and, honestly, we were extremely worried. All this while, we have been asking him to come along. Oh, Noosh, I want to hug you again, *beta.* God bless your child. We will soon be proud grandparents, and then Kabir shall be here, too."

"I am hopeful, mom, I am very hopeful, and I do not wish to give up."

"You need not get stressed out; it is not good for the child also. Please feel free. This is your home."

She served her water and tea, followed by food.

"Thanks, mom."

"Once Kabir's father arrives in the evening, we shall discuss this in detail and try to engage all our resources and contacts and find out about our son and your husband."

"Thanks, once again, mom."

Mrs Prakash told her that she was going to be in her room for some time, as she needed to finish her prayers.

She closed the room and only began to cry, looking at Kabir's photograph. Unlike any other moment where the emotions meant sharing together, for this time, she just controlled those, as she saw Noosh was already troubled. And, this was her first meeting. The mother-in-law did not want Noosh to show her weak side. She knew if as an elder she loses it, who will take care of Noosh and her son. She was very worried.

Noosh was still out in the living room. She dozed off in no time. She hadn't slept for last two weeks.

Mrs Prakash got Noosh up, and asked her sleep in the room comfortably.

As the day began to pass, Kabir's father arrived home.

It was going to be a very tough night ahead, and many equally or may be tougher days were in store for them.

The stark truth was yet to bite this newly developing family. As Mr. Prakash handed over Kabir's renewed life Insurance Policy to his wife, the obvious came to the fore.

He kept staring at the papers in his trembling hands as his wife began to slowly and steadily talk about things in detail, with much carefully chosen words. No matter, how well it could be articulated, the subject was not simple. Kabir was stuck in the war, and was now missing.

Chapter 23

"Sukh sagar ka sheel hai, koi na pave thha
Shabd bina sadhu nahi, dravya bina nahi shah."
"Politeness is a boundless ocean of bliss, no one can fathom its
depth
Person without money can't be rich, and can't be blessed
without politeness."

FOR KABIR, IN KABUL, MANY RECENT ATTEMPTS TO FIND HIS WAY out of the hotel were in vain. It was a curfew, all these days. The hotel had opened up only for a selected few.

Last two weeks had witnessed several acts of inhuman debauchery. Kabir tried very hard to establish contacts, and he failed each time. Nothing was working, or was even closer to being restored to normal. He could not speak with anyone outside the city. In fact, on occasions, not even within the city limits.

As he was continuing with his spree of enquiring about his beloved, over these days, he was able to gather multiple views from people about her, and the most convincing was that she and some people had left in the truck that day, which was supposed to cross over towards the eastern border. He wanted to believe it.

With that positive feeling on one hand, and on the other, insanity arising out of nearly three long weeks of separation, the news of curfew being lifted only added a big boost. Kabir had already paid the transporter to take them to Jalalabad.

Without wasting any time, they were moving on to the next phase.

"How far did he mention the residence of transporter is?"

"About 3 kilometres off Jalalabad old postal office."

They reached Jalalabad in a few hours. To their surprise, there was no disturbance on the way. As they reached the place, it was already dark.

"You think, this is the right time to meet this man?"

"Yes, we have no choice, and we cannot wait."

Within twenty minutes of reaching the town, it seemed straightforward. They finally managed to reach the lane. It might have been the best address in town. Kabir rang the doorbell without any hesitation. On attempting a couple of times, when there was no response, Babu knocked the handle at the iron made gate.

In no time, two well-built men showed up.

"Yes, what do you boys want?"

"We have come to meet Zahir *saab*."

"Who sent you?"

"Nobody, we just know that he has some transport business, and we wanted to gather some information."

"Police?"

"No."

"I card?'

'No."

"Then?"

"We have no gun."

"Okay, wait here."

One of those two guards returned in a minute.

"Come inside, and don't worry, the dogs have been leashed up."

He quickly frisked them both before allowing them inside.

Zahir came out, wearing an impressive leather jacket and an expensive watch, "What do you want?"

"Salaam sir, we know you are a big shot; you have a huge influence, and we need help."

"People come to me for guns and opium and cash in lieu, which one?"

"Sir, you are mistaken; I lost my wife."

"I am sorry to hear that."

Then Zahir came closer to Kabir, which surprised him. In some time, Zahir recognized the man he met once, "Hello, Journalist, where is my camera lens?"

"Oh, goodness, how the hell I could not recognize you. You run a transport company also?"

"Yes, the income from the hotel began to dwindle, so I thought it is better to do what works for the reason, and here I am."

They both met warmly. Kabir had not met the hotel owner after his Jalalabad visit. And now, it was a complete coincidence for them to meet in this manner. Even though this was just a second meeting, Zahir met him very cordially. For Kabir, this came as a blessing.

Zahir began to enquire about everything with much interest. Kabir told him the information he had from the locals in Kabul on Noosh, Salem and Meer.

It was very important for Kabir to give as much details as possible. He only waited with anxiety for Zahir to respond.

Zahir was only trying very hard to assemble all this thoughts, and how much further could he add value to the information that Kabir already possessed. The intensity and sincerity with which Zahir was making efforts, made anyone believe that these guys must have been great friends for long time.

He knew how to exactly approach this entire puzzle now. It was very pertinent to note that, once Kabir leaves the country, he might not be able to return for long. In case Noosh was still here, then the matters would get more complicated.

Therefore, the onus now lay on Zahir. He began to feel responsible. He was a family man and, therefore, he was able to relate to Kabir, apart from feeling anything else. He had to find a way out. After much thought and discussion and suggestions, it was decided to wait for Pasha to return, and he would be there anytime soon now. Pasha worked for Zahir in his company, and he had been taking care of carrying the people across the border.

"Talk of the devil, and the devil arrives," said Zahir. Pasha settled down after meeting everyone. He was fatigued, as he had returned from India, a while ago.

Kabir immediately handed out Noosh's picture to him. He only glanced at it briefly, and sounded sentimental "How can I ever forget this face? You are a lucky man."

Kabir jumped with joy, for it was an immediate confirmation of her life.

"She never wanted to cross the line without you, Sir." Pasha said firmly.

"Where did she go?"

Pasha explained everything, in detail. After being asked about Salem and Meer, Pasha told the truck that carried men fell in the deep gorge and they all died.

A great news was followed by a terrible shocker. Pasha continued, "You are blessed. If you had travelled with us that day, you wouldn't have been alive."

That got everyone around high and heavy on emotions. The news troubled all to a great degree. Kabir was consoled by the men around. In return, he hugged Pasha and Zahir.

They planned to leave the next afternoon for India, forever. Finally the moment he yearned for was only a night ahead.

Zahir and his family took great care of these boys, before seeing them off the next day.

==========

In Bombay, much action was planned at the residence of Mr. Prakash.

"Don't worry, I shall go to the embassy tomorrow. Then, I need to travel to Delhi. I will make the arrangements and take the train to the capital," Prakash announced.

"Okay, then, please do carry woollens; it is not like here, and this is October. It will be freezing cold in Delhi," his wife said.

"Yes, I will buy from Roopam."

"Then, plan your travel for a day later."

"There is an evening train. I shall be done with all the pre-work by noon."

"Okay, as you please."

She tried to peep inside to see Noosh. There was a photo album, by her side, hands still in the grip, and she was fast asleep.

"I feel bad for her; what all she had to go through."

Mr. Prakash stepped out to the balcony, the place where he spent time by himself.

Mrs Prakash put a quilt over Noosh, took the album from her hands, and placed it on the table in the living room.

"Come inside; see our kids' photographs." Prakash said.

"Really, I am coming."

Both were completely engaged, like kids themselves. They looked at all the photographs with utmost curiosity. Somewhere in their hearts, they knew it would have been a different treat to look at these pictures with a running commentary by Kabir and Noosh. However, for the moment, it would have been ok to have Noosh explain to them the photographs, but then they could not wait.

"Dinner time now," Mrs. Sen, the neighbour said as she came to their house.

"Mrs Prakash, how is Noosh now?"

"Oh, you know about it already."

"Oho, I was the one who guided her towards your house and briefly chatted."

"Thanks, Mrs Sen, as always, for guiding her right."

"Please, it is okay. She is like my daughter."

"Where is Kabir?"

The Prakashs knew these questions will be put forth with ease, so they were prepared with the honest answer and informed her of the actual events.

Around 9 p.m. in the night, most of their friendly neighbours were in the house. Noosh was still kept away from them, though, when she woke up, her sensitive mother in law decided for her to rest completely.

Right from the help in ticket reservation to finding contacts in the embassy was discussed with the neighbours. Possibly, someone was known in Doordarshan as well. This helped the couple a great deal. Prakash noted all the relevant phone numbers and the addresses and, in some cases, neighbour's phone numbers were given.

Some women did ask Mrs Prakash if Noosh was awake, and that they were very tempted to meet her.

The night seemed longer than usual and, with the winters setting in, the nights had gone longer anyway, but today seemed an extra stretch. The neighbours were seen off after a small tea session and the support of helping hands.

Much was talked about; much was being planned, and the next coming days would be all about execution. The family would be glued to television news, regularly. Most of the newspapers were subscribed to. They were doing all the intelligent things they could do to find out about their only son, whose wife was also in a bad shape.

Mr. Prakash left for Delhi, in the evening train. He was dropped by Mr. Sen's driver. Food was packed for the way. Hotel was booked by Siddiquis, and Delhi transport was arranged by Mr. Boxerwala, whose sibling was an engineer in Doordarshan.

Mr. Prakash took great care of himself as he had promised his wife. Therefore, he decided not to skip any tea nor any meal.

Upon reaching Delhi, he was welcomed by the local contacts, garnered with the help of neighbours and friends in Bombay.

A few days were spent in Delhi. The situation in Kabul had only deteriorated by the day. All the foreign embassies were shut down out there. The news was that some more foreigners were killed.

Mr. Prakash tried to gather as much information from them in these days. Mostly, the information that he could collate only pointed in one direction, that anything adverse could have happened.

"Mr. Prakash, I can tell you, if we had any information at our end, we would have contacted you. You know it already that Mr. Sen has been my classmate. He also rang me up. I assure you, I am taking personal interest here. I am looking into this as my own son's case." Mr. Arora, the official at Embassy said.

He continued, "In the previous three weeks, the fiercest and the severest attacks had taken place. The Soviets increased their presence many folds. Lot of damage had been caused to the machinery. I do not want to say anything just to please you."

"Is there any other way to get more info?" Prakash asked.

"Most of the info we get is through intelligence and any local who is out there. There is nothing official that is available. You can see these boxes; there are no letters. All we get every day is a physical attendance by someone like you, who would come and ask for their kith and kin."

"Prakash *saab*, if Kabir has not contacted you in last three weeks, in any form, then, I believe, either he is in some danger or you could think of the worst." Mr. Chawla, another colleague added.

"How can you say like this, Mr Chawla? I mean, have a heart. I came to you with some hope."

"False hopes?" Mr. Arora added.

"At least, you could say that there are a,b,c things you shall look into further."

"That goes without saying."

"Then say it."

"Prakash *saab*, please have tea; be calm and don't be tensed."

"Sir, do not mind, here I am talking about my son. You are laughing and listening to this India England cricket commentary."

"*Arey*, oh chawlaji, volume, please, little low."

"Thanks, Arora*ji.*"

"I am writing to the high commission further, that means the people higher than me and also seniors in the ministry of external affairs to probe this."

"Yes, I plan to meet them too. They must help us find our family members; a few thousands from our country reside there."

"We have already received a memo from the government about the steps they are taking. They are trying all political ways and means to help. India is using its friendship card with the Soviet Union to get the Indians out of the danger. The only trouble is Indians are like any other citizen in a war like situation that you cannot differentiate, and, since the extent of damage is high, you cannot say much."

Like a helpless father, he kept running around. Kabir's photo was also shown in missing people section on the television, and a message was also sent to Moscow.

The case was escalated, and picked up lot of attention; the message reached Kabul, and it was even broadcasted on the local radio.

There was some hope building up, similar to any action. Hope follows an action, and so was the case, but, so far, all this seemed to be going in vain.

Mr. Prakash spent a few extra days in Delhi, expecting some relief, however the results were not positive.

He thanked everybody, gained more contacts, established touch with the ministry, was assured all help and he could see the help coming his way, too.

If it was India, he would have been here by now. How do we control some other country which is trying to save its own ground? How would they find my son? What is the test now for us? How many more days and months like this? Mr. Prakash thought.

He checked out from the hotel in Karol Bagh, and left for Bombay via old Delhi railway station.

This was the worst journey of his lifetime. He was giving up. He reached Bombay.

He took a taxi from the railway station, and begin to talk to the driver. Then he asked the driver to turn on All India radio for the news.

The news did have some portion about the war in Afghanistan, and then he was disappointed again.

The driver mentioned to him that yesterday, the whole day, there were ads about missing people, and, he said, one name he remembered was Kabir.

"*Saab*, think about it; how can anyone find one person in a country that does not even know where its own people are?"

"Yeah, right."

"Wars should not happen."

"Yeah, right."

"They only kill people and wipe out humanity."

'Yeah, can you please drive now, and you may turn your music on, if you wish."

"When you reach near causeway, take a left from Gupta sweets, in case I doze off, and then stop at the second house to the left, at those tri level apartments."

"Yeah *saab*, I have seen those."

"Okay, great, now please drive safe and don't worry about Afghanistan."

Mr. Prakash had been thinking in his head, how will he face the family with no results? Being a man of the house, he held tremendous responsibilities, and he needed to be strong enough to control the foray of emotions and sentiments that might flow. As a matter of fact, he needed much control himself, and that was the fight going on in his head down to his heart. This was the reason he did not buy any favourite sweets from Delhi, else Mr Prakash never went without some stuff in his hand, even locally. But, this father returned empty handed. He returned without sweets and without his son.

Noosh opened the door, and greeted him. She could sense, well enough, from his expressions that he either has no news, or there is something horrific he is going to share. "Please have water, dad," she gave him a glass of plain water, hands were shivering and tone feeble.

"Where is your mother, Noosh?"

"She has gone to meet Siddiqui auntie. I believe there is someone in Times of India that they know of, and trying to seek help for Kabir."

"Okay. I will not have lunch; I had it in the train. You both may eat."

"Dad, if I may ask you, please tell me what the news is. Tell me whatever it is."

"There is no news, Noosh. No news. We announced in the radio, put it in the print, shown on television, engaged ministry but, they say, it is tough to trace a single person out in today's situation. Once the situation calms down they may be able to do something."

"I am realizing his worth much more than ever before. It is simply not easy to live like this."

"You need to relax and take care of your child too. We will do whatever is in our might and then, for the rest, we need to surrender to God."

"Yes, dad."

Over the course of next couple of months, everyone in the family and social circuit had Kabir as the top priority.

Noosh was also taking care of herself, and, then, the time came when she delivered a boy. That day, she missed Kabir a lot. It was very tough on her to be in the situation that she was in.

Overall, the news did bring a big change in the house. There was happiness as the grandparents celebrated the occasion.

Noosh remembered her father, her husband, and continued to give all her love to the child. Being a single parent was not easy, but there were beautiful memories that she wanted to remember. One great support that Noosh received was that of her in-laws. All this while, they had been the pillar of her strength. Also, she had made some friends in the area, where Noosh could discuss her life and things that she could not with her in-laws. That kept her strong, and, also, in times of her weakness, there were people of her age too. She even exchanged many letters with Nikita and Lisa. Over a period of time, her friendship with Nikita had grown strong.

As far as finding Kabir was concerned, it was never given up. There was not a single day when Kabir was not discussed in the household or with friends and the social circle. Never.

Time leaped forward, but it only felt like yesterday.

===========

While Sehar was growing up into a lovely child, it was observed that he had many of his father's traits and, at a very young age, began to learn photography. He had almost mastered it by the time he turned nine. He was pampered and protected by everyone in the family.

When asked what Sehar would want to grow into, he would talk about armed forces. Nobody was surprised, since, most of the time, the topics have only been war and Kabir. This seemed to have had its effect on the little boy.

In the kin, there was only one person who was in the army, and it was Kabir's cousin, Akash.

Akash specialized in commando training just before Soviet withdrawal from Afghanistan in 1989.

His goal was to go to Afghanistan and fight there, one day. Maybe, the time for this was round the corner. He was chosen for UN forces. When the news was announced, he met his parents, and immediately met his uncle, Mr. Prakash.

They did get worried for him. Also, they invited him for Sehar's 10th Birthday.

==========

Prakash mentioned the list of invitees to Noosh.

"Mom, hope you have invited the grandniece of Mr. Boxerwala. Last time, we missed to invite her, and they felt hurt."

"Oh, yaaa, she is here in the list. We all love that child; it was a slip up. In fact, many kids have grown up, so I am sure there will be more kids than the elders this time."

The Prakashs have been extremely social in the community. Any celebration, all would gather at their place. Most of the festivals including Diwali, Eid, Holi, Xmas, would be celebrated at their place.

This occasion was no less than a celebration. Sehar's tenth Birthday was supposed to be celebrated with zest and gusto. Also, big news of Akash's appointment added icing to the cake.

"Last ten years have flown by, and there has not been a single day when I have not missed you, my man," Noosh looked at their photo on the wall.

"Yes, Noosh, and such days bring pain and joy both," Mrs. Prakash said.

"Mom, it will take me a lot of time to understand what wrong I did that I had to go through the agony, the stabbing pain in my heart all these years."

Mrs Prakash put her hand on Noosh's head, "Come, you have suffered enough now. Let us plan the date we celebrate our little boy's birthday, so that everyone can make it."

"Mom, how does the weekend of tenth sound?"

"Yes, I was thinking of the same. It is a holiday, so most of the people would be able join us."

"So, I am considering this list as final."

"Yes, mom."

Noosh tied a black thread around Sehar's wrist. She took some *Kajal,* and puts it on his forehead corner.

"Oh, mom. My friends will make fun." Sehar remarked.

"Let them make fun, I will not stop."

"Haha, okay, mom."

Sehar left to play with his friends. Mr. Prakash was out in the neighbourhood. Noosh was busy, ensuring Mangla gave the house a complete makeover. Mrs Prakash was coaxing Noosh to go to the salon today and get herself a makeover, too. The house was full of activities, like never before.

Mangla was cleaning the house, and she spotted a packet of letters beneath the bed. Noosh mentioned she had been looking for these for many days, and that these letters are from their friends across the world who they spent time with while she studied and worked.

Letters written by Kabir were laminated and kept separately. The photo album had a specially designed almirah, and it was kept like a royal treasure.

Friends and neighbours had arranged for all the decoration. The house was brightly lit up, and the day of the boy's birthday arrived.

On the morning of July 10th, the newspapers mentioned about India's commandos' participation in the fight for peace. That was more or less the topic of discussion at home too.

The Prakashs had heard the entire life story from Noosh many times, but, today it was the first time that Sehar heard it from her in entire detail.

"Today, son, you have turned ten, and at this young age, you really understand human relationships and values. I know you shall make us all proud, like your father," said Noosh

"I don't think, mom, I can be any closer; but, yes, I will not let my family down, ever," Sehar talked like some elder.

"God bless you."

Chapter 24

"Sangati so sukh upaje, kusangati so dukh hoy
Kah kagir tah jaaiye, sadhu sang jaha hoy."
"A good company of people creates happiness and evil one
misery
To be good, one should always be amidst good people."

IN 1990, THE DAY ARRIVED WHEN AKASH LANDED in Kabul on his mission.

"Oh, God, this is the place that *Bhai* and *Bhabhi* lived. This valley looks different in those photographs, than what I see here." Akash said.

"Yes, Akash, it is. Your *Bhabhi* is from Kabul, right?" Mitra, his colleague asked

"Yes Mitra, but *bhai* never returned."

"Yeah, man, I feel sorry."

"Many years ago, I am sure, at the spot you and I are, the Soviets would have taken the charge."

"Yeah, true."

"And the only common thing is that the war within still continues here."

"It is sad, buddy."

"We need to be tough, man."

"We are."

"But I won't shoot at an innocent."

"We are here to protect."

"Like the protectors."

"Exactly."

It was a soldier-to-soldier conversation, between two men who had studied together, were great friends, and were connected like any normal person.

They were supposed to spend two months here in Kabul.

During the time they had at hand, along with the other army men, they would go around the city. In some pockets, life seemed fairly normal. In others, there was no life at all.

Akash discovered quite a lot during this experience. It was a different one for him. In everything he did, there was a fair bit of his brother who would come in his imagination. In fact, one day, he left all by himself to the terrains, and started shouting Kabir's name that echoed in the universe.

He was also fond of photography.

Sometime later, there was a release of prisoners from Soviet war era, and the entire battalion was invited.

It was a mix of inmates. Some were charged with treason, some with arms smuggling and all such big crimes. There were many prisons in the country that were built by the rulers and the Soviets to accommodate the prisoners who were arrested. Most of the people were killed in the war.

At a local prison level, there were achievements being discussed. It was brought to the notice how the inmates worked towards the economy of the country while they were engaged in many commercial activities. For some, their punishment was cut short due to the good conduct.

Akash was just busy taking pictures, as he wanted to make sure he did not leave anything unfinished.

It was a moment of celebration for the inmates. But they did not know how to celebrate yet, so preferred to remain quiet. Some did not even know where to go after this release, and nobody around them was interested, either.

The activities and formalities were done with, and the commandos left for their own work now.

"Mitra, *Bhabhi* mentioned there used to be white houses here, and the valley lit up in the night when these houses were glazed by the moonlight."

"Where?"

"Here in Kabul."

"Let us find out."

"Where?"

"We need to go to the city, tomorrow, to figure out."

"It is a good idea. Let us use our break day and go around."

==========

Back in Bombay, folks at home were worried for Akash. Noosh asked Mr. Prakash if he had any news on him, as he had not called in the last few days.

"Yes, of course kid, he is fine. He must be engaged in the duty."

"That I know, but, still, he ensures regular calls."

Mr Prakash checked with his brother over the phone, and they shared the same thought that Akash must be busy.

It was quiet natural for Noosh to get worried this way, especially in the situation that only she had faced.

"You are thinking too much; let us wait till tomorrow. Remember, he mentioned today he will be busy, and there is a break day tomorrow."

"Okay, sure, dad," she could only agree with him.

==========

The next day, Akash and Mitra went around the city and reached the hotel. They sat down for coffee.

There were some foreigners that could be seen, too.

Some people were attached to the embassies and others were on reconstruction duty. Many engineers from India had also gone to help build roads and infrastructure.

There were two men sitting behind Akash and Mitra.

One of them was quite old, and began to talk about the history of the country. Akash keenly kept listening to him.

"You know, I saw this country across generations; you were not even born then."

"But look at what has been done; it has been destructed."

"Yeah, at one point, this used to be one of the most beautiful nations in the world. It was called the heart of Asia."

"Really, I cannot believe it."

"Yes, that is true."

"This hotel used to be full of activities, and the women used to be very liberal."

Akash jumped in the conversation; he could not resist himself.

"Uncle, may I be part of this?"

"Yes, please come, ask your friend also to join this table."

"Uncle, my *Bhabhi* is a Persian; her name is Noosh, and my brother is Kabir. It is for love of my brother and country that I joined the Army."

The old man did not pay attention to the latter half and only stuck up with the name, "you mean Nooshafarin?'

"Yes, uncle, you know her? She is my *Bhabhi.*"

"Yes, but I will keep asking till I believe my ears. I am one of those survivors that you often see in documentaries; I have been filmed many times by BBC and your Indian channel Doordarshan."

"You are Noosh's relative, come here," he hugged him.

"Where is she? Where is her man? What is his name? I can't recollect?"

"His name is Kabir, and he is my brother."

The world of coincidence came clashing at the time, when one would least expect.

"I know her since childhood. She was my friend's daughter. She was doing great work for humanity here. We told her to go to India and settle down over there. After her marriage, I never saw her again. Kabir was a good man."

"Yes, we looked for my brother, all these years, but could not find him."

"What is your name, uncle?"

"I am Jehan."

"Okay, I will talk to *bhabhi* and my uncle, today, and convey the same. She will be delighted to hear this."

==========

There was somewhat chaotic scene in Bombay

"Noosh, did we not get today's newspaper."

"No, dad, I think Raghu has delayed it today."

"Oh, okay."

Newspaper came flying in the balcony, and Noosh grabbed it.

She opened it up, and attempted to give it to Mr. Prakash.

"See, this boy dropped the newspaper at ten today."

"It's okay, dad; I believe, he is preparing for some entrance exam, hence he must have delayed it."

"Okay, so what are the headlines, Noosh? Get my spectacles, please."

"Earlier, the print used to be bigger, but now the print is too small to read without specs. I can barely see this picture too."

"Here are your specs, dad. Do you want me to read the news out to you?"

"You always do that. Why don't you read it today as well?

Noosh looked at the front page, while it was still in Prakash's hand. Before she could begin reading, there was a pin drop silence. The world came to a standstill. Everything was halted. She kept staring at the front page. There was no finger movement, nor could anyone hear her breathe anymore. She seemed to have had a shock. A big shock. Noosh had a blackout. The next moment she began to shiver.

"He is there, dad."

"Who?"

"My man, your son."

"I do not understand you. Do you mean, Kabir?"

"Dad, that newspaper, get me that newspaper."

"Which one, Noosh?"

"The only one I could not read out to you in last ten years."

"Oh, ok, I will."

What happened, Noosh? Mrs. Prakash asked as she joined them.

"Mom, you see the newspaper first."

Mrs Prakash kept sitting quietly, as Noosh went into complete silence and the feeling that would take a lot of time to sink in; her tears won't stop now.

"Mrs Prakash, my wifey, look at this, look at this."

"Oh, God!"

Noosh spoke, "See, mom and dad, you look at this; what is in the headlines."

It says 'Good sign- Release of prisoners'

"This shirt that Kabir is wearing, it has 'Yogi' written on it; now, we don't know what all happened. But, I know this name was assigned to him to take part in some covert operations around that time.

Akash does not recognize him, and is happy posing for the photo ops.

Dad, you must get a connection to Akash at the earliest please. I don't want to lose him again."

"Oh, my goodness; yes that's him. I will ring up a few people. Need to talk to the high commission." The engagement was established. They mentioned that all the people who have been released were undergoing medical check-ups and all, at the moment.

This was a moment of euphoria, moment of bliss. It appeared to be a miracle. For those very moments, one would want those to stay with them for lifetime.

Noosh kept thinking everything. The visuals moved across her hyper active brains at a supersonic speed. She did not want to sleep till the time she met Kabir. She wanted to make up for these lost ten years; she wants to be twenty five all over again.

The parents kept thinking about Noosh and Kabir. They only had one thing on their mind, gratitude.

The same evening, both went to offer prayers before the God, and thanked the almighty for the miracle.

The next day, Prakashs were able to establish contact with Akash.

"Uncle, where have you been? I have been dying to talk to you. I called up, but nobody picked."

"Akash, stop talking breathlessly and listen to me."

"Okay, please tell me."

"Where are the men you took pictures with a few days ago? I mean which hotel and hospital?"

"Exactly, that is what I also wanted to talk to you about."

"What?"

"I met Uncle Jehan here; tell *Bhabhi* about him; he is her uncle. I want to speak with Auntie too."

"Okay, your Auntie is here, let me give the phone to her, but make sure you talk to me after you are done talking to her."

"Okay, Uncle."

"Hello Akash."

"Auntie dear, I love you."

"I love you too, *beta*."

"Auntie, before you say anything, I want to ask Bhabhi if she remembers Jehan Uncle."

Amidst all the natural confusion and excitement of varied kinds, Noosh was given the phone by now.

"Yes, yes, he is our relative."

"Okay, so I met him."

"Really, how is he? What a coincidence, kindly convey my regards and give our phone number to him."

"*Bhabi,* where have you been all these days? Was there a landline trouble, again, due to the monsoon. I tried connecting with the neighbors too, no response, so I assumed it could be a network wire issue yet again."

"Did dad mention anything to you?"

"He just asked me to talk to him, once you and I finish talking."

"Okay, I will give him the phone, let him speak with you."

"*Bhabhi,* before you do that, listen."

"Tell me."

Jehan uncle mentioned that I should go and check the list of prisoners who were just released, maybe I can find *bhai* or a clue, you know what I mean."

"Okay, talk to your uncle now."

"Yes uncle, I was telling *bhabhi* about the prisoners."

"I know, so listen to me very carefully, while the government is involved, yet it is about our family so we need to be ahead."

"Okay."

"Now, that set of prisoners has your brother also."

Akash could not believe what he just heard, "Really, I will figure that out; so, whatever Jehan uncle told me was true, then."

"Yes, listen to me; that is already figured out."

"What? Figured out."

"Yes. Akash, go; go and get your brother his code name; in fact, his name out there is Yogi."

"Uncle, I still cannot believe my ears. I am elated."

****

Akash jumped with joy, like a child, ran around like a bird flying freely, kissed a few men on the way, grabbed Mitra by his hands, "Bhai is here, my brother is here."

"Whoaaaaa."

Akash and Mitra informed all the units about the same. They went to meet the prison authorities who told them that the released prisoners were taken to the commanding area that was taken care of by the Afghan army units.

Both these men did not want to stop. They got all the relevant details from the officials about the prisoners. It was after some time, when they were directed by the local army staff, they found out the location where Kabir was kept.

He was shaved and given a new set of clothes. Kabir looked at Akash as he saw him coming inside the tent. He could not believe his eyes. He broke down and began to cry. Akash hugged him, and kept holding him firmly. They did not speak, at all. They just kept crying, and Kabir said, "I cannot imagine this is real. I have no words, Akash."

"*Bhai,* see your brother has come to take you. We missed you, a lot."

Kabir asked him about everyone right away. They talked in between their tears.

The entire unit came forward to Kabir, the community, the doctors, the para medical help, locals, cops, everyone. They all shared the emotions with this man.

It was clear that he was the only Indian who was held captive in this prison, maybe in the entire country.

There was a special aircraft arranged for Kabir. The entire unit saluted him as he entered the specially arranged plane that was flown from India. He had no words to express, just kept looking around and smiling at people, nodded his head in between, ate food when offered, accepted flowers and bouquets.

Then he went near the cockpit, "Hey captain, hope you know where I need to go."

"Yes chief, we all do, and, I believe, your entire nation does."

"Where are you from?"

"I am from Delhi."

"Aha, the capital city."

"Yeah, man, and you are safe now."

"Yeah, I can trust you, buddy."

"By the way, can you tell me where I need to go?"

"Yes, mister Kabir, you need to go to Noosh, and we are taking you there."

Kabir's emotions did not stop. His smiles were mostly artificial, as he tried hard to hide his emotions, but they could not be faked for long, and he kept crying out loud now.

"Akash told us about your love story, and we want to hear from you while we ride the plane."

Kabir went back to his seat and hugged Akash, who had been crying non-stop.

"You are a soldier, come on; you don't cry."

"You are a messiah; if you can, I am just an ordinary human."

The brothers kept talking, hugging, clapping and jumping on the way.

"Bhai, you are coming home, yipppeeee."

"Oh, God, I still cannot believe; miracles happen. I believed, the day I met your *bhabhi*."

As the plane hit the ground in Bombay defence airport, Kabir started getting very conscious and nervous.

"*Bhai*, please be calm, okay? It is all right."

"We have lots to catch up on."

Chapter 25

"Riddhi Siddhi mangou nahi, mangou tum pai yeh
Nishidin darshan sadhu ko, prabhu Kabir kahu deh."
"Kabir does not demand God for any material wealth
He asks for favor to have a good person in his sight forever."

AS THE PLANE LANDED AT BOMBAY AIRPORT, and the message reached the officers stationed there, the family of Kabir was informed, too. Everyone was high on emotions.

There was a very warm and celebratory welcome arranged for Kabir by his family, friends and lovely neighbours.

The moment he reached the lounge where his family was waiting for him, he broke down again.

He greeted his parents, hugged them tight and took their blessings. They were all quiet, and were letting the moment sink in.

Noosh was looking at the other side; she did not look at Kabir.

She was numb, and so was Kabir. They both were completely deafened out to any noise around.

Kabir fell down on his knees, and began to weep profusely.

It all came together like a dream, a beautiful dream. The only voice they wanted to hear now was their partner's.

Noosh was gathering courage to turn around and look at her husband, but she needed time. She kept murmuring his name.

Kabir lifted himself with the help of his parents, went and hugged Noosh from behind, then pulled her towards himself. She did not still look at him, and Kabir's eyes were also closed. For those moments, they both were in a state of complete transcendence. They were not connected to the rest of the world. All they knew was that they do not want anything else now. They felt each other.

"One life is not much for many, and I lived many lives in this moment alone," said Kabir.

"We will make up for these ten years," the moment Noosh said this in Kabir's ears, he kept asking her to keep talking. He wanted to hear her voice, over and over again.

"I am sorry for leaving you ten years ago."

"Thank you for returning, not many people do."

Both opened their eyes now, and started with the conversation.

Discussions began with the family.

He explained, in detail, what had happened after Noosh had disappeared.

He told that his truck was held captive, "Then the Russians came, and there were many soldiers, and we knew it could be a potential attack on us."

"I told them in Russian that I am going to look for you; they found it funny. They asked Babu his name, first.

He was so nervous, he took my name. I could not have repeated, else they would have thought something else, so I had to take some other name. Yogi name struck me.

They arrested us on charges of treason, and those are serious charges out there. I mean, it means we are against that country, so nobody shall support us anyway.

And that is how my name was also registered."

The discussion continued till they reached home.

The entire neighbourhood gathered at The Prakash's. Sehar tried to fit himself in Kabir's arms. Kabir could not stop holding Sehar tight. Sehar did not stop talking. He had so much to say. Kabir patiently listened and kept loving him.

Noosh did not leave Kabir's hand even for a moment. She kept looking at him, watched all his actions, and noticed everything about him. The folks were sensitive and understanding, giving way to privacy to the couple. In the room, Noosh and Kabir looked into the mirror together.

"You have not changed at all; you look the same." Kabir said.

"You asked me not to change and be the way I am. There was not a single day, when I did not look at this photo album, you know. I looked at it, every day, like a prayer book."

"Aha, you have put a name to this album too."

"Yes, we call it Kabira. It veils in the most beautiful moments of our life; in fact, it is life, and it has been my life. You must have gone through so much, Kabir."

"Less than what you did, Noosh."

"You are truly a Messiah, you know. How did you spend all these years suffering inside the prison?"

"Noosh, I used to make rugs over there, and I always told the people to ensure these get exported to India."

"Really, you were engaged in labor?"

"Yes, they make you work and give you some meagre pay too. I knew in some form or the other, I will be still connected with you all."

"I was always connected through my soul and through our son, parents, and all those who mattered."

"Did you know I was alive?"

"What about you?"

"Yes, I did."

"And you?"

"Yes, I always had a hope."

"There is the right time and right place, you know."

"I believe, there is something to do with God's mood here, if you remember."

"So true, and that we call destiny."

Over the course of next few days, the family planned holidays and travelled to many places together.

They returned around festivities time.

Weather was at its best in Mumbai, and the food and sweets could be seen all across the town.

"This is what I missed in the prison, apart from you all," Kabir said.

The atmosphere was all jovial, and the normal course of life had begun.

One fine day, there was a door knock.

"Let me open the door, dad."

"Yes, who is it?"

"Post Card for you," Postman said.

"Oh, okay."

"Are you Mr. Kabir?"

"Yes, I am."

"The address was of the older house, and this post card was in the post office for many years, with the older address. Today, I found it."

"Okay, sure. Where has it come from?"

"Somewhere in Peshawar, I suppose."

"Really, that is very weird. Thank you for finding us."

"Sure, Sir, these are human errors; apologies."

The Post Card read as below,

Dear Noosh Madam*ji*,

Do not worry about your husband. He is fine. You can work through your government, and get him out of here. I used to work for my owner in a transport company and, if you remember me, I dropped you to Pathankot, where you shared your Bombay address. And, that is how I know the address. I want to let you know that Kabir *saab* was caught yesterday by the Soviets, and he was taken to a prison in Kandahar.

Khuda Haafiz.

Sincerely Yours,

Pasha.

"See, this is what God's mood is," Kabir was stunned on reading the letter.

"Oh, God. I wish we had received this then," Noosh said.

Epilogue

In December, Mangla and Nur got married. Mary, Lisa, Jemima and Nikita attended their wedding. They extended their holiday to spend some more time in Mumbai and celebrate New Year's too.

Kabir ensured that the family of Babu, Salem and Meer received all possible financial and moral support from his side.

The family tried to trace Pasha, but could not find him.

Nikita confessed that, at some point, she was falling in love with Kabir. She gave up when she found out that Noosh prepared better food.

There were some talks amongst the friends, about getting Sehar and Rain married when they grow up.

Noosh is planning to write a book on war, titled 'The War that Nations Lost.'

----A New Beginning---

About the Author

Arvind Parashar hails from a beautiful valley in Northern India, Dehradun, capital of Uttarakhand. He lives with his family in Mumbai. In his free time, Arvind loves to paint oil on canvas. Most of his work has been gifted to friends and family. He enjoys traveling, and mostly does road trips with family and friends.

He decided to quit his sixteen year long corporate career for the passion of writing, and is now fully devoted to it.

He had been associated with Corporate Social Responsibility in the past-Give India and Junior Achievement, in particular. He wishes to continue with the philanthropic work more rigorously in the future.

He has held many guest lectures as a motivational speaker in various colleges and schools across India.

Be part of author's extended family on facebook or follow him on Twitter, Instagram and Google Plus. Also, visit the website www. arvindparashar.com

Keep visiting above, as there will be launch of contests and also many inspirational quotes and stories to follow. You may also click your picture with the book and send to the author. Let him know in advance if you would like it to be part of the facebook fan page and author's website.